"What's he doing feeling up your legs?"

Harper was steamed. As long as he'd fantasized about caressing Barbara, not just her legs, but all over, and another young man had his hands up her leg . . . he saw red.

Barbara sighed. "I'm hiring Trent to help in the shop. Not that I need to explain, but he's giving me a pedicure," she said patiently. But the way her eyes were sparkling at him, he could tell she did not like explaining herself.

"He feels your legs like that during a pedicure?"

"He's not *feeling* my legs, he's massaging them. And so did Vicky when she gave pedicures."

"Well, you already know his skills. He doesn't need to be feeling you up anymore."

"Yes, sir," Trent said.

"You haven't finished my pedicure," Barbara said to Trent. "I don't see any polish on my toenails."

"Barbara . . ." Harper started.

Other books by Candice Poarch

Golden Night
Long, Hot Nights
Bittersweet
Discarded Promises

Published by Kensington Publishing Corporation

ISLAND
OF DECEIT

CANDICE POARCH

Kensington Publishing Corp.

http://www.kensingtonbooks.com

DAFINA BOOKS are published by

Kensington Publishing Corp.
119 West 40th Street
New York, NY 10018

All Kensington Titles, Imprints, and Distributed Lines are
available at special quantity discounts for bulk purchases for
sales promotions, premiums, fund-raising, and educational or
institutional use. Special book excerpts or customized print-
ings can also be created to fit specific needs. For details,
write or phone the office of the Kensington special sales manager: Kensington Publishing Corp., 119 West 40th Street,
New York, NY 10018, attn: Special Sales Department, Phone:
1-800-221-2647.

Dafina and the Dafina logo Reg. U.S. Pat. & TM Off.

ISBN-13: 978-0-7582-3802-3
ISBN-10: 0-7582-3802-9

First mass market printing: June 2010

10 9 8 7 6 5 4 3 2 1

Printed in the United States of America

In loving memory of my father, the late Alfield Poarch, for being such a terrific man who gave with his heart. He was an inspiring role model, not only to his family, but the community as well. He influenced others to follow his untiring work ethic. We all consulted him and my mother for advice and guidance. When I think of romance I think of my parents' story. I couldn't have asked for a more loving father. Thank you, Dad.

ACKNOWLEDGMENTS

During a chat with RAWSISTAZ, I asked what type of story they'd like to see. Tee C. Royal responded that she wanted more stories with plus-sized heroines. So here's to you, Tee C.—a book that celebrates womanhood regardless of her size. Women are wonderful, creative, and sexy at any size.

I give my sincere thanks to readers, book clubs, book sellers, and librarians for their support. I also thank Sheriff Raymond Bell and Mary Porter for background information.

As always, I extend profound thanks to my parents, my sister, Evangeline, who travels with me to promote my books, and Sandy Rangel, for their unswerving help. Most of all, I'm deeply grateful for my husband's continued support for my writing. Thanks to my writer friends for keeping me sane. Many thanks for guidance from my editor, Selena James.

Last but not least, I am very grateful to have had the late Kate Duffy for my editor. We all miss her, not only for her editing skills, but for her friendship and as one who always offered great advice.

PROLOGUE

Dorsey McNair placed her fancy new Easter hat on her head and looked at herself in the mirror, hoping it would make her feel better. Nobody could say she didn't pull out all the stops for Easter Sunrise Service. She prided herself that she looked at least ten years younger than eighty-five, but she didn't pride herself in letting some young pup make a fool out of her.

At seventy-five, Elliot Stone should know better. At least he told her he was seventy-five. He could have been younger or older. Some men didn't age well. But she was going to fix his bacon if she didn't get her money back. Every single penny of it. He wasn't going to get away with waltzing into her life to steal her money.

She'd shampooed, cut, and permed lots of heads to make that money. Sometimes her back had hurt so bad it felt as if it would crack in two. But did she take a sick day? No. She took a pain pill and kept on working.

Right now as she lifted her hand to powder her nose, she felt every year of her age. Her face had darkened with age to a deep brown complexion. It was an old face with few wrinkles. There were more wrinkles on her neck. Even considering that, she'd held up well.

She'd never felt old before, not really. There was still too much to do. No, she'd never had time to feel old. Not until now.

Suddenly weak, Dorsey stumbled to the bed and sat down hard on the soft mattress. She needed that money. Her house was paid for, and she and Barbara had even had it renovated five years ago. But there were medical bills. Lots of them.

She'd never been a burden on anyone, and she wasn't about to start now. She'd saved enough to take care of herself in her later years, and she just couldn't let Elliot get away with stealing her life savings.

Every year, she contributed to the College Fund to give some child a boost in this tough world. When the Lord saw fit for her to leave this earth, what little was left over was earmarked for her granddaughter. Not that Barbara needed it. She'd done well for herself. But she certainly didn't want it to go to Elliot and his band of thieves.

Had she not gone to the bank to take out another CD, she would never have known he'd cashed in several of her CDs. Nearly $400,000. That's the trouble with bank branches. He'd sent someone to a branch where the folks didn't know her. At her local small branch, every last person knew her.

He'd worked fast, the scoundrel. How did he know how much money she had, anyway? And how did he get ahold of her things? He must have broken into her house and taken her certificates when she wasn't home.

She'd thought about it all night. She should have kept them in a bank lock box like Barbara had told her. But she liked to have them in her house, where she could put her hands on them.

She was going to deal with Elliot after church services. She'd pray on it. The Lord would find a way for her to work this through. He'd gotten her through many tough battles, and the deaths of her daughter and son-in-law. He'd let her live long enough to raise Barbara and to know that the girl would have a good life—and that she was self-sufficient. She only wished that Barbara could find a good man like her own late husband. A woman needed somebody who cared.

But she had to look on the bright side. Barbara was ready to retire and had done well. The two of them planned to travel together before they moved back to her birthplace in Virginia—Paradise Island. She was finally going home.

Yes, indeed. The Lord had surely blessed her. She had no doubt that he'd get her through this, too.

An hour later, Dorsey thought she might as well not have gone to church. She didn't hear a word of the preacher's sermon. After the service, she didn't linger to talk to friends. She drove directly to Elliot's house and punched the doorbell. No one responded.

Back at the car, she slipped off her heels and slid her feet into flats before she left the car again and eased around the side of the house. If he could sneak into her house, she could sneak into his. Before she rounded the corner, she heard voices coming from the back yard. She plastered herself against the side of the building and listened.

She could distinguish four voices, two female and two male. One was distinctly Elliot's.

She listened as they discussed moving to another location and setting up more "marks." They discussed how they needed more money before they could retire.

No kidding, she thought. But they willingly stole most of *her* retirement. And how many other people had they hoodwinked? Dorsey tightened her mouth into a thin line. Somebody had to stop them.

"Whatcha doing, lady?" a kid, no more than four, asked, squinting at her. He held a huge ball in his hand. And he had the prettiest brown eyes. Dressed in jeans, a long-sleeved knit shirt, and sneakers, he obviously hadn't been to church today. Even if folks only made it to church once or twice a year, most families attended Easter Sunday service.

"What's that on your head?" he asked, frowning up at her.

Dorsey put her gloved fingers to her lips. "Quiet," she whispered. Didn't kids know about hats anymore? Had he been a boy from her neighborhood, Dorsey would have sat on the front porch with him and told him stories about church and hats and appropriate attire.

She listened for the Stones while the boy regarded her curiously. But the Stones had quit talking.

"Can I have that feather? I never seen purple strawberries. Are they real?"

"No." Hurriedly, Dorsey raced to the car as quickly as her legs would carry her, started the engine, and drove off.

She'd traveled a mile before reason began to reassert itself. She couldn't deal with these people alone. There were too many of them and they were obviously skilled thieves.

At the red light, she fumbled for the cell phone Barbara had given her. She should pull into a parking lot to use the phone, but this was an emergency. And she didn't want Elliot to catch her in his neighborhood.

She didn't usually depend on other people to do things she could do for herself, but she realized she was in over her head. Elliot lived with an entire family of thieves.

Barbara's phone rang and rang until the answering service picked up. Impatiently, Dorsey listened to the long spiel until she could talk.

"Barbara, honey, I hate to bother you, but I'm in a scrape. Remember the man I told you I was dating? Elliot Stone? Well, he's stolen nearly half a million dollars of my certificates. I've met Elliot's son, Andrew, and his sister, Minerva, but it sounded like Minerva is really his wife. There are four of them. Two women and two men. I don't know who the other female is and I didn't get a look at her, only heard her voice.

"Elliot's like you in that he doesn't like taking pictures. But I sneaked one at a church brunch. It's in one of my jewelry boxes. Not the real one with my good pieces, but the pretty Valentine's box you gave me filled with chocolates a couple of years ago. I keep it in my bedside drawer. The picture is on the bottom turned upside-down with some heavy costume jewelry on top.

"Honey, maybe we can put our heads together to come up with a solution. I guess I'm going to have to go to the police. And they were talking about my family's golden bowl. He must have seen the picture I have or read the article in my scrapbook. I need to get my money back, and I need to save the bowl. I really don't want to be a burden . . ."

* * *

When Barbara Turner returned home that night, she listened to her messages. Fear and anger shot through her. She knew Dorsey. She'd try to handle this on her own.

She called her grandmother immediately, but got the answering machine. She dialed frantically for the next hour. Dorsey never stayed out this late. Without bothering to pack a bag, Barbara caught a train from Penn Station to Philly.

But when she got home, it was too late. She found Dorsey dead at the bottom of the stairs.

CHAPTER 1

Six months later

Barbara Turner had timed her walk along the beach perfectly. It was eight-thirty in the morning. Bundled up against the cold ocean breeze, Minerva Stone came outside for a breath of fresh air with Lambert Hughes.

In an isolated area off the marsh, Lambert's house had as lovely an ocean view as Barbara's. Only Barbara's shoreline was sandy.

Barbara felt like some lewd stalker peeping through trees and thick bushes. A wet leaf fell on her nose. Swiping it away, she glanced up. The limp brown leaves on the tree would fall with the next high wind.

She wiggled her toes. Mud squished beneath her feet and soaked through her shoes. Her next trip to Virginia Beach, she was getting herself a pair of Timberlands. Uncomfortable and cold, she glared at the couple through small but powerful binoculars.

Minerva urged Lambert to sit on the glider, and that tramp plopped her butt right beside him. There wasn't an eighth of an inch of space between them. Using her foot, she pushed the glider to set it in motion. Dorsey had had one painted in blue and white when Barbara was a child.

Minerva smiled up at Lambert and sidled closer, brushing her ample breast against his arm. Barbara watched with growing alarm when the woman took his wrinkled hand in hers and stroked it. Innocent lovers. She let his hand go and rubbed the inside of his thigh.

Lambert was ninety-something, for heaven's sake. Barbara watched with disgust as Minerva's hand worked its way closer to his groin.

Love between older couples was healthy and good, but this had nothing to do with love. Some massages *were* therapeutic, but not this one. Of course, if one had a sense of humor, this could be considered therapy of a sort.

Minerva was somewhere between sixty and sixty-five, and wore every year on her face. Lambert was in surprisingly good health, but what would it do to him when he found out that Minerva didn't love him, that she was out to get his money? Would he be too charmed by Minerva to believe she'd con him? The problem with situations like this was the victim was so enchanted with the swindler, he wouldn't even believe he was victimized.

Barbara shook her head. To the unsuspecting, they appeared to be a couple in love, a couple who'd weathered the pleasures and storms of a lifetime together and were now enjoying their sunset years.

If he only knew, Barbara thought grimly, that it was all an illusion, a pretense of caring and love that Minerva used to build trust. Barbara felt saddened, not just that Minerva would get the opportunity to fleece him, but the emotional baggage she would leave behind was much worse. She'd give Lambert's life purpose beyond golf and existing. His kids didn't live close by. Minerva was someone to love. And who didn't want that emotional connection even if the only pleasure he got was petting and touching? When you didn't have it, it was one thing. But to have that illusion suddenly snatched away . . .

Suddenly, Barbara felt sick. Her own life was as barren as Lambert's. Once she returned to New York, she'd have her friends and activities to keep her busy. Except there was no New York for Lambert. His lonely life was here.

But Barbara had woven her own illusions. Not only on the Stones, but on the island in general. She was known as the hot New York hairstylist and customers had come in droves. She had many more than she ever expected or wanted.

Most parents encouraged their girls to learn typing skills to fall back on in hard times, but Dorsey had insisted Barbara learn the hairdressing trade. While her friends worked retail during summer vacations, Barbara had used hairdressing for spending money and to help pay college tuition.

A beautician was a good cover. Everyone talked in hair salons. Most black women got their hair done. More than likely, Dorsey had bragged to the Stones about Barbara working on Wall Street. But Barbara didn't think she'd mentioned the hairdressing.

The phone rang and Barbara jumped. Fumbling in her pocket, she retrieved it before the sound carried to the house. A quick peek revealed Minerva hadn't heard it.

Barbara whispered a greeting.

"Where are you?" her friend, Liane Harding, asked. "In a conference or something?"

Barbara laughed. "I'm spying." Liane had worked on Wall Street with Barbara.

"So what's going on?"

"They finally found a mark. I was a little confused at first because Elliot usually does the cons, but this time he's using his wife, Minerva."

"Who did they set up?"

"My neighbor. His previous companion vanished a month ago. She was in her mid-twenties and people assume she left for a better job. And, of course, Minerva stepped right in to fill the void."

"You think they did something to her?"

"What else? They've done it before. More than likely, they'll be out of here by Christmas. The bastards."

"Calm down, girl. They aren't going to get away with it this time. You've got the old man's back."

"I hope it's enough." Barbara slid the small binoculars into her jacket pocket and turned, striding quickly down the beach along the Atlantic. After standing still long enough for her body temperature to drop, the breeze grew uncomfortable and she pulled the collar tight against her neck, still talking to Liane.

"It seems like such a coincidence they ended up there. Wouldn't they have more sense than to go to a place Dorsey mentioned?"

"What better place? This is the last place I would think to look for them. The only reason we were moving here in the first place was because Dorsey wanted to."

"Be careful, Barbara. It's a small town. Don't you think you can get the sheriff involved?"

"I'm not taking that chance. The police in Philly couldn't help. I don't see why it'll be different here. Besides, if I tell the sheriff, I won't be able to retrieve the money and distribute it to the people they stole from."

"I worry about you."

"I can take care of myself."

"Famous last words. I have a meeting. Keep me updated and let me know if there's anything I can do."

"Thanks, Liane." They disconnected and Barbara shoved the phone in her pocket.

After the Stones fled Philly, Barbara hired a private investigator to find them. It had taken him a month to find them. She hadn't expected them to be hiding out in Paradise Island, her grandmother's home.

Barbara lifted her face to the breeze. Although the Philly police hadn't taken her accusations seriously, she believed Elliot had pushed Dorsey down the stairs, killing her in the fall. Dorsey had left Elliot's address and Barbara had gone there with the police, but they'd already cleared out.

He must have caught Dorsey spying on him and knew she was going to cause trouble. Dorsey believed in confronting problems head-on, and she wasn't afraid to face adversity. Suddenly, raw and primitive grief overwhelmed Barbara. Dorsey was her only family and she missed her terribly.

Barbara closed her eyes, her heart aching with pain. Her grandmother had been filled with life, every day full of meaning. She didn't complain or bemoan her fate. She went out of her way to help others. The average person didn't have half of Dorsey's heart. Barbara wished she'd retired earlier so that she'd have had more time with Dorsey, but her grandmother wouldn't have stood for it. She'd urged Barbara to live her life.

The one thing Dorsey wanted had eluded her. She didn't make it back to her island.

Five women. The investigator had found five women Elliot had conned in the last two years: Ellen Marks, Mariam Jones, Thelma Louis, Ivy Russell, and Ruby Taylor. All of their lives destroyed by one thieving family. All left devastated and heartbroken.

No, she couldn't work with the sheriff. She'd get their money and return it to them.

Mud kicked up from the marsh as Barbara increased her pace. Having been here since July, she understood why Dorsey eagerly waited for Barbara to retire so they could move to Paradise Island together, and how devastated she must have been that much of her life's earnings had been stolen by con artists, changing the way she'd planned to live her life.

In reality, life wouldn't have changed for Dorsey. Barbara had made and saved more than enough money to take care of them both for the rest of their lives. Dorsey knew that. But it was the principle of the thing. The fact that someone could come into her home and steal her life's earnings without a care. That was totally unacceptable.

Barbara sighed. Her life had changed dramatically in the last six months.

In Philly and Manhattan, Barbara's existence had been a constant barrage of sirens, honking horns, corner delis, cramped condos, and droves of people around all the time. At times, even she wanted to be alone. She found this place enchanting.

Here her grandmother's childhood home offered a breathtaking view of the Atlantic with two acres of land around her. The flow of the water was soothing to the soul, she thought as she listened to the lapping of the water and wondered what life had been like for Dorsey as a child. Dorsey had left a month after she graduated from high school. What was it about this island that made her desperately want to return after being away so long?

Barbara guessed it was "home." No matter where life took Dorsey, the place where she was born and raised was always considered home.

The muddy path became too slippery for Barbara to walk, and she left the shore and headed to the country road.

It hadn't taken long for her to be enveloped into the community. The island matriarch, Naomi Claxton, had roped her into working on the Founder's Day committee and into the search for her family's golden bowl. Since the islanders didn't really know her true identity, Barbara wondered why she was chosen. You never could tell what was going on in Naomi's mind.

She couldn't refuse, though. No one refused Naomi. But shouldn't the woman have chosen one of the islanders? With all that was on Barbara's plate, the last thing she wanted was to get mixed up with the infighting that went with the monthly committee meetings.

The wind increased and Barbara's hat flew off her head. Before she could retrieve it, the sheriff's car drove up beside her, and although it didn't roll over her hat, the driver positioned the vehicle so that it was on top of it. She sent an irritated glance at the pain-in-the-backside sheriff.

The object of the game was to stay as far from the law as she possibly could. She wasn't exactly using lawful means to retrieve her grandmother's money. Her brief sessions with the Philly PD had taught her that the only closure she'd likely get was by her own means.

How many times had Dorsey told her that?

Unfortunately, the sheriff was always turning up, even though she didn't want to see him.

"Better hold on to that fancy hat or you'll lose it," Sheriff Harper Porterfield said, opening his door to retrieve her hat as if she were incapable.

That man, Barbara thought in exasperation.

"Honey, that wind's strong enough to blow you away," Harper said.

"Is that right, Sheriff?"

"Harper. Just Harper," he said.

Oh, he had such a sense of humor, did he? Though Barbara didn't take any crap about her weight, that little breeze wouldn't bulge a baby, much less her at size 18. The sheriff took his time to give her the once-over, and by the time his eyes lingered on her face, she felt unusually hot and her breasts tightened with awareness.

When he shifted his gaze to retrieve her hat, she felt as if the laser that had beamed on her had released its heat. With her hat in his hand, he stood up to his full height. Barbara looked way up, to at least six-three or four. She was only five-five.

It wasn't so much that he was large, and he certainly wasn't pumped-up-on-steroids bulky, but with his solid muscular build and the authority with which he wore it, he presented an imposing presence. The black hair around his temples was sprinkled with gray, but it only enhanced his sex appeal.

Barbara felt a tingling of awareness in her stomach. She reached for her hat, but Harper held it out of her grasp and leaned against the car, his arms folded over his amazing chest. Her hat dangled from his long fingers. "Is there a problem?" she asked.

"I'll say. Breakfast at the B and B is getting better and better. Have you sampled the new menu yet, Barbara? Heard Gabrielle added a couple of items. Thought I'd give them a try." He hit her hat against his hand. "How about joining me?"

As irritating as the man could be, she couldn't deny the attraction between them. Barbara would love to join him—under other circumstances. Harper was one fine-looking man who'd attracted her from the beginning. She didn't know what he saw in her, but she had no choice but to decline.

"I'm sorry, Sheriff, but I have early appointments. Besides, I'm already in a relationship." She nearly gagged. Just the thought of being in the same room with Andrew Stone made her skin crawl.

Harper scoffed. "That boy?" Harper moved closer, invading her space. "He wouldn't begin to know how to treat a woman like you. You need a real man, honey."

That was putting it mildly, but sacrifices for the cause must be made. "And you would?" Barbara asked, feeling mischievous. She shouldn't be flirting. Harper needed no encouragement.

"You can count on it." He sent her a look that said he knew exactly how to handle things. Suddenly, Barbara was grateful for the wind. She needed cooling off.

Um-um-um. The way he was looking at her, she could have melted into a puddle at his feet. And that was saying a lot for a woman immune to silliness.

Those melted chocolate eyes impaled her. Barbara

looked away. She was here for justice, not to be distracted by the handsome sheriff.

"Ms. Turner, I don't know why you're dating that boy, and I'm not going to stalk you. But I have to say, you're a fine-looking woman."

Barbara closed her eyes briefly. Why did he say things that turned her inside out? Why couldn't he have come along a year or two ago—five years ago or even ten? Why did he have to wait until it was too late?

"Have a nice day, Sheriff," she mumbled. "I have to get my walk in before I go into the hair salon."

It was several seconds before Barbara heard a car door slam and the car inch closer.

"You know I'm beginning to wonder about you. You aren't afraid of the law, are you? Or are you hiding out? Rob a bank, Barbara?"

He was hitting too close to the truth for comfort. Maybe she hadn't robbed a bank, but she planned to rob the Stones. "Of course not," she replied smoothly.

"You're not putting your customers under a spell and robbing them blind when their heads are tucked under the dryer, are you?" He was so corny, but he could get away with it.

"Heard any complaints, Sheriff?"

"They're under your spell. How would they know to complain?"

Barbara laughed.

"One day you'll let me have my way."

Barbara stumbled. Just the thought sent a pleasing ripple through her.

"I'm already under your spell," he said. "Be careful, you hear? Have a good day."

Harper pulled ahead and turned a corner before Barbara realized he still had her hat.

* * *

Three miles from Barbara, Trent Seaton cut the motor in his boat and paddled the rest of the way to shore. He'd rented the old house for four months and needed to get the lay of the land before he moved in. With his binoculars, he watched some asshole leave the house with a magazine tucked under his arm, scratch his belly, and amble to the outhouse as if he belonged there. What the heck was an outhouse doing there? The place had an indoor bathroom. But maybe the electricity hadn't been turned on yet. After all, he wasn't supposed to arrive for a few more days.

And the owner had said the house hadn't been rented out since the end of September. He'd also mentioned a brother-in-law who tried to sneak in freebees. Trent couldn't have that. He couldn't have some asshole walking in on him or spying on him. He was going to nip this shit in the bud right now.

Trent hunkered down in the marsh behind some bushes. Made him remember the old times when he was in the Marines. He waited ten minutes. A flock of birds flew south. A great gust of wind blew in, sending a shiver up his backside and bringing the stench of death with it. He shivered again. Must be a dead animal somewhere. Or else it was the unique stench of the marsh. He'd have to put up with it for the next couple months.

Was the guy going to read the whole friggin magazine in the stinking outhouse?

This had seemed the perfect place. Isolated. No houses in sight. Didn't have to worry about nosy neighbors getting in his business, trying to keep tabs on him, reporting his movements to what stood for pitiful law enforcement on this hick island. Now that part suited him just fine. He didn't need any jerkwater cop trailing him.

Trent took aim at the outhouse. It was time it came down anyhow. This was the twenty-first century for chrissakes, in the good old US of A. Trent fired over the man's head, peppering one end of the outhouse to the other.

The man yelled "Jesus H. Christ!" from inside. Was more than likely crouched on the floor. Trent emptied his gun, dropped the clip, inserted another one, and fired again.

"All right, for crissakes! I'm leaving," the guy hollered out.

Trent stopped firing, and after a moment, the man gingerly cracked the door, probably to test the waters.

Trent had already reloaded, but he wasn't going to shoot the guy.

Pulling up his britches, and without even bothering to pack his gear, the guy sailed to the truck and fumbled the remote to unlock the door, all the while looking around like a scared rabbit, expecting to feel a bullet any second. Once in the truck, he jammed the key in the ignition and sent gravel spewing as he pulled off.

Trent had paid good money to rent the cabin and no SOB was going to encroach on his time. As soon as the loafer was out of sight, he retrieved the motorboat from its hiding place and started the motor. Soon he was bumping across the choppy water back to Norfolk. Good thing he had a cast-iron stomach, else he would have upchucked the breakfast he'd eaten at the IHOP.

Okay, so maybe his mother wouldn't have approved. She was always whacking him upside his head, telling him to use the brains the Good Lord had seen fit to give him.

He didn't take drugs or sell them, and he didn't steal. But his mama disapproved of his career choice. He felt so laden with guilt and grief he couldn't stand it. His mother loved him. And he'd never been a good son. Only brought her worry and heartache. To make up for all the deeds that made Mama heartsick, he was going to pay the sonofabitch back who took Mama's money.

"You're gonna be proud of me, Mama. I'm going to get some justice for you."

He'd been away on an enforcement when some slick-talking dude had sweet-talked his mama out of her savings. She believed in putting away a little at a time. She'd attended secretarial school right out of high school. She'd waited tables to make the money to put herself through school and had started out working in a secretarial pool at a large corporation. She'd worked her way to the CEO's office.

"Hard work, Trent. That's the way to make it," she'd drilled in his head. Sure he worked hard, but it wasn't quite the work she was referring to. He wasn't exactly the nine-to-five type.

He'd done a stint in the Marines. That was as close to an honorable job as he'd ever had. It made him tough at least. Tough enough to be a bouncer in nightclubs or an enforcer when people didn't pay the bookie on time.

He never killed nobody. Just broke a few arms, bloodied noses. Stuff like that. The worst he'd done was shoot a guy in the leg. Once you'd gained a reputation, they went to any length to get the money for you. And if they were dead or too incapacitated to work, you couldn't get your money. He wasn't all bad. At least Mama could be proud he wasn't a murderer.

But when those suckers cleaned out her bank account, they might as well have put a bullet in her head. She couldn't live knowing she'd lost everything—that she'd have to depend on others for basics like food and medicine. Social security didn't pay enough for a person to live on. And although she had her company retirement, she felt that she needed that extra money for emergencies. You never knew what life would turn up. She'd always been proud of the fact that she'd earned her own way.

Pain pierced Trent's chest. When he got through with them, they'd wish they'd never heard of Lucinda Seaton.

Right now, she lay in her bed nearly comatose. His sister was looking out for her. Maybe if he could get her money back, she'd come back to them.

He'd been monitoring the Stones for a month now. What he couldn't quite figure out was how Barbara Turner fit into the equation. His mother told him the old guy had a daughter. At first he thought Barbara was the daughter, but she wasn't a young chick and she was dating the guy's son. That didn't make sense to him unless she was really his son's girlfriend all along and just told his mother another lie. Elliot had said his son's girlfriend was younger than he was, but then, how could you count on anything Elliot had said being true? Still, why would Andrew want to date a woman so much older than he?

It also surprised him that Barbara worked, really worked hard. That lot wasn't known for hard work, only stealing. Anyway, he was going to try to get a job in the shop with her. That way he'd get the low-down on everything. Nobody talked like a bunch of women in a hair salon. It wouldn't take him long to learn everybody's business.

A man came barreling into the police station to report a shooting. After listening to him, Harper brought him back to his office and pulled out a form.

"Did you see anyone?" Harper asked. He knew who the guy was—the cabin's owner's brother-in-law. He'd stayed a week during the summer. The cabin's owner had asked Harper to keep an eye on things. Had even sent Harper an e-mail telling him he'd rented the place out for a few months to Seaton. This was not Seaton and the man had no business there.

"Are you staying on the island?" Harper asked.

"Oh, no," the man said, shaking his head. "Like I said, I was just passing through. Thought I'd report what happened, though."

"We're going to check it out. In the meantime, why don't you wait around?"

The deputy on duty saw to the man's comfort with a cup of coffee, and Harper called John Al-dridge, his day-shift assistant.

"Scott, why don't you drop by there, too? Just in case there's trouble," he said to Scott Lowell, a re-tired officer helping out while their lone detective was away on training. The place he mentioned was close to Barbara's. It disturbed Harper that some-one was shooting that close to where she lived, espe-cially since she went walking in the mornings.

He sighed. They'd just solved a string of murders. A funeral home owner who'd married one of the islanders had been a necrophiliac, and it turned out he was also a serial killer.

It was the end of October. Thanksgiving and Christmas were close. It would be nice if the island went back to its normal peaceful state when the sheriff's department's worst offenses were neighbors arguing over fences and speeding tickets. This was a small town—too small for all the activity they were having lately.

Now that Harper had dispatched Scott and John to the site, he was rifling through paperwork. And thinking about Barbara. He'd be the first to admit that he'd become complacent and uncompromising with the dating scene. Sure he spent time with women on the mainland—never on the island—because marriage wasn't on his mind and women here wanted marriage and expected marriage. They had families, voters actually, to back them up, and he had to run for office. When a relationship ended, he didn't want irate relatives knocking on his door, bringing up his dating experiences when election time came around every four years.

He'd given up on finding someone who interested him enough to bring him out of his isolation. And then Barbara had appeared and set his blood on fire. Made him dream of things he'd long forgotten, like having a woman in his home, a permanent fixture in his life. Someone who cared. He started to think bachelorhood wasn't all it was cracked up to be. Saying that she'd knocked him for a loop was putting it mildly.

Barbara was a big girl, but a beautiful woman. Her black hair had grown longer due more to lack of time to get it trimmed, he suspected, but it was always well-coiffed. Her face was the rich brown of gravy poured over chicken or turkey. And her warm eyes—he just wanted to see them light with desire for him.

Harper sighed in frustration. By the time he'd decided to pursue her, the island was riddled with murders and he was up to his neck in trying to solve them. It was the wrong time to pursue a new relationship, especially with a woman as skittish as Barbara. He needed time to woo her.

By the time they'd caught the funeral home owner, some snot-nosed kid had caught her attention. Harper shook his head. What a sophisticated woman like Barbara saw in that boy, he didn't know. But there it was.

It had been many years since Harper had had to work to get a date. Hell, since high school, women approached him. He stifled a groan. He had his work cut out with Barbara, though.

He wasn't giving up. He wasn't a stalker either, but as far as he was concerned, Barbara was his. The relationship she was in was doomed to failure. He was a long way from thinking of a permanent relationship, but Barbara wasn't from the island and wasn't encumbered with the problems islanders presented.

"John's on line one, Harper," the dispatcher said on the intercom.

Harper picked up the phone.

"Got a dead body here."

Harper tightened his grip on the phone. "Who is it?"

"Don't know. It's been here a while."

"Shit." Harper scooted back the chair. "I'll call the coroner."

His second call was to another retired deputy to keep any crowd at bay so that he and his deputy could actually work the scene. Harper got there ten minutes ahead of the local doctor, who was also the coroner. Slipping on crime scene bootees and plastic gloves, he waded through the marsh to the water's edge, focusing on the scene around him.

John was snapping pictures and Scott had set cones out, blocking the driveway, but stayed well away from the body.

Harper looked for old tire tracks or footprints, wondering how the body had gotten there. It was a woman. Had someone merely dumped her off a boat? Even from ten feet, he could see red polish on her long nails and wondered if someone was walking around with scratches from when she fought him off.

There was one set of fresh footprints, made by John. Any older ones had long ago washed away with the rain. But something was there. There always was. And they'd find it.

Harper went closer and stooped near the body. One arm was caught on a bush—as if the bush had grown around her. Up close, the pungent odor of death and decay rose to his nostrils, the scent mixing with the natural decay of the marsh. Caught in the underbrush, the body had decomposed enough that the face was unrecognizable, although most of her body was intact. Birds had obviously attacked it, and animals, too, but not enough to drag parts away.

"If I hadn't been checking out this area, the corpse could have gone a lot longer without discovery," John said. "Maybe eventually work loose in a storm to disappear into the ocean." At six feet, John wore his uniform and a yellow county-issued coat identifying him as part of the Paradise Island Sheriff's Department.

"I'm thinking she's that missing woman, the one who worked for Mr. Hughes," John said. "Sarah Rhodes."

Harper nodded in agreement. She was the only one missing that they knew of. And since she wasn't from the island and her family hadn't pressed the fact that she was indeed missing when Hughes called them, they'd believed she had simply stopped working for the older man.

Harper glanced toward the house and called the deputy who worked the night shift to get out of bed and get a search warrant for the house. Afterward, they began to process the scene. They had a long day of charting, measuring, photographing, and collecting evidence before them.

Dusk fell by the time they were ready to leave the scene. The corpse had been taken to Norfolk to the medical examiner's office, and the coming and going of the curious stopping to gawk had stopped with it. The woman's purse was missing, as well as any form of identification, but they'd gotten good fingerprints.

Harper began assigning duties. Since Sarah Rhodes was the only missing person on record, they would work under the presumption that the corpse was hers until a formal identification was made. Either way, a woman was stabbed.

"John, I want you to interview the ferry captain and

docking captains at the ferry. Find out everything you can about Sarah Rhodes. Whom she associated with. She's been riding that ferry for months and the workers get to know regulars."

Then Harper focused his attention on the other officer. "Scott, interview people in town. See if we can get some leads. I'm going to interview Lambert Hughes."

Scott had worked for the department for thirty-five years before he retired three years ago. Harper didn't need to spell out every tiny detail for him. The two men left for their cars and Harper went to his. He'd opened the trunk to discard his bootees and gloves when he heard a stringent voice.

"Harper?"

In annoyance, he focused on Tracy Moore as the island's lone pest of a reporter jogged toward him.

"I need a statement. Who was that? What condition was the body in? What can you tell me?"

"We were unable to identify the body. It has been taken to the medical examiner's office for an autopsy and identification."

"So you think it was murder?"

"We can't make a determination until the medical examiner does an autopsy."

"Come on, Harper, give me something to work with here. Do you think it's Sarah Rhodes who worked for Lambert Hughes?"

"I can't make any assumptions. After we identify the body, and contact the family, we'll release the information to the public. You already know that, Tracy. Now, I've got a job to do."

"Harper . . ."

"That's it, Tracy."

Sighing, she left for her car, trying to flag down John. But John had pulled off; dejected, she left.

Harper headed to Lambert Hughes's place, just a mile away. He'd confiscated four knives on the property. They'd all been placed in evidence bags, dated, and sealed.

Who was she? Harper wondered at her story. Did she know her abductor? Was it rape, robbery, an irate boyfriend? Was it a stranger or someone familiar?

Hughes's housekeeper answered the door.

"We saw a lot of traffic up the road. What's going on, Sheriff?" the woman asked.

"And you are?"

"Minerva Stone. My brother and I moved here a few months ago with his son."

"A body was found in the marsh," he said. "I'd like to speak to Mr. Hughes."

"Come on in," she said, directing him to the kitchen where Lambert was eating dinner.

"Evening, Sheriff. What brings you here?" Lambert asked, struggling out of his seat. He was an ancient man, though he was still rather fit for his age. He was slim with a medium brown complexion. Probably close to five ten or eleven at one time, but no more than five seven now. Harper often saw him on daily walks.

"Don't bother to stand. I have a few questions about Sarah Rhodes."

"Is she the one you found in the marsh?" Minerva asked.

"The body hasn't been identified," Harper told her, then focused on Lambert.

"My Lord."

Harper started again. "Could you tell me the last time you saw her?"

"It was a month ago. I called it in. Just didn't show up for work one morning. I wrote it all down because I don't remember the way I used to." He struggled from his seat and started pulling out drawers.

"I'll help you," Minerva said, busily searching through the drawers.

"Do you know the people she associated with on the island?" Harper asked.

Lambert's hand hovered over some papers as he shook his head. "I don't know. We never went anywhere except to the golf course at the base and to my doctor's appointments."

"She never took you grocery shopping, Lambert?" Minerva asked, outraged. "Or riding around?"

Lambert shook his head. "She shopped for my groceries each week."

"You poor thing," she said, patting his arm. "Kept you closed up in here like a prisoner."

"She wasn't nearly as good as you, Minerva, but she was a nice girl," Lambert said, smiling at Minerva as if in a lovesick daze.

What the heck? Did Lambert have the hots for his housekeeper? "Did she mention any of her friends?" Harper asked, bringing the conversation back to Sarah. "Anybody she had problems with?"

"No. Never," Lambert said, tearing his gaze from Minerva.

"Anybody ever pick her up from here?"

"Sometimes she caught a ride if her car was in the shop. That was often. She needed a new one."

"Who did she catch rides with?"

"I never saw the cars and she never mentioned

names. But I had written down some things to refresh my memory just in case and now . . ." He started digging through the drawers again and so did the helpful Minerva, who spent more time listening than working.

Although Lambert searched, he couldn't find his notes. Handing him a business card and telling him to call if he remembered anything, Harper was forced to leave with very little information.

At least he knew Sarah often caught rides to the house. Maybe she'd caught a ride the day she disappeared. The cottage near the body was rarely used in the fall and winter. But islanders knew that.

Two miles away, Barbara spritzed on perfume and sighed. The last thing she wanted to do was go out on a date with Andrew Stone. But for her plan to work, she had to pretend to be involved in a relationship with him.

Her cell phone rang and she looked at the number. Andrew. Perhaps he was canceling.

"Barbara?" he said when she answered.

"Yes?"

"I can't get the car tonight. You think we can take your car?"

Barbara took the phone from her ear. Was she dealing with a high-school boy? This man was thirty-five years old and he had to go to his daddy for a car?

"I'll be happy to drive," Barbara said sweetly. "I'll pick you up in a few minutes," she said, then disconnected.

Honestly, it was easier working a legitimate job than to go through the nonsense Andrew's father put him through. If he'd had a job, he wouldn't have to ask his father's permission to use a car or for spare money. He'd have his own. He was a single man with no responsibility. It wouldn't take that much for him to find a place to live, especially in a place like Paradise Island, where prices were still reasonable.

Maybe it was a good thing she was picking him up.

She donned a Chanel pantsuit and paired it with a Louis Vuitton purse and Gucci shoes, then went to her jewelry box. She slid a diamond ring on her finger, large diamond earrings, and a matching necklace. Let them see she was well off.

If it was one thing the Stones knew, it was the cost of designer goods. She'd put herself through the trouble of trooping to some of New York's famous sales outlets before she left. The places were packed with businesswomen fighting over designer discounts.

Quite frankly, she thought it was a waste of good money to spend it on high-priced designer wear when that money could be invested. But she knew it would impress the Stones, and she had to play her role. So she'd been one of the women shoving and pushing, trying to get to the best choices. It was worse than a day on the stock market. But it had paid off.

The Stones lived on the other side of the island near Mrs. Claxton. The kitchen light was on in Mrs. Claxton's house when Barbara exited the car.

Andrew slammed out of the door as Barbara walked toward the house. His light brown face disclosed the early ravages of a drunk. He was no more than five nine or ten and his clothes drowned him.

"I'm ready," he said.

"Can't I at least greet your aunt and dad?" she asked.

"I thought . . ."

"It won't take long. I don't want to be rude coming in their yard and leaving without speaking."

Andrew stopped as if the thought had never occurred to him. "Oh." He was used to being led so she didn't have to work to get him to follow her lead.

Jesus Christ! For this she gave up breakfast with the sheriff?

She hid her exasperation as she perused his jeans and sweater. They were designer, but still jeans. He had the audacity to wear a jean jacket over that. She hoped he had enough money on him to pay for dinner, because she planned to select the most expensive items on the menu.

She opened the door.

"Hello . . ." she called out.

"Barbara?" Minerva responded. "It's so good to see you."

Barbara crossed the floor and kissed the woman on the cheek. "It's good to see you, too. Hi, Elliot," Barbara said as he entered the room. Both of them dressed far above what one would think they could afford with Minerva working as a companion. Even Elliot's shoes were made of soft expensive leather.

"Oh, doesn't she look pretty, Elliot," Minerva said, checking out the goods.

Elliot looked at her as though he was calculating to the penny what everything cost just as she'd been. "Does that."

Barbara grabbed Andrew's arm and moved close. "Andrew's treating me to dinner in Virginia Beach. Thought I'd dress for the occasion."

"I like that purse," Minerva said.

"This old Louis Vuitton? I'm almost embarrassed to carry it, it's so old. But it matches the outfit. I need to update the wardrobe, but I'm always working and don't get to New York as often as I'd like."

"I've always wanted a Louis Vuitton purse," Minerva said, still checking out the goods with an envious sigh. "But they're so expensive. Never could afford one."

Barbara bet she owned more than one Louis Vuitton, but she'd play the game. "Well, my friend told me about this sale coming up after Thanksgiving. I'm going to New York on a spending spree. Get myself a few new things for the holidays," Barbara said. "I've worked hard enough to deserve a little splurge. Let's see what Santa can do about that purse."

"You were telling me about this stockbroker friend of yours," Elliot said, shaking his head. "Stock market isn't doing too well right now. Risky business to be in."

"It's all a matter of choosing the right ones. My friend gets the news ahead of time. I know inside trading isn't quite legal, but it's how the real money is made," Barbara almost whispered, then looked fearful. "You won't say anything about this, will you? She could get in trouble with the Securities and Exchange Commission."

"Oh, no. No," Elliot said, shaking his head. "You don't have to worry about that."

"Those diamonds are something else," Minerva said, glaring at the stones on Barbara's ears and neck, not to mention the rock on her finger.

"A girl's best friend."

"Ready?" Andrew asked impatiently.

"I'm sorry I took so long, sweetie." She feigned

an affectionate smile. "I didn't want to be rude to your family."

"You picked yourself a winner this time," Elliot said. "Y'all have a nice evening."

Barbara smiled up at Andrew. "We will."

Elliot approached Andrew and slipped folded bills to him.

Pocketing the money, Andrew led her out. When he started to the driver's side, she let him get the door for her.

He looked disappointed. "I thought I was going to drive."

"No, honey," she told him pointedly and pinched his cheek. "I love the power behind a wheel," she added, and slid into the smooth leather seat.

Barbara didn't bother to look his way as he made his way around the car. Was he crazy? Let him drive her brand-new Cadillac SRX Crossover? So new it still had the new-car smell. She stifled a chuckle. Not in this lifetime.

CHAPTER 2

Andrew's gaunt face was flushed with anger as he scraped change from the bottom of his jean pockets to pay for the food and tip. Barbara counted the money to make sure he left the appropriate amount.

"Don't know why we had to leave all that money. He just served us. Didn't make the food."

"If you expect good service the next time we come here, you have to tip generously."

"We ain't coming back."

"This food was worth every penny," Barbara assured him. "We are coming back."

Andrew had suggested they eat at a fast-food joint, but Barbara had driven to an upscale restaurant. She didn't understand him. The Stones were used to living large. Andrew must be accustomed to tipping well. And now they were acting as if they were scraping the bottom of the barrel. Barbara guessed it was part of the role they played.

"I wasn't going to spend that much money," Andrew said.

"One of my customers recommended this place."

"They sell good seafood at cheaper places." Andrew

sulked in his seat. "I thought we'd go to a bar or something afterward, but I'm broke."

"Maybe another time," Barbara suggested, heading to the ferry.

"Well, you could . . ."

Barbara glanced at the illuminated clock on the dashboard. "It's late and I have to work tomorrow." As if she would buy him drinks. She didn't think so. And since he'd spent all his money on her dinner, he certainly couldn't afford to buy any.

Neither of them got out of the car to catch the breeze on the ferry. Andrew sulked and Barbara turned the radio to an R&B station.

As the DJ's seductive voice came on, Barbara leaned her head against the headrest. She couldn't help thinking the music was better heard between the sheets with a lover. God, wouldn't it be nice to be seduced by a live man rather than the vocalist's mesmerizing voice.

Sometimes . . . Barbara swallowed around the dryness in her throat. The music took her to a more intimate and giving place in her soul. Sometimes she wished she had somewhere to go with those thoughts. That she didn't have to keep all her feelings bottled up. There were times her toys just weren't enough. But when you had nothing else, this would have to do.

"I shoulda let you come back to the island alone and stayed in Norfolk."

The shock of Andrew's grating voice was like a glass of icy water thrown in her face.

"You should have," Barbara murmured, glad the ferry was pulling up to the dock. She was ready to kill him.

Once they disembarked, Barbara drove directly

to the Stones' house, and since the light was on, to Andrew's dismay, she went inside again.

Wearing a smoking jacket and silk pajamas, Elliot was reading the paper in the living room as if he were waiting up to make sure his high-school child didn't break curfew. He placed the paper on the badly scarred coffee table and stood when Barbara entered the room.

"Ya'll have a good time?" he asked, nodding at Barbara.

"Just wonderful," Barbara said, smiling brightly, but Andrew merely grunted.

"You and Minerva have to try out this restaurant. The food was excellent, wasn't it, Andrew?"

"Expensive . . ."

"We will," Elliot said, ignoring Andrew. Barbara noticed he often ignored Andrew. "Have a seat."

Barbara settled as comfortably as she could on the badly sprung army-green sofa. Andrew elected to stand in the doorway, sulking.

Minerva joined them with a silk scarf tied around her curlers and wearing expensive off-white lounging pajamas.

"How do you like your new job, Minerva?" Barbara asked as the older woman settled on a cushioned ladder-back chair across from her.

"This isn't my usual lifestyle. I only took it because Lambert needed someone so badly. He's all alone, poor thing. I'm blessed to have a brother and nephew so close. But Lambert is nice and not demanding. Otherwise, I simply couldn't work for him."

"We lost a lot in the stock market," Elliot said. "Everybody's cutting back with the downturn in the economy."

"You heard about the body they found in the

marsh?" Minerva asked. "It was so close to where I work it just gives me the shivers."

"Some of my customers mentioned a lot of activity near Mr. Hughes's house."

"Well, the sheriff asked Lambert questions about that girl, Sarah Rhodes."

"Was it her?"

"He wouldn't say. Said he couldn't identify the body. But he wouldn't ask questions if he didn't think it was her."

"That poor girl," Barbara commiserated, saddened, even though she believed all along that Elliot had gotten rid of her. She'd hoped Sarah had found another job, but if Elliot did kill her, what was one more murder to him?

"Andrew said you paid for your shop outright with the money you made from investments," Elliot said after a brief comment about Sarah's untimely demise.

Barbara nodded. "I've always invested well. I have a very good broker I've used for twenty years," she said, noticing Elliot was hanging on to every word like it was the Gospel.

"We've been friends since I started working in New York. You know, I considered retiring instead of opening a shop here, but what would I do with all that time on my hands? I may as well make more money."

"You're a smart woman," Elliot said.

Andrew moved toward the door that led to the back of the house.

"Where you going, boy?" Elliot asked. "You got company. Sit down."

Mouth pressed tight, Andrew sank into a chair

in the corner, even though Barbara had the couch to herself and there was plenty of room for him.

"I tell you one thing," Minerva said. "I'd travel if I didn't have to work. I'd find plenty to do. Shopping would be at the top of my list."

"You've got a point there, Minerva. I've done a lot of traveling, but there are still places I haven't seen yet. Maybe I'll retire in five years. Fifty is still young. Maybe someone will want to buy me out, or I could rent booths to other hairdressers and just manage. Which shouldn't take up much time," she said. "I've saved enough for a very long retirement. I'm going to use my profits from the next few years strictly on entertainment," she said. "You know how I like my designer things."

"You've got a brisk business in that shop. Ever thought about hiring help? Andrew . . ."

"I've thought about it. But I can only offer my customers the best. They expect quality. Sometimes quality falls when you get other people in the mix. Just look at the stores now. You ever tried to find help when you need it? I've seen a man screaming for some help at the top of his voice. Stopped everyone in their tracks. And I commiserated with him because I needed some help, too, but management has cut back so much, quality service is a thing of the past."

"Oh, girl," Minerva said, nodding. "Isn't that the truth?"

"Everybody's got nothing but good things to say about your shop," Elliot agreed. "You know what you're doing. I tossed around the idea of investing in the stock market, but it's too iffy right now. Shoulda done it while it was still going up.

Right now, you're better off putting your money in the bank."

Barbara shook her head. "Interest rates are way too low to make a decent profit. I work hard and I need my money to work just as hard for me. And you know that's not happening in the bank," she said. "You know they charge a mint on loans and credit cards, but they don't pay you squat on your money. No way I'm putting large sums of money there," she assured him. "It's just a matter of knowing what to invest in and having the right broker." Barbara stood, knowing she'd said enough to keep stringing Elliot along. "I better get going. Have to work tomorrow. Thanks for dinner, Andrew."

"Umm. Yeah," he said, and escaped to the back room.

Deep in thought, Elliot walked Barbara to her car. Even opened the door for her and closed it after she got in. She waved as she backed up. He was still watching her as she drove away.

Designer clothes and poorly sprung sofas. What a contradiction these people were.

The next day, Harper skipped lunch and dinner, and had consumed just half an egg sandwich for breakfast. His hunger increased with his temper and frustration.

They all gathered in his office after the interviews.

"What did you find?" he asked.

John checked his notes. "Sarah was seen with lots of people from the island. Car always broke down and she was always catching rides," he said, which confirmed what Hughes had said. "She knew lots of people here. Very friendly. Was dating Ben at the bar for a while. Hung around the bar many nights waiting for him to get off. Some nights didn't go home. Don't know how long ago, but they've broken up." John glanced up. "We all know none of Ben's relationships ever last."

"Scott?" Harper asked.

"She was seen regularly at the Greasy Spoon, with Ben, too, especially on his days off."

"Did she date anyone else after they split?"

"No, she was friendly with a lot of people, though."

Harper glanced at his notes. "Was Ben at the bar?"

"He went to South Carolina to visit his family for a couple weeks," John said.

"In the meantime, let's interview some of these friends of hers and find out whom she was getting rides from. One of them could have killed her. And her purse was missing. So we can't rule out robbery. See if any of the rides were from addicts."

"I've got a couple more leads I'm going to check at the bar later on tonight," John said.

Harper sighed. He was going to head to the Greasy Spoon before it closed, but first he called the local real-estate agent who rented out the house to ask for identities of the people who stayed there around the time Sarah went missing.

Another murder. His chances of getting with Barbara were growing slimmer by the minute.

Around seven, Barbara led her last customer to the door. The hair salon had been busy, as usual, and her ears had burned all day about the woman in the marsh. The location had been so close to

Barbara's house that shivers ran up her spine just thinking about it.

"Take care of yourself, Vanetta," Barbara said, locking the door. She went to the cash register and began to count the day's earnings.

Since her husband was found dead—and naked with another woman—Vanetta Claxton Frasier was quickly disintegrating into a recluse. She'd asked Barbara if she could come in when there weren't other customers. Barbara had agreed to fix her hair after her last customer left. She didn't usually work this late on Saturdays, but the high-school children had a party that night and she was working late anyway.

Finished with the counting, she recorded the amount in her ledger and padded to the storage room. She placed the money in the zippered pouch before stuffing the bundle in her oversized purse. Back in the salon, she straightened up and disinfected the surfaces before she swept the floor.

Vanetta was still suffering from her husband's death and betrayal. It was the same old thing—her husband was screwing around with other women. Men created all kinds of havoc in women's lives, Barbara thought.

As much as she wished for someone special in her life, she wondered if men were worth the trouble.

Truth was, she was absolutely heartsick about Sarah's death. Would reporting the Stones' activities to Harper have prevented it? *If* the woman was Sarah, Barbara had no doubt the Stones killed her. Since Andrew didn't have the balls to kill anyone, Elliot was her main suspect.

Even if she'd reported what she knew, Harper couldn't have prevented the murder. She was unaware they had chosen Lambert as their next mark until Minerva began working for him. She thought they'd choose someone in Virginia Beach.

Barbara rubbed her forehead. Guilt had eaten at her insides like acid all day. She had a screaming headache. It was a good thing she didn't have a date with Andrew.

God, how many people had that family killed?

Andrew was getting on her nerves so badly her stomach cramped just thinking about him. He tried to kiss her once. Eventually she'd have to let him, but she didn't know how she'd tolerate it without throwing up. If she could trick that bunch of thieves any other way, she would.

Barbara stopped for a moment to gaze around the room. It was a lovely place. Cheerful peach walls with white borders and wainscoting. She knew her grandmother owned property here, but Barbara only found out about the retail space after her death. The last lease to this building had ended more than a year ago. Naomi Claxton's sister, Anna, had handled the rentals for her until she'd died in February. Dorsey was waiting until she and Barbara moved to the island to make a decision about renting it again.

Barbara straightened the magazines in the rack, feeling sad at Dorsey's loss and that she never got to enjoy her island again.

She debated whether to drop off the day's earnings in the bank's night deposit box or wait until tomorrow. Tomorrow, she decided, too weary to go tonight. Her back was killing her and her feet were so tired the only thing she wanted was to get naked and slide her whole body into the tub. And she had a meeting to attend in an hour. Maybe she could shower quickly and soak her feet for just a few minutes.

Someone banged on the door and Barbara glanced sharply toward it.

Why would anyone be knocking on her door this time of the night? Thinking it might be the sheriff returning her hat, she eased around the corner.

It was only Andrew. She realized then how much she wanted to see Harper again. But what was Andrew doing here? They didn't have a date.

Barbara groaned and summoned a smile she was far from feeling. "Hi, Andrew. I wasn't expecting you," she said, opening the door. "I have a meeting tonight, remember?"

"Yeah, well, I've run into a little problem. I have a cash-flow situation and wondered if you could make me a little loan."

"I loaned you a hundred dollars a week ago. You spent it already?" She was not giving that sonof-abitch another red cent. The first loan had nearly killed her.

"How long do you expect a hundred bucks to last?" he asked. "I spent that in no time. I'll pay you back when I get some money."

Like never. "I have my own bills to pay and the month has been slow."

"You work from sunup to sundown at this place. You've got to be raking in the money."

"That's none of your business," she said, nudging him toward the door. "It's been a long day and I was on my way home."

"All I'm asking for is a small loan. I've taken you out to dinner. Showed you a couple nice evenings. Woman, you're not cheap, you know. You cost me all the money Daddy gave me last night just to pay for your dinner."

"And I've cooked you a fine meal. But I didn't ask for payment for services rendered." He had some nerve. She opened the door. "It's time for you to leave. Like I said, I have a meeting. Maybe you should consider getting a job."

His brows slammed together. "Listen here. No reason you can't give me that money. You're lucky I'm taking time out for you. Look at yourself. I try to overlook a few extra pounds. Not all men are that generous. Now you get over there and get me some of that money."

She pointed to the opening in the door. "Get out of my shop. Now."

Before she could see what was coming, he slapped her face so hard her head reared back with the impact. She balled her hands into fists.

"Are you crazy?"

"Don't even think of hitting me," he said, leaning close. "I'll whip your tail good for back talking me. You get yourself to that cash register and get me that money. I'll take everything you earned today. Teach you a lesson to get smart with me. Who do you think you are? As a matter of fact, I'll keep the books from now on."

Barbara's eyes widened. Her cheek throbbed and the pain in her head escalated until it pounded with her heartbeat. But the pain didn't touch the rage sizzling through her. Andrew was a damn idiot if he thought she'd let him get away with hitting her. No damn body hit her. *Nobody.*

Barbara breathed deeply. "Just give me a minute. The money's in back," she said with amazing calm.

"Hurry up." He whacked her on the backside.

Fury almost choked Barbara. He definitely needed to be taught a lesson and she was just the one to do it. Tell her she was lucky to have him. And he actually thought she'd let him control her money! A thirty-five-year-old man who couldn't even stand up to his father? Who didn't even work?

Damn it. Her cheek throbbed and her head exploded.

"Hurry up," he shouted.

With quick steps, she made her way to the storage room/kitchen combination. It took her only seconds to find what she needed. "I can't open the drawer. It sticks sometimes in this damp weather," she called out.

"You're about as helpless as they come." Grumbling, he approached her. Barbara moved to the side and got into position. As soon as he poked through the door, she swung the bat and hit him— and heard the bone in his arm crack with the impact.

He howled and she hit him again. Screaming curses, he fell to the floor, rolling and thrashing about.

Barbara stood over him, the bat ready to swing.

"You crazy bitch."

"Shut up," she shouted.

He quieted, his eyes buggy and wide with pain.

"Just a warning for the future. Fat doesn't equate with stupid or helpless."

He groaned.

"Shut up. I'm not finished. You are one sorry excuse for a man. The way I see it, I'm a better catch than you. I can support myself. I don't go begging to you or anybody else for money. You should be grateful I spend time with you. Remember that the next time you take a decent sista out."

She picked up the wall phone.

"If you so much as breathe aloud while I'm on the phone, I'll break your other arm. And you know I will." She dialed 911.

When the dispatcher came on, Barbara inhaled. "Oh, my God. I'm being robbed. Help me, please!"

"Ma'am, tell me who you are and your location."

"Barbara Turner at the beauty salon." She rattled off the address.

"Barbara, are you okay? Are you hurt? This is Shirley." Shirley Langley was one of Barbara's customers.

"Not yet, but I'm scared for my life. He may get up and kill me. Please send help! I don't know what to do."

"Just hold on, honey. Someone will be there soon. Stay on the line with me. Can you get to a safe location?"

"If I move, he may get a gun and try something. Just get somebody here fast."

Andrew started to get up. Barbara gripped the bat and glared at him, daring him to move, daring him to speak. With a moan, his head thumped on the floor.

Harper was getting ready to leave for the Greasy Spoon. When he heard the report of the robbery, he hopped out of his seat so fast, he got dizzy. "What the hell's going on?" he asked the dispatcher. "Is she hurt?"

"She said she isn't, but she's afraid. She keeps a lot of money there, Harper, with all the heads she does."

He had to catch himself. "Anyone at the salon yet?"

"John is on his way."

"So am I," he said, rushing out the door.

He couldn't believe it. On his island, the woman he'd been pining for for months had been robbed. He turned on the siren and burned rubber out of the parking lot. He was only a short distance away, but it might as well have been a hundred miles the way that worst-case scenarios were zinging through his head.

He parked near John's patrol car and slammed out the door, mere footsteps behind John.

Both of them came up short when they spied the squirming man on the floor and Barbara with the bat standing guard over him.

"Ma'am, we'll take it from here," John said.

Barbara lowered the bat and used it for support as she took several steps back. Her gaze met Harper's in a nervous gesture. Suddenly, she got all fluttery.

Andrew managed to stand, but he kept well away from Barbara.

"What happened?" Harper asked.

"He tried to rob me. I was closing up shop when he came by. I thought he just wanted to talk, so I opened the door. But he threatened me and tried to force me to give him today's receipts." Her hands were trembling as she placed one to her chest. She approached Harper with tears glistening in her eyes. "When I refused, he attacked me."

"His arm's broken," John said. "And his shoulder might be dislocated."

"I didn't attack her . . ." Andrew started.

"Call Doc," Harper told John, "and tell her we're bringing him in." Then he focused on Barbara again.

"That crazy bitch," Andrew screamed. "She . . . she broke my arm."

"Shut up," John said.

"I had to protect myself. Look at my cheek. He hit me hard and my face is swollen. And it hurts," Barbara countered.

On closer inspection, her cheek was a little red and puffed. He wanted to knock the hell out of the man for touching Barbara, but Andrew was bawling over his arm.

"I wasn't trying to rob her. I asked for a loan. That's all it was and she made it into a big deal."

"He hit me and told me I had better bring him all the money I made today. Does that sound like asking for loan? If that isn't robbery, I don't know what is," Barbara said, her voice gaining strength. "It wasn't a choice. I work too hard to just give money away like that."

"You damn straight you do," John said.

"She broke my fucking arm!" Andrew screamed.

"I have a right to protect my person and my business. I don't stand on my feet nine hours a day for my money to be taken without my consent," Barbara continued, tears forgotten.

"Mirandize him," Harper told John, and he did.

"Are you saying you didn't hit her?" Harper asked Andrew.

"She was mouthing off at me. Man got a right to put his woman in her place."

"You see? He's got no right to strike me. Look at him. He's taller and stronger than I am. I can't fight a man hand to hand."

"Be quiet. Both of you," Harper said. "We'll take both of your statements. Take him to the clinic, John," Harper said, then peered closely at Barbara's face. "Do you need to go, too?"

"No," she said. "I'll put ice on it when I get home."

He glared at Barbara. "Did he take anything?"

"I stopped him. As soon as I could, I got some protection and used it on him. But he hit me first."

"I just slapped her with my hand. I didn't knock her out. And I didn't break anything."

"You had no business slapping her," John said. "That's assault."

"Will any of his fingerprints be on the money?"

"No, like I said. I stopped him before he could take it."

Harper nodded. "I'll take you to the station and you can charge him for attempted robbery and assault."

"That's not fair," Andrew wailed.

"Think about that next time you try to rob someone," John said.

"I can drive," Barbara told Harper.

Harper quirked an eyebrow. "You sure?" Of course she was sure. She beat the heck out of her boyfriend, didn't she? "I'll just wait outside for you to lock up."

Outside, a couple of spectators had stopped and Harper sent them on their way. He leaned against his car, and waited for Barbara to lock the door and get in her car. His anger simmered as he followed her to the station.

Behind the wheel of her car, Barbara seethed. It couldn't have gone better if she'd planned it. She was reeling Elliot in. She could tell he was very interested in the investments. And now this.

She'd wanted to take the bat and beat the living hell out of Andrew. When she parked in front of the station and got out, Harper caught up with her at the door and took her in back for her statement.

"Okay," he said, "let's start from the beginning."

"I was getting ready to leave because I have a meeting with the Founder's Day committee tonight. Mrs. Claxton put me on it."

"She must have accepted you in the fold, then. That's a real honor," Harper said. "What happened next?"

"Andrew showed up at the door. We didn't have a date tonight, so I didn't understand why he was there." She didn't have to lie. Andrew had admitted to slapping her and he'd attempted to take her money. He'd just failed.

By the time they finished, Elliot had arrived at the station.

"I'm real sorry about this, Barbara," Elliot said with contrition and sympathy. "It never occurred to me he'd do such a thing."

Barbara summoned up tears and let them spill over. "I thought he was a nice young man. It never . . . It was so frightening. You have no idea how stressful the ordeal was."

Elliot patted her hand. "I know. But . . ." He cleared his throat. "If you can find it in yourself not to press charges, I'll see to it he'll never bother you again. Boy's too dumb to know a good thing when he sees it."

Barbara wanted them to arrest Andrew and throw away the key, but she couldn't have him arrested. As much as it went against the grain, she had to let him go. She only hoped he'd learned his lesson, but she knew better. His kind didn't change. Look at his father. What kind of role model did he have?

"You don't think he'll come after me?" she asked Elliot, her eyes wide and feigning fear.

"I'll see to it he doesn't bother you again."

Leave it to a man to screw up a good plan.

Barbara nodded. "Well, in that case . . . if you're sure."

He patted her hand. "I'm sure."

Elliot left and Barbara told Harper she wasn't going to press charges.

"What do you mean not press charges?" he snapped. "This is an attempted robbery and assault." Harper was looking at her strangely, but what could she do? Barbara couldn't afford the publicity. She had to maintain a low profile. And for her plan to work, she had to find a way to stay in Elliot's good graces.

Barbara excused herself to call Naomi to tell her she'd be late for the meeting, but Naomi told her not to come. She'd update her later. Then she went to face Harper and the fallout for her decision not to press charges.

"I just don't understand it," John said. "What if he tries to rob someone else and uses a gun next time?"

"I'm trusting Elliot to control his son. Anyway, he'd get out on bail even if I pressed charges."

"Still . . ."

"There are too many of our men in jail as it is," Barbara defended.

"He committed a crime," John pressed.

"Let it go, John," Harper cut in.

It was apparent John wanted to press the issue further and Barbara couldn't blame him.

"I'm off," he said to Harper with a tired sigh, leaving Harper and Barbara in strained silence.

"Any news on the woman found in the marsh?" Barbara asked.

Harper shook his head. "They'll be doing the autopsy soon, but the DNA results will take longer."

He wanted to pursue her decision further, but a reluctant witness wouldn't make a good witness on the stand. Pick your battles.

"I take it the relationship is off, or do you plan to give Andrew another chance?"

She scoffed. "Are you kidding?"

He leaned back in his chair. He'd caution any other woman, but Barbara wasn't a novice. She was smart and she seemed to have a good reason for not pressing charges.

"You tell me," Harper said. "You refused to press charges—why did you even call me?"

"You know why. And whatever we had has ended."

"Glad to hear that." Harper turned a paperweight in his hand. "The last time we had murders on the island, against my better judgment, I decided to wait to pursue a relationship with you. But I'm not waiting this time."

"Harper, I'm not ready to start a new relationship."

"One thing I've learned is to grab the opportunity when it's presented. I don't intend to let you slip away this time." He stood. "But I understand you've been through an ordeal tonight. We can deal with us another day. I'll see you home."

"That's not neces—"

"For my peace of mind," he said, leading her out the door.

CHAPTER 3

Back home, Barbara took aspirin for her headache, knowing it would only dull the pain. She then took a shower and warmed up some leftover chicken. She was exhausted. She'd had to squeeze in two extra people that day. Everyone was complaining because she now worked only three days one week and four the next. But she just didn't have the time to work five days, nor did she have the inclination to do so.

She looked at herself in the mirror and touched the tender area. Her face was still slightly swollen. She'd probably look like a blow-up clown in the morning. She got a package of frozen peas from the freezer and put it against her jaw. In her bedroom, she stretched out on her bed and watched CNN.

Barbara closed her eyes, grateful it was Saturday. She'd planned to attend church in the morning. She couldn't show up with a swollen jaw.

Harper's words made her uneasy. Now that Andrew was out of the picture, he considered himself in. And she had no intention of dating the local sheriff. He was just too much—too imposing, too demanding, too everything. She couldn't lead him by the nose the way she did Andrew. Couldn't tell him what to do and expect him to follow. That man was like a hound dog with his nose and ears to the ground.

As much as she'd like to sample a relationship with him—Lord knew she'd had all kinds of fantasies about him—she couldn't afford to have him sniffing in her business.

John and Harper attended the autopsy Tuesday morning.

"Do you know the cause of death?" Harper asked.

The pathologist squinted as she examined the body, her demeanor serious. Harper had worked with her several times in the past. He'd even considered asking her out for a date, but was glad he hadn't.

"She has several stab wounds, but the wound in the back pierced the lung and killed her."

"What kind of knife?" Harper asked. Both John and Harper were taking notes even though they would get a report from the medical examiner's office.

"Something sharp, long, and narrow, like an ice pick or a fishing gaff."

"Was she sexually assaulted?" Harper asked.

"No, no recent sexual activity; she wasn't pregnant and she shows no signs of STDs."

So the boyfriend didn't go crazy on her for giving him a sexual disease. The woman didn't earn a mint.

A special contact lens with an identifying mark was stuck to her blouse. The crime lab was doing a search for the owner of the prescription, but it could take a few days.

Harper and John headed back to the island, talking about the case most of the way and how they would proceed.

"Let's question some of the fishermen," Harper said. It was easy enough for someone to pull a small boat into the marsh and dump the body, but he still believed the murderer lived on the island.

Now that enough time had passed that he wouldn't be blamed for the shooting at the outhouse, Trent took the first ferry over from the mainland and drove directly to the house. The key was under the potted plant on the front porch, exactly as the real-estate agent had promised. Who in their right mind would leave a key in such an obvious place? Everyone on the island probably knew about her hiding place. He was going to have to fix some way to make sure nobody got in the house while he was sleeping.

He'd quickly unpacked his gear and put up his exercise equipment. Couldn't afford to get out of shape while he was here.

He was hungry and figured he'd get the lay of the land early on. He headed around the island. It took no more than twenty minutes—and that was due to a tractor moving slower than an old woman. The asshole had waited for a car to approach on the other side of the road to pull to the side and wave Trent around. By the time the car passed, the driver had maneuvered the damn tractor to the center of the road again.

Trent wanted to beat the hell out of the old man. When he'd finally turned off, the old geezer had the nerve to wave and holler, "Have a nice day." It took considerable restraint for him not to flip him off.

There were two—two—places to eat on the entire island. Trent finally stopped at what passed for the heart of the town and found a place that actually had the nerve to call itself the Greasy Spoon. Several vehicles were parked in the gravel parking lot. Across the street seemed to be the town center, with the sheriff's office and the courthouse and administrative offices—a one-floor building with a million steps leading up to the front door.

Trent found a parking space in a free area where he was sure he'd escape dings in his truck. The Greasy Spoon seemed to be the jumping place in the morning. Trent shook his head. He missed D.C. already.

He already knew he'd have to trek all the way to Norfolk to find anything approaching civilization. The last thing he needed was some country bumpkin pulling out his shotgun when he went to bed with one of his daughters. And this looked just like one of those places.

But this wasn't like the fast-food places he usually frequented. He scanned the food on the tables. Although the faire matched its greasy name, the eggs were real and homemade. He ordered two sausage-and-egg biscuits and coffee.

As soon as he opened the door, he heard talk about a robbery. But everyone had stopped talking by the time he made it to the cash register and all eyes were glued on him. The person standing beside him in line actually spoke. Trent glanced around, then realized the man was greeting him. Trent managed a "Good morning" a beat late. The buzz started up again.

The hairdresser's robbery got equal gossip time with the corpse found near Trent's rental house. The crime scene tape was still up near the marsh. He hadn't killed the man who was staying there, so what the hell was going on?

The people here acted as if one robbery and one corpse was big news. Hell, that was nothing compared with the crime in D.C.

Trent paid for his food and snagged a table when four guys got up to leave.

Trent dug into his food and closed his eyes to savor it. Real homemade biscuits, full of flavor and dripping in butter. And the best sausage he'd ever tasted.

He listened intently to the local gossip while he ate. These people didn't mind telling all their business to strangers, either. They were still talking when he finished eating, and he engaged in a conversation with a couple of men who'd gone fishing the previous day. He got himself a second cup of coffee just to stay in the conversation.

"Robberies don't happen here very often. How's somebody gonna get away?" someone said. "No roads outta here." The man cracked up and hit his thigh at his wit. "That's a foreigner for you. Islanders know better." Trent had already gleaned that foreigners included all who were not born on the island. As if islanders were a nation among themselves. And at least they were talking, even to foreigners.

Trent hated when someone messed with his plans. He'd planned to approach Barbara today. He knew her manicurist died a couple of months ago and the position hadn't been filled. But with the robbery fresh in her mind, on top of the corpse found near his place, Barbara wouldn't be willing to hire anyone new, especially a stranger. Correction, foreigner.

But Trent was puzzled. Why would Barbara break her own boyfriend's arm? In the past, they worked their schemes together. He shook his head. None of this made sense. He needed that job so he could get the 411. He scrubbed a hand over his head. He could use a cut.

"Is this Ms. Turner any good at cutting men's hair?" He wanted a cut, but not to look like some country hick.

"Oh, yeah," someone said, nodding. "Or you can go to the barber shop. Barbara's better, though. Got those New York styles. She charges more than the barber shop. You short on money, you go to the barber shop."

"She charges a lot more," another islander grumbled. "Wife 'bout to put me in the poor house."

"You get what you pay for," Trent said, and headed home in his ass-kicking SUV. God, he liked the power behind these machines. Too bad he was on an island and couldn't really let go. Even this baby couldn't roll across the Atlantic.

But when he turned into his driveway, he got nervous. The sheriff's car was parked in his yard. He hadn't done anything illegal here. There weren't any warrants on him—anywhere. Like the guy at the Greasy Spoon said, there was nowhere to run on an island, even when you owned an ass-kicking SUV.

Trent rolled into the driveway and slowly got out of the truck, pocketing his keys and approaching the sheriff. It wasn't so much that the sheriff was big, but he was solid, all lean, not an ounce of fat. He knew he worked out daily. Not many men intimidated Trent, but he wouldn't want to get on the wrong side of this guy.

"Morning, Sheriff. Is there a problem?"

The sheriff unfolded his thick arms. "Just wanted to stop by and welcome you to our island. And to tell you there was some shooting out here a few days ago. A body was found nearby in a marsh."

Trent looked uneasy. "I heard about it at the restaurant this morning. But I didn't know it was near here. Seems like such a peaceful, quiet place, which is the reason I decided to stay here."

"Crime is everywhere."

"That's the truth. Appreciate your stopping by, Sheriff."

"Harper Porterfield," the man said.

"I'm Trent Seaton."

"Where're you from, Trent?"

"D.C." But Trent had the feeling the sheriff already knew that.

"You have any problems, just give us a ring."

"Will do. Thanks again for stopping by."

Trent watched the sheriff reenter his car and pull off. He exhaled a long, slow breath. When you skated around the edge of the law, you didn't feel comfortable about an officer of the law waiting on your doorstep.

Once inside the cabin, Trent changed into sweats and watched the satellite channel while he worked out with his weights. Then he took a long shower and left for the salon. He arrived exactly at ten when Barbara was opening the door.

"Ms. Turner?" he asked.

She eyed him nervously.

"Name's Trent Seaton, ma'am. I was at the Greasy Spoon this morning and folks said if I need a good haircut, you were the one to see. I'm new in town. Be here a few months at least, if not longer."

She eyed him sharply. "I see."

"I was wondering if I can get a cut today."

She glanced at her watch. "Let me take a look at my schedule. I may be able to fit you in if you're not in a hurry."

"I'm not."

Barbara had a tough day ahead of her. She was supposed to be retired. She hadn't meant to work this hard on the island. But once people found out she was from New York, and once customers started bragging about her styles and cuts, they poured in like rain during a monsoon.

"Have a seat," she said once they were inside. She was still a little nervous about this newcomer.

The thermostat was on a timer, so it was already warm inside. The message light on her answering machine was lit and she pressed the button. There were four messages. Her ten o'clock was going to be a half hour late. Was the woman out of her mind? When a customer was late it put her behind all day. That's the other thing. People thought they could just whiz in and out at their convenience, without a thought of inconveniencing other customers.

She felt like kicking all the Stones' butts. She and her grandmother would be on vacation somewhere . . . Barbara stopped her train of thought. She didn't want to break down in tears. But they'd made so many plans. She was reminded of the old salt that if you wanted to make God laugh, make a plan.

Barbara wrote down the numbers of customers who wanted to schedule appointments. She'd call them after she finished cutting Trent's hair.

"I can take you now," Barbara said.

Trent smiled. "Thank you."

"What do you want done?"

"The works. Wash, cut."

They discussed what he wanted while Barbara tied a plastic cape around his beefy shoulders. She led him to the shampoo bowl. He had nice hair. Soft, and since it was short, she washed it quickly.

"How long will you be with us?" she asked.

"Three or four months at least."

"Are you working nearby?" She always engaged her customers in conversation, not that she wanted to know their life's history, but it was hard to work on someone in silence.

"I needed time away. Had some tragedy in my family."

"I'm so sorry." Barbara could understand that. "It's a good thing your job will let you take time off," she said.

"I'm in your line of work, so I can easily find something when I return."

"My line of work?" Barbara asked, frowning.

"I've worked as a shampoo person. Worked in the nail salon doing pedicures and manicures. Do massages, too."

"You have a license for nails and massages?"

"Yes, ma'am. Even brought my massage table along just in case I decide to do a little work while I'm here."

Barbara felt like she was sixty with the man. But how often did you meet young men with manners these days? Somebody had taken the time to teach him some things.

She squeezed conditioner in his hair and thought of her tight schedule. "I have more customers than

I can comfortably handle. From the time I opened the shop I've been overscheduled. I have Sunday through Tuesday off, if that's any consolation, and every other Saturday."

He opened his eyes. They were midnight black. "Let me think about it and get back to you."

"If you decide to work with me, first I have to see what you can do. And I'd like a look at the certificates, and references."

"No problem, ma'am."

"You can call me Barbara. Everyone else does."

"Yes, ma . . . I mean Barbara. If I decide to take the job, when do you want to test me?"

"Tonight will be good. I'll need a pedicure after this day."

"What time?" he asked.

He was actually considering it? "Seven." If she was lucky.

Every time Harper passed Barbara's place there were several cars in the lot. This time there were just two. He took a chance at stopping by.

Two heads were under the dryer and Barbara came to the door that led into a storage and kitchen combination area when the doorbell chimed.

"Afternoon, Sheriff." She wiped her mouth with a napkin.

"Are you eating on the job, Barbara?"

"Trying to squeeze lunch in."

"A little late for lunch, isn't it? What're you having?"

"Just some fried chicken."

"I haven't had lunch either. And that chicken sure does smell good."

"Do you want a leg? I can share the macaroni salad, too."

Harper nearly swallowed his tongue. He'd love to have a feel of Barbara's leg. "You got enough to share?"

Barbara nodded and put a chicken leg on a paper plate along with a dish of the macaroni. "Here you go."

"My hands are dirty." He shoved both hands into his pockets.

"The bathrooms . . ."

"You can feed me. I trust your hands." He took a bite out of the chicken leg she was holding. She had already eaten half of it.

Speechless, Barbara glared at him while he chewed. Incredible.

Harper shook his head. "That's the best fried chicken I've had in years. Woman, you can cook. And I love good food." Harper smacked his lips. "You sure you aren't from the South?"

"I'm sure." He actually stood there waiting for her to feed him. Barbara shook her head, and dished a forkful of macaroni to him.

While he chewed, Barbara peeked out of the room to take a look at her customers. Racine Hammerfield's mother had actually taken the dryer up, her ears cocked and listening. Racine was frowning in the next seat.

"Please lower the dryer hood so your hair can dry," Barbara said. She had customers lined up and she couldn't afford to waste one minute.

Reluctantly, the woman lowered the hood, but both her eyes and her daughter's were glued to Barbara. Ignoring them, Barbara went back into the kitchen, where Harper had eaten his share of the macaroni and was gazing at hers. He'd attacked that chicken leg with his fork.

"Um, um, um, um." Moving a step closer, he invaded her space and she inhaled his woodsy soap scent a second before he slipped a kiss to her cheek. "I don't know. Hard to distinguish which is better, the chicken or you. But I'm betting on you."

Barbara couldn't help but laugh. "You are crazy, absolutely mad."

"Out of my mind for you, baby." His mouth covered hers hungrily and the unexpectedness of it rendered her motionless. He was caressing her mouth more than kissing it, sweeping her in and storming her senses as he teased her. As his overwhelming presence filled her with need and desire—that over the course of time he'd slowly awakened— she responded with abandon that would later surprise her.

Much too soon, he moved back. He swiped a hand across his face, then tilted her chin with his hand, stroking it while she longed for him to kiss her again. "Definitely you."

"What?" Barbara was completely confused. The knowing smile playing at his lips and in his eyes made her want to hit him when her brain cleared enough to realize what he was referring to.

"Don't go mean on me now."

She shifted her gaze and realized her right hand was pressed against his chest. His shirt hung close to his washboard stomach. Suddenly, his presence seemed to soak up all the air and space in the room. What in the world did he want with her?

"Breakfast at the B and B Friday morning?" he asked. "Pick you up at seven-thirty," Harper said, backing away and not giving her an opportunity to refuse. He'd make it to work by nine. He nodded to the ladies under the dryer and held the door for Lisa Claxton, who was arriving.

"The sheriff getting a haircut here now?" Lisa asked. "Lord it's been quite a day."

"He's taking Barbara out for breakfast Friday," Racine's mother said.

Racine looked at Barbara askance. "He's dating you now?"

"Go on, girl," Lisa said, smiling. "The sheriff's quite a catch. He's a nice man, too."

"What's he doing dating you?" Racine asked, looking Barbara up and down as if she was the last woman to catch a man's eye.

Barbara didn't dignify her question with a response.

But Lisa wasn't known for tact or holding her tongue. "What's wrong with him dating Barbara? You think you're the only one who can catch a man? Please." Lisa sank into the chair Barbara gestured to.

Barbara ran her hands through Lisa's hair, feeling an inch of natural root. "You need a touch-up," she said. "Your hair's breaking off because you're waiting too long between touch-ups," she scolded, ending the debate about her dating life.

It was nobody's business. Besides, she wasn't dating Harper, though she couldn't help the dip in her stomach when she thought about that kiss and his very nearness. But from what she'd heard, he'd never been married—and must be set in his ways. He'd be hell to live with.

Of course, feeling that time was passing at lightning speed and she was standing still, out of desperation, she'd married at twenty-nine. It lasted only a year.

Good thing her fiancé had insisted on a prenup. Her career had taken off and so had his, but he didn't know how far ahead of him she'd progressed and was the one to insist upon one. Which had been a good thing for her. Her salary and commission was double his. So when the marriage was over, he came out of it only with what he brought in.

There was nothing about that marriage that made her want to repeat the process. The dates she'd had afterward were even more disastrous. Unwilling to put up with the crap men put her through, she spent her spare time building her career. And by the time she'd hit forty-three, she'd saved enough money to retire. Her grandmother wanted to return to her beloved Paradise Island. She'd left there years ago when she'd married the "love of her life."

Barbara shook her head. She wouldn't deny she was very attracted to Harper and would actually like to date him, but she was too old to believe in that nonsense of ever finding the "love of her life."

She guessed men would think that *she* was too difficult to live with at this point. But men often wanted women to change to suit them, not the other way around.

Barbara had mixed feelings about the breakfast, but Harper had been coming on strong for a while. It wouldn't hurt to spend one morning with him just to test the water.

Harper had brought the State into the investigation to make it easier to move among jurisdictions. As soon as they'd found the body, Harper had contacted the DMV for Sarah Rhodes's address.

They'd gotten a warrant to check her apartment in Norfolk, and he met the officer from the state police there after his brief lunch with Barbara.

The apartment had a closed-in smell, but it was neat and the inexpensive furniture was fairly new. Located in an upscale area, Harper wondered how she could afford the two-bedroom apartment on a companion's salary.

The policeman and he covered their shoes with bootees and tugged on gloves before they crossed the threshold.

"Nice digs," the younger man said. "Wish I could afford a pad like this."

Harper frowned. It reminded him of a hotel room rather than a home.

The living room was small but freshly painted, and with the new furniture, carefully placed knick-knacks and magazines on the tables, it resembled a showroom. The kitchen was tucked into a corner to the left as they entered. All the appliances were new, although dust covered the surfaces. No dishes were in the sink, but a few were scrubbed of food and stacked in the dishwasher.

Harper hit the button for the answering machine. It was full of messages. He jotted down names and numbers as he listened. He played back the last number she dialed. It was to an islander. Robert Freelander.

The younger officer opened the fridge. It stank from month-old milk and meats. He quickly shut the door.

Her bedroom was just as neat as the rest of the apartment. Even the closet, filled with bargain finds, was neat, everything stacked up in precise piles or perfectly hung. Did people really live like that?

Harper wondered, thinking of his trousers and shirt lying across the chair in his bedroom.

Did she have a compulsive disorder? Who was this mysterious Sarah Rhodes?

"Sarah, are you back?"

Harper opened the door to a white woman with light brown hair. She had a deep tan, as if she'd just come from a Bahamas vacation. "May I help you?" Harper asked.

"I thought I heard movement in Sarah's apartment. Is she here?" she asked, trying to glance around Harper.

Harper extended a hand. "Sheriff Harper Porterfield," he said. "And you are?"

"Kristin Howard."

"Did you know Sarah well?"

"Nobody knew her well, but I knew her better than most. Why? Is something wrong?"

"I'm sorry, but Sarah's dead."

Kristin dropped her packages and Harper steadied her. "How? What happened?"

"Could you give me a few minutes? I'd like to ask you a few questions when we finish in here."

She pointed to a door across the hall. "Just come on over. I'll be there."

Harper bent to retrieve her packages. With trembling hands, Kristin took them from him and staggered across the hall.

"Are you going to be okay?" he asked.

She gave a jerky nod and twisted the key in the lock.

Back in the apartment, Harper thumbed through a thin photo album and perused the few pictures there. A few group pictures. One of Sarah at each age. Just a scant few more.

A couple of pictures were on the dresser tops. But

there was nothing to tell him who Sarah Rhodes really was. He took her small address book, added the most recent photo of her, and went to talk to Kristin.

Kristin dabbed her eyes with a tissue.

"What happened to Sarah?" she asked.

"Unfortunately, she was found in the marsh on Paradise Island."

"That's where she worked. She'd talked about visiting friends in Atlanta. I thought maybe she went there when I didn't see her for a couple weeks and then I left for a vacation. I'm just returning from Costa Rica."

"How long has she lived here?"

"Almost a year. She grew up in foster care, moving from home to home."

Her lips quivered. "She was so proud of this apartment. She invited me over to tea sometimes. Her place was the cleanest place I've ever been in. She was just so thrilled to have her own place, and she took very good care of it."

Kristin's place, while not unkempt, looked more lived-in. Wasn't quite so . . . perfect.

"Did she mention friends on Paradise Island or here?" Harper asked.

"She had more friends on the island than here. She often returned late from work. Never hung out too much. Her employer was more a grandfather figure to her. That meant a lot. Especially for someone without family. I think he helped her with the rent," she said. "What's being done about her burial?"

"We're trying to locate family."

"If you can't, please let me know. I'll see to it." She handed Harper a business card.

"If you think of anything, please call me," Harper said, extending his own business card to her.

As Harper returned to Sarah's sterile home, he couldn't help comparing his life with Sarah's. One who lived on the outside looking in. He felt a kinship. He had friends, he had family who lived far away. But his work was his life. And for some reason, lately he'd begun to feel hollow inside.

He didn't want to be one of those lost souls without a purpose when he retired, without someone to share life with, to brighten the days.

And then there was Barbara. He smiled. Already she had begun to fill the emptiness.

Trent arrived at Barbara's place and asked if it was okay to begin the evening's cleaning. Barbara was glad to comply. She pointed out the location of the cleaning supplies while she finished up her last customer. Ten minutes later, the customer left.

The man was punctual and didn't need to be directed. Two points in his favor.

"You can do the manicure and pedicure, but I don't feel like curling my hair tonight."

"I can do it all," Trent said. "I don't have a beautician's license, but I do my mother's all the time. I can blow-dry your hair and curl it in the style you have now."

"You sure?" She would like to have a new hairdo for her date with Harper—correction, breakfast. This wasn't a traditional date.

"Yes, ma'am . . . I mean Barbara."

Barbara showed him where she stored the shampoo, conditioners, and hair coloring, and told him about the supplies and general information about the shop.

Barbara closed her eyes after she was settled over the shampoo bowl. Warm water showered through her hair. He squirted shampoo on his hand and rubbed it on her hair. Barbara stifled a moan. As his strong fingers massaged her scalp, she thought she'd died and gone to heaven. The women were going to love this.

With a shampoo person like Trent, she could do more heads. It would seem curious if she continued to turn customers down.

He blow-dried and curled her hair like a professional.

At the manicure station, Barbara's mind wandered back to Vicky Michaels, who had worked there until she died. The station had not been used since her death over Labor Day weekend. Loss and nostalgia hit Barbara, but Trent began to talk until she calmed down. In no time, he'd painted her nails and she was sitting back in the pedicure chair with her feet soaking.

They talked about some of the places he'd worked as he ministered to her feet.

And then he was massaging her feet and lower legs. Have mercy. He had magical hands. Barbara closed her eyes to enjoy.

"What the hell!"

Barbara jumped. Her eyes snapped open and her feet fell into the foot tub with a splash.

"What's he doing feeling your legs?" Harper asked.

Trent had jumped, too. He let out a long breath. He was no longer massaging her legs. "Evening, Sheriff."

"Harper, you scared the shit out of me," Barbara scolded, clutching a hand to her chest.

"What's he doing feeling up your legs?" Harper was steamed. As long as he'd fantasized about caressing Barbara, not just her legs, but all over, and another young man had his hands up her leg . . . he saw red.

"You can continue, Trent," Barbara said, but Trent didn't move.

Barbara sighed. "I'm hiring Trent to help in the shop. Not that I need to explain, but he's giving me a pedicure," she said patiently. But the way her eyes were sparkling at him, he could tell she did not like explaining herself.

"He feels your legs like that during a pedicure?"

"He's not *feeling* my legs, he's massaging them. And so did Vicky when she gave pedicures."

"Well, you already know his skills. He doesn't need to be feeling you up anymore."

"Yes, sir," Trent said.

Barbara rolled her eyes. "He's not feel . . . What are you doing here?"

"I saw your lights on and your car outside. You don't usually work this late. Of course I was concerned."

"Thank you, but I'm okay." Trent was beginning to pack up his things. "What do you think you're doing?"

"I thought . . ."

"You haven't finished my pedicure. I don't see any polish on my toenails."

"Barbara . . ." Harper started.

"This is business and you will not interfere." They weren't even dating and he was becoming possessive already? This didn't bode well for the future.

He looked as if he wanted to argue. Barbara could tell by the play of muscles on his face, but with the look on *her* face, he obviously changed his mind.

"I'll wait and see you to your car." Harper pulled a chair where he had a clear view, much too close to Trent. The poor guy was nervous. Barbara could have whopped Harper upside the head for being so ridiculous.

"You know, Trent can see me to the car."

"I'm off duty," Harper said. "Got nothing but time on my hands." Sure he did. With a murder on the island, he had nothing to do? Barbara elected not to call him on it.

"If you have to stay, give Trent room to breathe," Barbara snapped. When Harper didn't move, she said, "Move your chair three feet to the side. He has to be able to move. I want a proper pedicure."

Trent wiped the cream off Barbara's legs, smoothed lotion on them, and got to work completing her pedicure.

Harper sat right there, in the way, because he'd scooted his chair back no more than a couple of inches.

Trent quickly painted her toenails and slid sandals on her feet. He switched the heat lamp off without suggesting she put her feet under it to speed the drying process. He really was nervous about Harper.

When Trent was finished, Barbara said, "You can start working Wednesday next week."

"Yes, ma'am."

Trent helped her clean up and the three of them left.

"You headed home?" Harper asked as he walked her to her car.

"First I'm going to stop by the night deposit box

at the bank." Trent had already left. "Harper, don't interfere with my work again."

"I wasn't. . . ."

"Yes, you were. I wouldn't dare interfere with your police investigations, and I'm not having you meddling in my work, either."

"Can you blame me?" he asked defensively and full of outrage. The coat he wore made him look even larger and the frown was enough to send a lesser woman scurrying. But Barbara had spent a career working with men with overblown egos. She wasn't easily intimidated.

"I know how you like young men."

Barbara gaped at him, incredulous. "Trent's in his twenties, for God's sake."

"And how old is Andrew? He might be in his thirties, but he has the mindset of a teenager."

"Andrew isn't twenty years younger than me."

"At least ten years younger."

"This is ludicrous. I can't believe I'm discussing age with you. Especially when men date women twenty, thirty years younger. I'm through with this ridiculous conversation. I'm having second thoughts about even having breakfast with you." Barbara unlocked her car door with the remote. Springing tight with anger, Harper opened her door and she slid into her seat. He marched to his own county-issued sedan.

Barbara was seriously considering canceling the breakfast. She wasn't going to let him snoop into her life or dictate what she could or couldn't do.

And then it hit her. *He's jealous.* Her mouth curved into an unconscious smile. *Unbelievable.*

* * *

True to his word, Harper saw Barbara home. He parked behind her car. She expected him to get out and come inside, but he didn't. As soon as she closed the door behind her, he backed out of the driveway. Through the window, she'd watched his taillights as they disappeared down the road.

In her bedroom, Barbara rummaged in the closet for a long, comfortable knit dress she often wore at home, then went to the kitchen. She chose leftover steak and prepared a salad.

After she showered, she noticed a message on her answering machine. Liane had returned her call.

"Any more robberies?" Liane asked. Barbara had told her about it the night before.

"I am so angry with myself. I should have just loaned him the money. If my plans had worked out, I would have gotten it all back."

"Your temper always gets the best of you, especially when you're tired. It's a wonder he only got a broken arm when he hit you."

"I was thinking about poor Sarah Rhodes. That Elliot killed her so that Minerva could take her job. I just lost it. And on top of that, Andrew had the nerve to whack me on my backside."

"The corpse isn't necessarily that young woman."

"Yes, it is. It was on the news."

"Do you have a contingency plan?" Liane asked.

"Elliot has been staying rather close to home. I'm still walking every day near Lambert's house. Minerva's advances are getting more forward. She's all touchy-feely. She rubs Lambert's arm or hand when she talks to him—always seated close beside him. Feeling his thigh. They kissed this morning."

It just sickened Barbara that people with no heart would take advantage of the elderly, especially ones without family close by to care for them. It was a form of elder abuse.

Barbara gave Liane the address. "Think you can find out something about him? See if he has family."

"I'll do my best. What do you plan to do with the information?" she asked.

"I'll contact his relatives and let them know what's going on. I just might have to go to the authorities, but just like in Philly, they can't make an arrest until they can prove something, or suspect Minerva or Elliot actually committed a crime. Proving it is very difficult. And they have a way of disappearing before the authorities get to them. I want to get that money."

"You don't need it."

"Not for me, but for others they've scammed. Most of those women were left destitute. If they've scammed five people in the last couple of years, think of the number of lives they've destroyed. Somebody has to put a stop to it."

"Okay. I'll get back to you as soon as I find some information."

"I thought I'd be back in New York by Thanksgiving, Christmas at the latest. And now . . ."

"Maybe I'll spend Thanksgiving with you."

"Oh, Liane, thanks. I have plenty of space."

When Trent left the salon, he went to the bar and ordered a whiskey neat. The last thing he needed was some country sheriff getting up in his face over his girlfriend. The old man didn't have to worry. Trent wasn't attracted to Barbara. He was using her.

A woman sidled up next to him. She was smaller than Barbara, but not by much.

"Hey," she said, and ordered herself a martini.

Trent started to ignore her, but he should be polite to the locals. He nodded.

"This is one dry place," she said. "You're new here."

"Just got here," Trent said. "How about you?"

"Been here a while. All the action's in Norfolk, but can't go there every night."

Trent chuckled.

"My name's Sonya." She extended a hand.

"Trent." Trent took hers in his for a brief shake.

"Well, hi, Trent. Nice name."

She wasn't Trent's type, and the conversation wasn't exactly enlivening, but he settled back to enjoy a few minutes with her anyway. If the sheriff thought he was interested in someone else, then he'd leave him alone about Barbara.

Sonya Davies stayed long enough for Trent to pay for a couple of her drinks before she left. She was sick of staying in her room. Her housemate was helping someone fashion a bowl, a replica of the pre-1600s. Why, Sonya didn't know. They were always doing something strange.

Boyd should be getting off the ferry soon. She bid Trent good-bye and went outside to call Boyd.

Boyd Xavier was a good cover. She liked this island. The artist colony was isolated with new artists coming and going all the time. The islanders didn't pay much attention to them. The workers at the colony didn't ask a whole lot of questions if you were talented, and Sonya was talented.

She introduced Boyd as her husband. She didn't have to worry about Elliot hearing about a Sonya. She was supposed to be in the Bahamas. They were fools if they thought she was going to let them get away with keeping all the money and live on the piddling Elliot dolled out. She'd told Elliot about Dorsey, and what did he give her? Another job in the Bahamas. And he expected her to bring him the money from that, too.

Did she look like Andrew? Did she look like some woman he could lead around by the nose? She already had the money, and she wasn't turning over shit to him. It wasn't nearly as much as he'd gotten from Dorsey. But she was going to remedy that.

CHAPTER 4

Harper picked Barbara up a few minutes before seven-thirty. He was captivated by her purposeful stride. She moved as if her life was full of meaning and she meant to get every drop of satisfaction out of it. When she passed him on the way to the car, he caught a whiff of delicate perfume and inhaled a deep breath of pleasure.

What a fine note to start the morning on.

He got her door, making sure to move close for another whiff, but she whisked herself inside and closed the door quickly, nearly catching his fingers. He strolled around to the other side and slid in beside her. He was finally going out on a date with her.

"I wish I could spend the day with you, but I have to go in to work," Harper said.

"I understand that."

Harper nodded. "So what will you do for the rest of the day?"

Barbara sighed. "I missed the Founder's Day meeting, so Mrs. Claxton volunteered me for research on the Rochester family. I have the dubious task of gathering information for the celebration in May. I wish I had my bat and Andrew before me now. I'd break his other arm. That lady must have it in for me."

"She's accepted you," Harper said around a grin. It was good to know he wasn't the only person who irritated her. "She wouldn't put you in charge of things if she felt you weren't capable."

Barbara groaned.

"You could always tell her you're too busy," Harper said, knowing very well nobody turned down Naomi Claxton's requests.

"Why are we just sitting here?"

"You haven't buckled your seatbelt. And I'm enjoying your company."

Barbara made a production of buckling in, and he started the engine and drove slowly to the B&B. The place was packed. They were lucky enough to grab a table as a group was leaving.

The B&B's owner, Gabrielle Long Price, Naomi Claxton's granddaughter, approached them with menus. She'd taken over the management of the B&B when her great aunt, Anna, couldn't run it any longer. In the end, Anna had left it to her when she died. "Can I get you coffee?" she asked.

"Do you serve mocha?" Barbara asked.

"After a fashion. If you don't like our blend, I'll fix something else. Topped with whipped cream?"

"You're killing me, but, yes, thank you."

"Make that two," Harper said. "Bring a couple of juices with it. Orange okay with you, Barbara?"

"Sure."

When Gabrielle left their table to take orders from other customers, Barbara and Harper scanned the menu. "See anything you like?" Harper asked her.

"It's been a while since I've eaten here. But I remember everything being delicious."

"The omelets are great. Maybe some French toast or pancakes to go with it. They serve it with maple syrup and whipped cream."

Barbara was trying to be good, but Harper wasn't making it easy.

When Gabrielle returned with their drinks, they gave their orders. Harper leaned back in his seat, surveying the faces around them. Many were familiar, some were strangers. He spotted Trent. The murder occurred long before he arrived or Harper would have questioned him.

He'd already interviewed Lambert Hughes, but he wanted to interview the older man again without the presence of his new housekeeper. Harper sighed. He was going to give himself an hour to spend with Barbara before he returned to work mode.

She was pretty in her black slacks and vivid green top. She wore just a little makeup, but it looked just right, not overdone. She sipped her mocha and wiped the whipped cream mustache away.

"Good?" Harper asked.

"Perfect."

He was glad she wasn't one of those women who nagged him about being afraid to eat for fear of gaining an ounce or munched on salads when they went to dinner. He enjoyed food and preferred a wide-ranging conversation, rather than one that dealt with her gaining ten pounds by just inhaling the scent of a cinnamon roll.

"So tell me about yourself, Barbara? Why did you settle in our town?"

"My grandmother wanted to move back here.

She even had the house renovated," she said. "Unfortunately, just before she was ready to move, she died. I visited the island and fell in love with it." When lying, stay as closely to the truth as possible, she thought.

"Where're you from?" he asked.

"Manhattan."

"Nobody's from Manhattan."

"I am."

Harper leaned forward, took her hand in his. "Now, why is it I believe you've left out a lot in this abridged version?"

She shrugged. "I haven't. I'm rather plain and uncomplicated."

Harper rubbed the back of her hand. "There's nothing uncomplicated about you."

"Tell me about yourself," Barbara said, wanting to shift the focus.

"My father was career Navy. His last tour was Norfolk. I graduated from high school here, got a football scholarship and messed up my knee. I finished college, worked in the Baltimore PD for a while, and became a detective before I returned here to run for sheriff."

"I have a feeling you've left out a lot in that abridged version. So where are your parents?"

"They retired to North Carolina. Raleigh. They both grew up there."

"Any siblings?"

"A brother and a sister. Both live near my parents."

"Any nieces or nephews?" Barbara sipped her mocha. It was fabulous.

"Two of each. You?"

"I'm an only child. And I have no children. You have to try this. It's fabulous."

He sipped his mocha and pronounced it delicious. "Ever been married?"

"It didn't last long," she muttered, annoyed with all the questions. "You like getting the facts up front, don't you? I feel like I'm in an interrogation room."

An easy smile played at the corner of his mouth. "Do you have anything to hide?"

Barbara regarded him with amusement. Going out with Harper was absolutely foolish. She reached over and stroked his hand. "I'm sure you have your ways of convincing me to divulge all my secrets."

Harper inhaled a quick breath before his hand came down on hers purposefully. Kissing the back of it, his gaze never left her eyes. It was a slow, lingering kiss, and she felt his tongue stroke her just before he let her go, forcing her to admit how much she wanted him. Was he that slow and thorough in lovemaking?

"There are some secrets worth exploring," he said softly, his voice stroking her in the middle of the crowded dining room. She shivered as goose bumps sprinkled her arms. Nervously, she ran her hand through her hair.

"Ha . . . Have you ever married, Harper?" God, he was turning her into a babbling idiot. An easy smile played at the corner of his mouth. He knew very well the effect he was having on her.

"Once, when I lived in Baltimore. It lasted about two years."

"So you're pretty much set in your ways by now."

Harper smiled. "Don't worry. I'm adaptable," he said. "And house broken, too."

A waiter appeared with their food, giving Barbara a chance to catch her breath. She ordered the ham-and-cheese omelet with a blueberry muffin and fresh fruit.

Harper ordered the French toast and omelet. He poured syrup on his French toast and topped it with the whipped cream. He cut a piece and held the fork out to Barbara. "Try this."

Barbara closed her mouth around the food. "Oh my gosh. I've died and gone to heaven."

"Told you it was good."

She glanced around. Many townspeople were here, but visitors were present, too. They more than likely stayed at the B&B. One slim woman across from her was dressed in tight designer jeans and a sweater. She was eating fruit and drinking a glass of bottled water. Sometimes Barbara wished she could be satisfied with a meager meal, but she'd long ago stopped beating herself up for lack of control.

"Why aren't you eating?" Harper asked.

She picked up her fork. "I'm eating."

He glanced over his shoulder. "Don't let that skinny woman ruin your appetite. I'm going to enjoy my food. Every mouthful."

Barbara realized she was being silly. She was acting like those stupid commercials. Everyone wasn't the same. Wasn't built the same. Americans were going crazy with weight. Sure there were health issues. Bulimia and anorexia were eating disorders, too, weren't they? But the tube wasn't filled with commercials exploiting those issues.

People had issues in all sizes. Women more so than men. They spent too much time worrying if their butts were too big or too small. Plastic surgeons were making a mint with breast implants, tummy and thigh tucks, eye lid and chin tucks. Whether we liked it or not, we were all going to get old if we were blessed to live long enough, and pressing out all the wrinkles wasn't going to change that.

Barbara always exercised and tried not to overeat—too much. But she could damn near starve herself and still wouldn't be a Paris Hilton or Beyoncé look-alike. And she didn't hate herself. Those women were the worst. *Ooh, my thighs are too big. I hate myself.* So she was going to stop acting stupid. She began to eat and enjoy her food.

"How are you progressing on Sarah's murder investigation?" she asked. "Can you talk about it?"

"We're working a few angles," he said, his face tightening. "You mind if we don't talk about the case? I want to enjoy some time with you before I go to work. All of us have to work overtime on this case and the budget is tight."

"I understand," Barbara said.

She liked him. From their past encounters, she knew he cared about his job. He wasn't just putting in time until retirement.

She wished she could divulge the information she knew, but they had nothing on the Stones. He'd indulge her but wouldn't take her seriously, no more than the Philly police had done.

Besides, one breakfast didn't entitle him to her life's history or alleviate her caution of men. What did she really know about him? Not nearly enough to trust him with her secrets. And she couldn't tell him about her plans to rob the thieves. Even if he took her seriously, she'd get thrown into jail for robbery while they moved on to their next victim.

He leaned close to feed her another forkful of French toast, and the sweet taste of the food mingled with the subtle scent of his woodsy cologne. He was a handsome man.

And he didn't seem to mind living in a fishbowl. Many eyes were watching their movements. To heck with it. Barbara fed him some of her omelet and he smiled. He had a nice smile. Barbara was glad she came to breakfast with him.

They discussed current events, everything from how Obama was doing to Condoleezza Rice. When they were halfway through breakfast, Harper's cell phone rang.

"Not now," he said as he retrieved it from his pocket and answered it. Barbara watched him closely as he listened intently. When he disconnected, he said, "I'm sorry, babe, but I've got to go." He dug into his pocket for his wallet. "I'm going to leave enough for you to get a cab home."

"Don't worry about it. I can get home. And I'll take care of the bill. Just go."

"One of the problems with dating a sheriff in a small town. I'm never completely off duty." He wiped his mouth and stood. "But I invited you to breakfast and I'll pay for it."

"We'll be happy to drop her off," Lisa said from behind Barbara.

"Thanks." Harper tossed bills on the table; then he kissed Barbara, startling her and probably everybody else in the room, before he strolled out with long, quick steps. Barbara watched him leave. Lord, that man knew how to make the most of a few seconds.

She wondered what was so urgent.

"Mind if we join you?" Lisa asked. "It's pretty busy in here." People were standing around waiting to be seated. Lisa was here with her sister, Vanetta.

"I don't mind at all," Barbara said. "How are you, Vanetta?"

"I'm fine." Vanetta's husband had been murdered on Labor Day weekend along with the manicurist who'd worked in Barbara's shop.

"I didn't expect this place to be so busy this weekend," Lisa said. "We had a small convention all week. Some important people from a corporation up north. Some of their families are joining them today and they're staying over for the weekend."

"It is a nice little vacation spot," Barbara agreed.

"Did Harper mention anything about Sarah Rhodes?" Lisa asked.

"Not yet."

"Does he have any ideas who did it?"

"I don't know. What have you heard?" Barbara asked to steer the conversation away from Harper.

"Not much."

Barbara noticed Vanetta was agitated. The pain of her husband's murder was still fresh.

Instead of her usual ponytail, Lisa wore her hair down around her shoulders for a change. "You've got the day off?" she asked. Lisa was one of the cleaning women at the B&B.

"Thank God."

"I've been trying to convince Lisa to start her own cleaning service," Vanetta said.

Lisa groaned and glanced toward the ceiling. "Don't start that again. I don't have a head for business, much less the money."

"I could teach you what you need to know. And I have the money to back you," Vanetta said. "I'd like to help you, Lisa."

"I can't start out owing money. I'll always be playing catch-up. If I decide to take that step, I want to do it on my own."

"Lisa, what do I have to spend money on? If nothing

else, Matthew left me very well off. The house is paid for. I get an income from the businesses."

"Usually our greatest limitation is our own fear," Barbara offered. "Good cleaning services are always in need. Why don't you write up a business plan, even if you don't actually go through with it? It will give you some idea of what you'd be getting into. Start with cost of supplies and getting bonded, things like that. How would you train your cleaning staff? Where would you set up shop? How would you get the word to customers?"

"Oh, my God." Lisa's eyes had gone wider with each question.

"It's what you would have to do with any business. At least a business plan will tell you if it's feasible. All that will cost you is time," Barbara said.

Vanetta seemed to come out of her trance and reached over to touch her sister's hand. "I can help you with that," she said.

"I'd hire you, Lisa, and I'd like to have someone once a week to give the shop a thorough cleaning."

"You see," Vanetta said with a smug look. "You'll have more customers than you even thought about."

"Maybe after I find Grandma's golden bowl."

"Golden bowl?" Barbara asked. Dorsey had mentioned something about a golden bowl, but Barbara had forgotten about that.

"It's lost. Jordan has a list of suspects. I'm going to find out who they are and search for it."

"You better leave that to Alyssa," Vanetta said. "Our ancestor acquired the bowl in the early sixteen hundreds, and now it's lost," she explained to Barbara.

"How long has it been lost?"

"I have no idea. Our Aunt Anna kept it. She died

in February, and when Grandma searched for it, it was missing."

Anna had died in February, before the Stones stole Dorsey's money. Maybe they didn't have it yet.

Harper drove directly to the Stones' home. Someone had broken in. They lived next door to Naomi Claxton.

Naomi stood in the yard with a knit hat pulled over her hair. Lumps underneath outlined her hair rollers. Alyssa often said her grandmother began her day later than she used to. She was in her 80s, so she deserved to take as much time as she needed.

John was already on the scene and talking to the Stones as Harper approached Naomi.

"I offered for them to come to my house to get out of the cold, but they certainly are an unfriendly lot," Naomi said, nodding toward the Stones. "They aren't as friendly as Wanda was. God rest her soul. Wanda Fisher was a wonderful woman."

Harper reserved judgment on Naomi's opinion and elected not to comment. "Nice" Wanda Fisher had chopped up her husband to fit in the chest freezer. Naomi and her granddaughter, Gabrielle, had found him there after Wanda had died of a heart attack and Naomi went looking for pies she had given her.

Naomi had been arranging a wake for Wanda. She was famous for her pies. Earlier in the month she had given Wanda several of them and Wanda hadn't had an opportunity to eat them before she passed away. Wanda's relatives didn't live in the area and had refused to give her a memorial service.

Naomi was so upset over her friend's death and knew her friend wouldn't mind her using them. She went to Wanda's house to retrieve them. The pies were sitting on top of Harvey Fisher's frozen corpse. Of course, Naomi had commented that he hadn't been a nice man, as if that was any excuse.

"Mrs. Claxton, have you seen anything unusual in the area lately?" Harper asked her. "Anything out of place?"

"I try to mind my business," she said. "I just got back from a cruise, you know. It was a gift from my grandchildren."

Harper tried not to smile. "Yes, I know. Did you and your husband enjoy your vacation?"

"Oh, yes. There was so much food. And the Bahamas was so warm and nice. One of my grandsons arranged a guided tour for us. He goes to college with a friend from there. The boy's father works for a tour company."

"I bet that was nice." Harper considered that maybe he should take Barbara on a cruise if things ever calmed down. For a small town, they were having a record crime spree. This year alone, they'd had more homicides than in the last twenty years.

After John finished talking to the Stones, Harper started in while John interviewed the neighbors.

"Has anything unusual occurred recently?" he asked.

"No," Elliot Stone said. "We told your detective that."

"I bet it was Barbara getting revenge," Andrew said. "She did it."

"Her whereabouts are accounted for," Harper assured them. She was with him.

"She's got money. She could've paid someone to do this," Andrew insisted.

"Shut up, Andrew. It wasn't Barbara. Why would she break in here? Can you see her trying to climb in that window?" Elliot plucked Andrew's head. "Think, boy."

"We'll look into that. In the meantime, do you have any enemies?"

They glanced at each other.

"None," Elliot said. "We must have come back in the nick of time. They didn't get a chance to steal anything."

"So you're saying they broke in and stole nothing at all?" Harper reiterated.

"It's the damnest thing," Elliot murmured. "I can't figure it out." But Harper didn't believe him. Elliot was very upset even though he tried to conceal it.

"We're going to lift prints."

"They didn't get inside, Sheriff. And any thief with a lick of sense wouldn't leave prints behind. All you'll find is ours. They got as far as the kitchen window. That's it."

Why don't they want their prints taken? Harper wondered.

"It's procedure. And an insurance matter. I'm sure the owner would want prints taken, at least at the point of entry."

"Suit yourself," Elliot said.

Harper approached John. "I'm going to let you all tie this up." He left him with instructions to get some of the prints from inside the house, too.

John glanced up from his pad. "With everything going on, are you still having the teen meeting this afternoon or do you want to reschedule?"

"It's the one thing we have to do."

John nodded and Harper started to his car. What disturbed him most was the number of second- and third-generation families tangled up in the criminal justice system. He used any excuse to get their teens in his program, not to harass them, but to try to steer them in a different direction. All the teens, boys and girls, were in after-school activities. He had monthly talks with each of them individually to discuss school, grades, home, any problems they needed to discuss. His door was always open, not that they actually brought their problems to him, but hopefully it would make a difference.

It was one of the reasons he preferred a smaller town versus a large city. Here, he felt he could make a difference. He couldn't give individual attention in a larger area.

He didn't reach everyone, but his record was good, and he felt a sense of accomplishment. He was very proud when he took one student shopping in August for his college wardrobe and saw him off to Hampton.

As he backed out of the driveway, he focused on the Stones. What was it about these people that made him uneasy? They were here when Sarah went missing. But there was no connection between them. It was a stretch to think the two could be connected, especially since Sarah was ten years younger than Andrew and the Stones' name was never mentioned during the investigation.

He checked his watch and headed to Lambert Hughes's place. Minerva was home and he could talk to Hughes without her input.

Barbara should be home by now. He'd like to spend more time with her, but it wasn't feasible.

As he passed her house, he noticed her car in the carport, but he couldn't tell if she was there.

Another two miles and he stopped in Lambert Hughes's yard with its well-kept white Cape Cod with green trim. For years it had been neglected. When Hughes bought it, he'd restored it to its former beauty.

"Mr. Lambert? Sheriff Harper Porterfield." Harper rang the doorbell three times before it was answered.

"I know who you are." He opened the door wide. The man looked sad. He still wore his robe and hadn't shaved. Maybe Minerva did all that.

"I want to ask you a few questions about Sarah Rhodes. Do you have time?"

Lambert stepped back. "Come on in."

They settled in the living room.

Lambert's café au lait complexion was a shade darker with age.

"How are things working out with your new helper?"

The older man's eyes lit up. "Minerva's very good. She never misses a day. Even calls on the weekend to make sure I'm okay. And I never have to remind her to do things. I'm lucky to have her."

"Very good. I'd like to talk about Sarah."

"She was a nice girl. A little young and sometimes scatterbrained, but a nice person."

Harper took out a notepad and pen, and began to make notes. "Did she report to work regularly?"

"For the most part. Not as stable as Minerva, but she kept the place clean, cooked my food, did all my shopping. I'm so sorry she was killed. She was so young. Do you know what happened?"

"Not yet. Did she talk about people she socialized with?"

"Not really. She talked a lot on her cell phone, though. I didn't listen in. Young folks are always yakking about something. I'm military. We had to work. Couldn't talk on the phone all day."

"I understand," Harper commiserated. "Do you remember what she was wearing the last time you saw her?"

"I wrote it down when she didn't show up and I couldn't reach her. I found the notes last night." He went to retrieve them.

What Harper couldn't figure out was why she was found away from the ferry instead of toward it. Even the bar and the fast-food places were toward the ferry.

Hughes returned. "One thing I learned was to record the details. She wore blue jeans and a red blouse that buttoned down the front." He told Harper about the last day she worked for him.

"Did she work all day?"

"Yes, she left at four-thirty." He folded his notes and placed them on the coffee table in front of him. "Oh, and I forgot to mention that Sarah told me someone ran her off the road on her way to work. She couldn't catch a ride that morning and she walked. She fell into the ditch. It rained that day and her shoes got muddy. She was some kind of angry. Good thing she wore tennis shoes. She put them in the washer."

Harper frowned. "Did she know this person and could she describe the car?"

"Only that it was dark. It was real foggy that morning and hard to see."

"Did she show up for work the next day?"

Lambert shook his head. "No, that was the last time I saw her."

"Did you help pay her rent?" Harper asked.

"She couldn't afford a nice place. Had no family. I wanted to help her."

"Did you loan her money any other time?"

"The day she went missing."

"How much?"

"Five grand to buy a car."

"Five thousand?" Harper asked, his pen stalled over the pad.

"She needed a new car. Always catching rides. It was dangerous. And I needed her to take me to play golf and do my grocery shopping. She didn't have family to help her out."

"What was she going to buy?"

"Someone at the base was going to sell her a Camry. He was getting shipped out for the next few months and planned to buy a new car when he returned. He was going to deliver it to her apartment the next day, but she wasn't there."

This put an entirely new spin on the thing. Robbery moved to the top of the list.

Lambert looked at his hand. "I feel guilty. I thought she'd taken the money and ran off."

"Why didn't you give her a check?"

"She didn't have a bank account. I always paid her in cash."

"Let me make sure I got this right. You gave her the money the day she disappeared."

Hughes nodded. "That very afternoon."

"Thank you for your time," Harper said, pulling out a business card. "If you think of anything, even if it seems minor, please call."

Lambert looked at the card and put it with the

paper he'd written the other information on as Harper left.

The bartender hadn't returned from his vacation the last time Harper tried to reach him. It was time for him to try again. And to interview the people who gave Sarah rides.

As Harper neared Barbara's place, he debated stopping for a few minutes, but too much was going on for him to indulge himself. He sighed and headed to the office.

CHAPTER 5

"Oh, God. I can't believe they took our money," Minerva wailed.

"They took the money from the fake bottom in the suitcase," Elliot said. "All of it. Damn it, that's half our stash." Elliot slammed his fist on the table, eying Minerva and Andrew. "Five hundred grand. Gone. Just like that."

"You idiot. I told you not to put it there," Minerva said. "But do you listen to me?"

"Who talked?" Elliot glared at Minerva and Andrew.

Minerva glared right back. "I didn't tell anyone."

"Look, nobody waltzed in here and got that money out of a false bottomed suitcase," Elliot snapped. "They knew where it was. We weren't gone long enough for them to search the place." Elliot pointed his gaze at Andrew. "Andrew, did you tell anyone where it was?"

"You never told me where it was. Who would I tell?"

"What about Sonya?"

"She's in the Bahamas."

Elliot glared at him. "Are you sure?"

"She's working there. You set it up."

"You want a bourbon?" Minerva asked, slumped in the chair.

"Bourbon? Bourbon? Our freaking money is gone and you're talking about bourbon?"

"Well, I need one."

"Did you call Lambert to tell him you were gonna be late?" Elliot asked. "You've got to work. You can't go there smelling like liquor."

After Minerva called Lambert, she poured herself a soothing cup of tea and sat at the table, her hand twisting the napkin in her lap.

"You can't go in too late either," Elliot told her. "You've got a reputation to uphold."

"I can't believe they stole half our money," Minerva said. "What are we going to do?"

Elliot shook his head. "I don't know. I've got to think." He was the one who always had to come up with solutions. It would be nice if he had some help for a change. He stood a better chance at winning a hundred million dollar lottery.

"We've been living really low—no luxuries. You won't even let me get a manicure," Minerva whined. "Why would anyone think we had money stashed away? Nobody here knows us. Or do they? Is our cover blown? What did we do to make people think we had money?"

They both looked at Andrew. "You been talking, boy?" Elliot asked.

Andrew leaned back in his chair. Elliot pressed a hand to his chest and held him in place. "Not me. Not a word. I don't know anyone here to talk to. If Barbara had known we had money, she wouldn't have loaned me that hundred bucks. And I do all my socializing in Norfolk," he admitted. "They don't know where I live, and you don't give me enough money to flash around."

"Barbara loaned you a hundred bucks?" was the only thing Elliot picked up on.

Andrew looked sheepish. "I just needed a little spending money, Daddy. You're so tightfisted. I never have any to spend."

"Don't you understand we're trying to build up our stash so we can retire? When we get to Mexico we can live like rich folks, but not now. It blows our cover. You have food on the table and a roof over your head, don't you? What more do you need?"

"I'm tired of this work," Minerva cut in. "Ever since you got involved in that investment scam, everything has gone downhill. You never should have invested our savings."

"I didn't lose it on purpose. It was a mistake anyone coulda made."

"I'm getting too old for this scam. It gives me the creeps when that man touches me."

"I had to do things with women I'd rather not," Elliot complained. "You think I liked having to suck up to crones? They get bitchy and like to tell me what to do. You know I don't like that, but I had to suck it up for the benefit of the family. We all have to do our part."

"But, Elliot . . ."

"You've had a good life up 'til now. You've never had to work. It's time you did your part and quit complaining. I didn't complain when I had to pull the hours for thirty years, did I?"

"All right. Working is better than listening to you grumble."

Andrew just looked at him as if he thought going

to bed with women was okay in his book. Some of them were, but he wasn't going to let Minerva know.

Elliot pierced Andrew with a glare. "You got it easy, boy," he said. "You don't have to lift a finger. When's the last time you talked to Sonya?" Sonya was in the Bahamas as a companion for some really rich guy. They should make a killing off him.

"A week ago."

"How did she say it was going? She close to getting that money yet?"

"She said the old coot was coming around. But she has to work slowly. She can't do much with his family getting in the way. She expects to have something after Christmas," Andrew said. "His family is going oversees for the holidays and she'll have him to herself. She's going to work on him good before they come back."

Elliot nodded. "She should do okay." Although he reserved judgment on Sonya. She wasn't as malleable as Minerva and Andrew.

"But, Daddy, I don't like my women. . . ."

"Boy, you do what you have ta do to make ends meet. It's a tough world out here," he bemoaned. "Just because you don't have to work doesn't mean the rest of us don't. And now that the economy's shot to hell and folks have lost so much money, they're tightfisted as hell."

"But with half our money gone, we still won't have enough to retire on," Minerva said, wringing her hands. "And we can't keep doing this. We almost got caught the last time. That woman put up a fuss. She was spying on us. I still wonder if she talked to anybody. My face is the one on the security cameras."

"With all that makeup and sunshades, your own

mama wouldn've recognized you under that big floppy hat."

"But still, Elliot, my signature is on record at the bank," Minerva pointed out.

"I know, I know. But they've got no evidence that she didn't cash out the CDs herself. If somebody was coming after us, they would've done it by now. Just let me think," Elliot said. "The mark you have now is rich as sin. He made a mint and he saved plenty. Thirty-five years in the Navy. Retired as an Admiral. Then he worked high up in some corporation for eighteen years. Maybe we can get enough out of him to make up the difference. His family is clear across the country. They don't know what's going on here."

"I don't know, Elliot. We've always gotten a certain amount and no more. We can't get too greedy. That was your rule. Rich people have resources."

"That was because the people we usually go after didn't have but so much. The mark you have now is ten times as wealthy as the others."

"Could be ten times as dangerous, too." Minerva stood. "I have to go in to work. Elliot, you've got to come up with something. I can't make up the difference in what we lost. And I'll say it again. I'm getting tired of scamming people. I've got a really bad feeling about this. Everything's going wrong. I can feel something out of kilter in my bones."

"Your bones? Bunch of nonsense, woman. You listen here. Just quit your griping, right now," Elliot snapped, hitting the tabletop. "It's nothing but this damp weather messing with your arthritis. I'm tired of your bitching and moaning every single time you have a job to do. Nothing's going to happen. You work on getting that money and we'll be out of the country before his family knows what hit him. Let's aim for leaving here right after Christmas—New Year's, latest."

Minerva's mouth trembled in anger, but she knew better than to sass him. "Well, are you going to drop me off at work or are you going to let me drive the car?"

"I'll take you."

As Elliot drove to Lambert's place, he pondered the robbery. It had to have been someone who knew them and about the money. Otherwise, they wouldn't have found that stash. A regular thief wouldn't have thought to look in that false bottomed suitcase. They had a pile of old quilts and boxes over it.

"The only person I can come up with is Sonya," Elliot said. "For all we know, Sonya could've already robbed that old guy and come back here for our money. We can't tell where she is. Either that or she never went there in the first place. For all we know, she coulda been here waiting for her chance to grab the suitcase."

"You really think Andrew would do that to us?"

"A woman can turn a man's head, Minerva. Give 'em what he wants. Andrew goes to Norfolk nearly every night. What if he's meeting up with Sonya there?" he asked.

"Oh, Elliot."

"She coulda found out about your grandma's trust fund he's coming into at forty. Could even be planning to snatch him away from us. He doesn't need us to get it." Elliot parked in Lambert's yard.

Minerva's hand hovered over the handle. "We've got to stop her."

"I'll come up with something," Elliot said.

"You need to put the money we have left in a safety deposit box, Elliot. We can't afford to lose it."

"They won't find it. I've already moved it to a place nobody will get to it."

"You said that the last time."

After he dropped Minerva off, he headed to the ferry. He couldn't just let it go. Not that much money. He was going to hire his buddy in Norfolk to retrieve the money and find out if Sonya was here. That guy knew people for a hundred miles. Didn't anybody just walk off the street and choose his house. Not when they coulda hit somebody like Barbara or some of the rich islanders like that Jordan Ellis fellow who was loaded for sure.

Elliot drove an eight-year-old car. His house was a rental. He didn't work, nor did his son. Somebody was at the house most of the time. They lived like paupers. Yet, somebody had chosen his place.

Someone was watching their house, damn it. He'd have to give this guy a ten percent finder's fee. He hated like hell to give up that much. But if he got his stash back, it was worth it.

Then, too, he wouldn't put it past one of Minerva's good-for-nothing brothers to have stolen it. Never seen such a sorry bunch of men. He could put all four of their brains together and it still wouldn't make up a whole one. Andrew was more like them than him. Minerva must have been fooling around. No way that boy came from his seed.

But Elliot wasn't going to gripe. Andrew was coming into five million, enough for them to live off for the rest of their lives. Right now they needed enough to live off until Andrew turned forty.

He passed Barbara's place and shook his head. If Andrew had a lick of sense . . . Elliot's pressure shot up just thinking about how that boy messed up with Barbara. If that boy had played his cards right, the two of them could have married, and Elliot and Minerva would have been on easy street living in her house. That place was big enough for all four of them. He'd even manage the shop and money for her while she did the work and they wouldn't have to move. He didn't want to move to Mexico. They were having all kinds of trouble over there, but they couldn't afford to live large here.

Elliot sighed, looking at that new Cadillac parked under the carport, and pressed the gas pedal of his own ancient sedan.

Even he knew Barbara was too much woman for Andrew. He should have played the single man and courted her himself. He could have gotten rid of Minerva and married Barbara, and the two of them could be living in that house right now. And he'd have none of these worries.

Lips crimped together, Elliot made his way to the dock and waited in the ferry line.

When Harper left Hughes's place, he drove directly to Robert Freelander's house. At twenty-seven, Robert owned a tiny two-bedroom cottage on inner island property. After obtaining a degree from Norfolk State, he got a nursing job at a hospital in Norfolk.

His car was in the yard, and Harper rang the doorbell several times before it was answered. He'd been in bed.

"Sheriff?" Robert wiped his bloodshot eyes and drew his hands through his mussed hair.

"I have some questions about Sarah Rhodes."

Robert swiped a hand across his face and moved back. "Come on in."

"Late night?"

"I worked the night shift—twelve hours." He sunk into the leather sofa. "It was a tough night. Understaffed. The usual. What about Sarah?"

"When was the last time you saw Sarah?"

"The week before she disappeared. I give her a ride to work when I work the night shift and her car's in the shop. She doesn't live that far from the hospital."

"Your number was the last one she dialed."

"I'm not surprised. She called that week asking if I could give her a ride, but I was working the day shift."

"Did you socialize with her?"

"No, I met her through Ben at the bar. They were dating. And I started giving her rides when she needed them and our schedules jibed."

"Were she and Ben still dating?"

"They broke up a while back, but she still hung out at the bar sometimes."

"Who else gave her rides?"

"Don't know. I guess anyone going in her direction."

"Who can I call to verify your schedule for that day?"

Robert gave him the information and Harper left for the school gym to meet with the teens.

Most of the department employees volunteered time with the kids, and the secretary was taking roll when he got there. One kid was missing.

Mrs. Claxton and Lisa's mother were setting out snacks the church offered each month. Harper didn't know how Naomi Claxton did it. If it was a cause worth its salt, she volunteered. He hadn't asked for snacks for the kids, but as soon as she found out about the program, she stepped up to the plate.

"I don't know why we have to come here every month. This ain't doing no good. This is a bunch of shi . . . garbage." Harper didn't allow the kids to curse in his presence.

One of the kids was more out of sorts than usual. Sly's father, uncle, and older brother got caught robbing a bank three years ago. They got twenty years each. His twenty-four-year-old brother would spend his life in prison. There were four children in that family. Sly's brother was the one at Hampton. Harper wanted to turn the outcome for Sly and his sister as well, but ultimately that decision was theirs.

"What happened?" he asked Sly.

Sly slumped in his seat. "I did everything you told me and I still didn't make the basketball team. I won't even qualify for a scholarship."

"I'm taking a chance on you. I believe in you. But even more importantly, you've got to believe in yourself. Sly, I'm proud of you for working hard to make the team."

Sly slumped again. "For what? I didn't make it."

"If it's that important to you, try again next season," he said. "What's your next step?"

Sly blew out a frustrated breath. "Reevaluate. But I wanted to make it this year."

"What's the next step after you reevaluate?" Harper asked.

"Come up with an alternate plan. I know all that junk, but I have to wait out a whole year."

"For that team, but that's not the only team."

"It's the only one that counts," Sly said.

Harper understood his need to look good in front of everyone.

"Let's give Sly applause for trying."

Embarrassed, Sly ducked his head. But as everyone clapped, Harper could tell his words were sinking in. Harper wanted the kids to know that even if they failed, they'd made progress by just trying. They weren't going to succeed at everything, but they still had to try.

After the meeting Harper would talk to Sly about alternatives and his next step toward his goals.

The meeting lasted two hours, and at the end, Mrs. Claxton talked to the kids about their Christmas program.

On Sunday, Barbara was getting ready to leave church when Naomi flagged her down. She'd tucked her salt-and-pepper hair under a hat that was much more subdued than Dorsey's choice would have been.

"I'm sorry you missed the meeting."

"Me, too. I'll try to attend the next one," Barbara said.

"Well, we'll have one in a couple of weeks. It will be the last one before Christmas. People are getting busy preparing for the holidays. I've got a million cookies to bake."

"I didn't know people actually baked cookies anymore."

"Oh, yes. My grandchildren look forward to it. My children, too. Well, I won't hold you. I'm going to dig up some more information for you. I'm a pack rat and save everything, but when it's time to find something, I can't put my hands on it. When I do find it, I'll bring it by."

"More information on the Rochester family?" Barbara knew they were some of the original islanders who arrived in 1617.

"Yes, they're your family, of course."

"My family?"

"Of course. Didn't you know? I've been the town's historian for many years and I have all kinds of information. My sister, Anna, had some things, too. I'm going by her old house and I'll see what I can find there."

"If you need any help, let me know," Barbara offered, wondering if what Naomi said was true.

Barbara didn't give anyone details about her background. How was Naomi going to dig up information about her when she really didn't know who she was? But Barbara wouldn't deny or confirm her identity just in case Naomi was searching for information.

"No rush," Barbara said. "Like you said, the holidays are almost here."

"I'll find it when I least expect to. Don't worry; it will eventually come to me."

She started to leave, then came back. "Oh, don't forget you're working on the Thanksgiving food baskets with me."

"I am?" This was the first Barbara had heard of any Thanksgiving baskets.

"For the seniors and the families who need them. You're supposed to help us put them together Tuesday of Thanksgiving week. Harper is one of the delivery drivers. It's an all-day affair for us."

"I see."

"I'll get with you later on the details."

With a parting greeting, Naomi left.

Was the woman senile or wily? Barbara didn't remember offering to do baskets, although she'd gladly participate. She'd mark it on her calendar at home. She better start attending meetings so that she could control what she volunteered for.

Maybe she should offer Naomi some of her grandmother's hats. With the funeral, trying to find Dorsey's murderer, and her retirement, Barbara hadn't packed up the house yet. Dorsey had a million hats around the place and someone should use them. Barbara would keep only one or two.

Barbara was finally headed home. It was rather pleasant outside. The church was more inland and it was a little warmer than near the water. She rolled down her window to enjoy the warmth.

Harper had called her Saturday while he was still at work and they'd talked for half an hour, but he didn't stop by and she doubted she'd see him today. With a murder case to solve and only a handful of people in the sheriff's department, he had no time to spare. Maybe that was a good thing. Less chance of him sticking his nose in her business. Besides, the Stones were enough to keep her busy.

Barbara got up too late for breakfast. She drove to the Greasy Spoon for lunch instead. At least seven cars pulled into the parking lot right after her.

Inside, the first group she saw was Elliot, Minerva, and Andrew seated at a table eating. It was the first time she'd seen them since Andrew attempted to get her money. Andrew's arm was in a cast. Barbara ordered her food to go.

She was glad she'd worn a rich-looking ensemble, with Chanel jewelry, too. Another of her New York bargains.

She debated whether she should approach them. That and the dead woman had been the talk of the congregation. She'd been quiet about Andrew's attempt at robbing her. At least she could keep the communication open.

"Hello," she said, on her way out. "I just wanted to tell you how sorry I was about your break-in. Was anyone hurt?" Barbara made sure her diamond-studded watch was showing.

"No," Elliot said, rising from his seat. "We were very lucky."

"That's good, at least."

"Andrew told us he borrowed money from you," Elliot said, digging into his back pocket and pulling out his wallet. He selected some bills and handed them to Barbara. "Here you go. Will this cover it?"

Barbara counted. "Exactly. You're a good man, Elliot," she said, patting his shoulder. "I've always paid my debts and I can see you do, too. That's the mark of someone who's gotten somewhere in life."

Elliot nodded. "Me and Minerva do our best."

"I know. But there are bad influences everywhere. What can you do?"

"You got that right," Elliot agreed. "Looks like you've been to church. You look very nice, doesn't she, Minerva?"

"It's a very pretty outfit," Minerva said, smiling.

"You have a wonderful day," Barbara said. "Good seeing you again, Minerva."

Elliot stopped his wool gathering to speak. "You, too, Barbara."

When the door closed behind Barbara, Andrew said, "Daddy, why you give her all that money? I could use some myself. And you had that big doctor's bill for my arm. We don't have insurance."

Sitting abruptly, Elliot took a quick look around and leaned across the table. "We have to appear to be good citizens," he whispered. "Folks in small towns talk. You want them saying we don't pay our debts? You've given us a bad enough reputation as it is."

"I was just trying to teach her a lesson," Andrew defended himself, scowling.

Elliot leaned closer as not to be overheard. "How many times have I told you, you lay low where you live? You don't want folks yakking and wondering. You got the sheriff suspicious now. Boy, does anything I tell you sink in to that brain of yours? We're lucky that what you did hasn't spread all over town."

Andrew frowned at his sandwich.

"We won't be able to stay here too much longer. I've got to think about where we're going from here or what we can do to salvage this situation."

They resumed eating. Maybe they should send Andrew away, or at least let the boy keep a low profile for now. Elliot shook his head. He didn't know what Minerva was thinking to bring him to lunch with them. But he couldn't send him away. If Sonya snatched him, their futures were doomed.

He spotted Detective Alyssa Claxton's boyfriend walking in wearing an Armani suit. There was a lot of talk going around about how wealthy Jordan Ellis was. He was probably the only man in town wearing a suit that expensive.

Every time Elliot drove by that big house Ellis was building, jealousy roared up his spine. Even with all the money they'd stolen, they'd never be able to afford a house like that.

Elliot wished he could come up with a scheme to relieve Jordan of some of that money. But he was too young and sharp. Definitely not the type to be played for a fool.

The word was, he was building the castle to impress Alyssa, but she'd thumbed her nose at him until lately. Some folks had all the luck. Elliot had a good mind to plan something to lighten Jordan's pockets anyway, but he'd have Alyssa on him then. Alyssa had a reputation for being a hard ass, and they couldn't afford to have the law chasing them across the country.

"Hey, Jordan," someone called out. "Alyssa make any progress with finding her grandma's golden bowl?" someone asked.

"Not yet, but she's still searching."

The guy shook his head. "She's not going to give up on that."

Golden bowl? Elliot perked up. What about this golden bowl? How valuable was it? Was it solid, heavy gold? He tossed that idea out of his mind. He'd come up against Alyssa again. She wasn't just a deputy. She was a detective. Computers. ID checks. FBI crime info. That would bring on more trouble than he wanted to think about. He didn't want people tracking them down after they left. For the most part, they'd tried to stick to families with women in charge of them. Women were easy marks. They weren't coming after them like men would, too embarrassed to admit having been scammed.

He'd have Minerva visit Mrs. Claxton, though. Cover all the bases at least. Maybe the old biddy would open up about that bowl. If she didn't have it, maybe they could find out who did. He was thinking they weren't exactly acting like good neighbors, even when Mrs. Claxton offered neighborly gestures.

"Let's go," Elliot said.

They stopped at the door. The sheriff was talking to Barbara all intimate like. Elliot frowned. What was that all about?

"What is she doing with him?" Andrew asked.

"You're the one who messed up a good thing." Elliot felt like popping his son upside the head. All that money Barbara had—they could've made out like bandits. Hairdressers make a killing. Black women spent a fortune on their hair. Barbara charged fees like she was still in New York. He knew because Minerva went there and his pocket felt lighter every time. And that place stayed packed.

Elliot shook his head. His son never took advantage of opportunities. "You're such a fool, boy. When are you going to learn to think?" That's why Elliot couldn't give Andrew jobs. He messed up every time. Boy acted half simple.

He should go after Barbara himself. Men could always get away with dating younger women. He was only twenty years older. That wasn't so bad. Elliot crimped his mouth. Too bad it was too late now.

Before Barbara got into her car, Harper approached her, closing the distance between them with purposeful strides.

"Hey, pretty lady. Don't you look lovely today? And without me." Slowly and seductively, his gaze scanned her from head to foot. Barbara's heart jolted and her pulse pounded. When most men spoke that way to her, she waved it off as "some fool with a lame come-on," but when Harper spoke those words, it was as if they came from the heart and she was by no means blind to his attraction.

She laughed but couldn't stop the flash of desire flowing through her.

"You're full of stuff, you know that?"

"I tell it like I see it." He bent over her as his mouth hovered over hers a second. He kissed her softly with fluttery nips, slipping his hands beneath her coat to grasp her waist. This was far from the quick little peck he gave her the other morning, she thought as the butterfly strokes urged her to open up to him.

And when she opened to him, his hot tongue caressed hers, drawing a moan that reached her core. She was lost in the sensations he produced until she heard tires squeal.

She glanced up. One of the deacons was approaching the Greasy Spoon. "Take it home, Sheriff. Take it home."

"See what you're doing to me?" Harper asked, his gaze drilling Barbara.

"Me? I didn't . . ."

"You take away all my common sense and reasoning."

"I was perfectly fine until you invaded my space."

"I want to invade more than that," he said, leaving no doubt what he was referring to. Before Barbara could recover from that, he said, "This doesn't nearly make up for leaving you on your own to finish breakfast."

"Duty calls."

He wore a suit that fit as if it was tailor-made for him. It was obvious he went to services at another church. "I should have invited you to church with me," he said.

"You should have," she murmured, still recovering from his touch.

"Why don't I take you to dinner to make up for breakfast?"

"You don't have to. I still have your leftovers."

"I want to. Besides, leftover French toast just doesn't turn me on."

Barbara nearly groaned. "I've got a better idea. Why don't I invite you to dinner?"

"Even better. What time?"

Barbara told him and left. She didn't have a clue of what to prepare. As she drove away, her conscience started bothering her. At church, she'd discovered the retired deputy, Scott, had interrogated the bartender at the local bar.

Was it possible Elliot didn't kill Sarah? Was her death a coincidence? Could one of her boyfriends have murdered her? Barbara doubted it. She was pulling straws to make her feel less guilty for withholding information.

Barbara sighed and pulled into the parking lot of the local grocery store.

She couldn't tell Harper about these people yet. No one else was in danger of being killed by the Stones. As far as she knew, except for her grandmother, they usually didn't kill their marks. Dorsey was a fighter. She went after them. If only her grandmother had waited for her.

It usually took a few months for a scam artist to gain a mark's trust. She still had time on her side.

She hoped.

CHAPTER 6

Harper watched Barbara drive away. At least she wasn't fighting him.

He slid into his car just to people-watch. Sooner or later, most strangers in town ended up at the Greasy Spoon. So far all the faces and vehicles were familiar, and he went back to thinking of Barbara.

She looked so good in that burnt orange outfit. The color matched the fall leaves. One thing he could say about Barbara was that she always seemed effortlessly put together. Even when she was in her shop or just grocery shopping. Come to think of it, even in her walking clothes, with the cute hat that was still sitting on his dresser. He should give it back to her. He was holding on to it until later.

He was so accustomed to moving at his own pace, he'd completely forgotten to ask Barbara to attend church services with him. *Have to do better than that.*

After his divorce, he'd dated, but none of the relationships amounted to anything. It was a pretty crushing blow to find your wife in bed with another man. If he'd been some half-cocked crazy, the results could have been disastrous. He had just taken his jacket and shoulder holster off, and the thing was dangling from his fingers when he'd heard a masculine grunt and the mattress springs shift.

When his wife looked over the guy's shoulder and saw him looming in the doorway, she'd screamed. He'd never forget it. She thought he was going to shoot her. He'd just come from the scene of a drive-by shooting where an eleven-year-old had been killed. And he'd just witnessed the wrenching tears of a mother's agony.

He admitted to being an ass when he wanted to be. He'd stayed right in the doorway while the guy dressed and left, and he didn't even have to ask his wife to leave. She left on her own, all the time begging him not to shoot her.

She didn't have to worry about him shooting her. She wasn't worth the bullet or the effort. After that, he didn't expect or search for love. Just sex, thank you, to scratch an itch.

When he moved back to Paradise Island, he steered away from the local women. There were too many problems associated with dating in an old community with several generations of families. It was safer in Norfolk and Virginia Beach. But he got tired of that scene, too. At one point, he wanted more. But as hard as he searched, he could never find anyone he thought of as a partner. Someone he could settle down with, could trust.

Lately he'd been solo. The senseless dating scene wasn't cutting it and his mind had moved in a different direction. He was holding out for all or nothing. He wanted to be with someone who offered him more than an itch to scratch.

He'd been alone for a year now. He was beginning to think he'd never find that perfect match.

And then Barbara blew into town like a tropical storm and knocked not only him, but the island women off their feet. The women wanted her new hairstyles. And him, well, he wanted her in every way imaginable.

Only she wasn't interested.

He was still sitting and watching when the Stones made their way to their car. Nothing to stand out. A regular American sedan.

Andrew seemed disturbed about something. Elliot, as always, seemed to be calling the shots. After Andrew attempted to hold Barbara up, Harper had been keeping an eye on the family.

Something about them made his neck itch. An indication something was off kilter. Andrew was thirty-five. Why was his sixty-something aunt working while he sat at home watching the tube and playing Nintendo? Now, he knew households where the parents tried to kick out grown sons who wouldn't budge, but why did Elliot put up with it? It was reasonable that Elliot was retired, but hadn't the man worked during his lifetime? Why would he let his grown, healthy son live off them? What was he teaching him? He'd spotted Andrew half-drunk walking off the ferry a couple of times. He was withering away to nothing. And his family let him.

Here strangers were nothing new. People needing to get away from their everyday, hectic lives. An example was the guy who'd been rubbing on Barbara's legs. There was something nagging at Harper about Trent, too. But he allowed for his prejudice. If only men knew what went on in nail salons.

Harper gritted his teeth. He hoped the guy had enough good sense not to go feeling up Barbara's legs again.

The Stones drove off, Elliot at the wheel. A minute later, John tapped the top of his car and he rolled his window down.

"Got somebody under surveillance?" John asked.

"Just watching. See who's coming and going. The Stones just left. They're a weird bunch," he said. The window sill of their house had been wiped clean when they'd dusted for fingerprints. And he'd pulled nothing up on the computer. Not a traffic ticket, nothing. "Afternoon, Jordan."

Jordan nodded on his way to his SUV.

"Is Ben back in town?" Ben was the bartender John had gone to interview several times. His employer told him that he still hadn't returned from his vacation.

"I'm going by there in a couple hours. He's working this afternoon. I talked to the investigator in Virginia Beach. Nothing new there."

"I'm looking at the money angle."

"We'll see." John tapped the top of his car. "Check you later," he said.

Harper couldn't help wondering if they were missing something vital. A sudden surge of crimes usually had some common factor. And they were missing pieces here.

Harper stayed for another fifteen minutes before he headed home to change clothes.

Barbara decided to prepare the dough for the fruit croustade first. For the filling, she used canned peaches Naomi had given her at the end of the summer, and added fresh blueberries and plums she'd picked up at the store.

As soon as she put the scallop dish together and before she got it in the oven, Liane called.

"Sorry it took so long to get back to you. Lambert Hughes has a daughter and a son. The daughter lives in California and the son in Chicago. Couldn't find out if they knew Minerva was taking care of him," she said and rattled off the phone numbers. Barbara picked up the pen near the phone and scribbled a note.

"Thanks, Liane." Barbara was getting nervous about Minerva, especially with the robbery. If they got desperate, they would move.

"So, how are things going with the sheriff?"

"Can you believe I actually invited him to dinner? What on earth was I thinking?"

"Wow. He doesn't waste any time, does he? I'm dying to meet him."

Barbara moaned. "You probably will. This is the craziest thing I've ever done. I'm committing an illegal act and dating the sheriff at the same time. I could end up in jail."

"With what you have in mind, we both can," Liane reminded her.

Barbara's anger surfaced. "We're just acting on the same principles the Stones use. And they get away with it every time."

"That should be a great bed warmer when we're in jail. Think we'll be roommates?"

Barbara chuckled at Liane's dry sense of humor. "You can pull out anytime you want to."

"No, I'm in until the end. Just so you know, we both had better be prepared to return to work afterward, since we're going to spend our life's savings on lawyers."

"That'll take care of future years of boredom. We're too young to retire anyway. What were we thinking?"

"Sunny beaches, perhaps? A trip around the world? The temperature hit thirty-five here yesterday. I could soak up some Hawaiian sun."

"Haven't you heard? The dollar is down. The worst possible time to travel," Barbara assured her.

"Bargains are everywhere. I just saw discounted tickets to Hawaii for a steal. Keep me posted, woman. I'll see you soon."

Barbara decided to call Lambert Hughes's family immediately. It was Sunday, the best time to find them home. She first tried his son. No response, but she didn't leave a message. She dialed the daughter next.

"Ms. Houston. My name is Barbara Turner," she said when someone answered. "I recently moved to Paradise Island, Virginia. I'm calling about your father. He—"

"Is he okay?" the woman interrupted.

"Oh, yes. As far as I know. I'm not calling about his health." She paused, debating how to handle this without sounding like a lunatic. "I thought you should know your father's companion is known for fleecing senior citizens out of their life's savings. I know this because her husband stole hundreds of thousands from my grandmother less than a year ago. I couldn't save her, but I'm hoping that this information will help you save your father from the same financial nightmare."

"Did you report this to the police?"

"There's no concrete proof. As far as the authorities are concerned, the Stones haven't committed a crime here. There's nothing they can do. They couldn't help me with my grandmother after the fact, and I've decided to take matters into my hands, but it takes time."

"My God. She should be in jail."

"Like I said, they don't leave evidence behind. And they change their names all the time. I've found five people who have been fleeced by that family within the last two years. I'm sure there are more. In my case, Minerva dressed up to look like my grandmother and cashed out her savings. She wore a huge floppy hat and averted her face from the security camera."

"This is all so hard to absorb. Minerva seemed so kind and caring. I interviewed her myself. And I felt comfortable with Dad being so far away from my brother and me having someone responsible and so caring with him each day. Someone he can call if he needs help. She's always calling me with updates. His last companion wasn't quite as reliable. Many days she didn't show up for work at all. Minerva never misses a day."

"It's how confident people work. She's there. None of your father's family is close by, so he begins to rely on her. Also, you should know the police recently found the body of your father's previous companion, Sarah Rhodes."

"The one we thought ran away?"

"Yes, her body was found in the marsh a little over a mile from your father's house. They think she's been there since her disappearance."

"They killed her?"

"I think Minerva's husband killed her."

"Minerva's husband? But she told me she was single and living with her brother and his son."

"The man she introduces as her brother is, in fact, her husband, and Andrew is their son."

"Then my father's life is in danger."

"They can't get money from him if he's dead. So, physically, I think he's okay right now. She hasn't gotten the money yet. If she had, they would have left."

"Thank you so much for calling me. My brother and I will come to the island immediately. This time I'll convince him to move to California with me. It's going to be difficult, but I can't monitor him closely from this distance."

"I'll give you my number if you need to talk to me. And since I'm spying on them, I'd appreciate it if you didn't use my name. These people move from family to family, and I plan to put a stop to it. They leave their victims devastated."

Barbara couldn't help but wonder if there was another way to solve this situation. She wished she could go to Harper. Although Grandma always said she was strong enough to handle her own problems and not to look for anyone to solve things for her. But look what happened to her.

Harper was already peeved that she wouldn't testify against Andrew, but what would it accomplish? Minerva and Elliot would still be free to rob unsuspecting seniors. No, she was doing the right thing. They needed to know they could be as easily scammed as the next person.

Barbara slid a few CDs into the player and listened to music as she cooked. Harper had a huge appetite. At the grocery store she'd selected steaks and salad fixings. It didn't take long for the scallops she'd taken from her freezer to thaw. She'd serve them with baked sweet potatoes. Tasty, yet simple.

She still wasn't certain dating Harper was a sound idea. At first she was glad Andrew was in the

way to keep temptation at bay. She could feel herself
weakening for Harper and had been on the verge
of giving in countless times. He seemed to be a
genuinely nice person. But when it came to men,
she wasn't a good judge of character.

Barbara wanted what any woman wanted. She
yearned for intimacy with a caring, loving man.
What would it cost to at least test the waters with
Harper? What did she have to lose? An inner warning told her the cost could be very high if things
went wrong. Secrets and lies could blow up in her
face. But this was a temporary stopgap. Her heart
saddened. Now that her grandmother was gone,
there was no reason for her to move to a place full
of strangers. This was not her home. But she'd been
away from Philly so long that it wasn't home either.

She'd focused on her career and her grandmother her entire life. Dorsey had taught her self-
sufficiency. Barbara's mother and father had died
when she was a baby, leaving her with her grandmother, her only other relative. Fearing that Barbara might be left alone when she was still young,
Dorsey had raised Barbara with a strict hand.

She made Barbara stand up for herself. If Barbara
had a problem with her teacher, she'd tell Barbara
how to fix the problem—the first time. The second
time Barbara was to come up with her own solution.
It was only after Barbara had resolved the problem
that Dorsey would go to the school and have a talk
with the teacher. And the same effort went with
dealing with troublesome classmates.

It wasn't that Dorsey wasn't loving, because she
was. Barbara got forty-five years of hugs, kisses, and
care. And Dorsey always told her she loved her with
every beat of her heart, but Dorsey always said, *Life*

*was a series of picking up your boots and moving on until
you find someplace to plant them.* She'd always said she
was a grandmother, not a mother, and if she died,
she didn't want Barbara in the grave with her. She
wanted her to be able to deal with life's trials and
make a meaningful life for herself, whether Dorsey
was here or gone.

Tears ran down Barbara's face. She knew Dorsey
wouldn't want her dwelling on grief this way, but
she couldn't help it. The tears wouldn't stop rolling.

When she calmed down, she thought Dorsey would
like Harper. Besides, what was wrong with her deriv-
ing some pleasure for a change?

Barbara took in a deep breath. Dating after a
long absence was like rowing upstream. You never
forgot. Or like diving into a cold ocean. Dip your
toe first to test the temperature before you dove in.

If only it were that easy.

Harper glanced up when John strolled into the
office. He was wearing a blazer over his jeans.

"Just came back from interviewing Ben."

"What did he have to say?"

"According to him, he broke off the relationship.
He's been sniffing after Lisa Claxton and thought
he could get something going with her. I know he's
had a crush on her for a long time."

"Did he start a relationship with Lisa?"

"She wouldn't give him the time of day," John
said, sinking into a chair across the desk.

"What's your gut instinct?"

"Ben's telling the truth."

Harper nodded. He'd never thought Ben was a

viable candidate. But now they'd come up against a dead end.

"The old boyfriend from Norfolk could have come here to kill her. That rental cottage is rarely rented out this time of year."

"It's possible," Harper mused.

"Was there a connection between Sarah and Andrew?"

"Why don't you check it out?" Harper flipped through the folder. "I ran a check on the Stone family. There are no speeding tickets, parking tickets, no professional licenses. Nothing."

"Not one ticket among the three of them? Not even a speeding ticket?"

Harper shook his head. "Nope."

"That's strange. Most teens get a few. At least one or two. You gave Alyssa a few."

"I haven't forgotten," Harper said. "She was worse than her brothers."

"You could have given her a break," John said, chuckling.

"I did, but she showed no compunction to improve. She was a spoiled brat." But Harper admired the fact that Alyssa was a hard worker and didn't take crap from anyone.

"She wouldn't agree. She always says you ticketed her for spite."

Unrepentant, Harper nodded. "Especially after she told me I was just filling my quota."

John chuckled again. "She still gets pissed every time she talks about it. Her mother took her car away for an entire month. She could get away with murder with her dad, but not her mom. And she made her use her allowance to pay for them."

"Her mama was a smart woman."

John shook his head.

"I didn't have to worry about her speeding after that, did I?" Harper asked, sliding his chair back. "I have a feeling we're missing something big on this case. The islanders are getting nervous and I don't like it. I just haven't put my finger on it yet, but stay on the Stones. Andrew hit Barbara. This can't be the first time he's hit a woman, yet he's never been arrested."

"His record is too clean," John agreed, walking to the door with Harper. "You got all decked out. Got a hot date or something?"

Harper ignored him and opened the door.

"With Barbara?"

"None of your business."

"You're allowed to date, you know. All the women want to save you from yourself. You don't have to be so secretive about it. It's all over town anyway that you kissed her at the B and B."

Harper groaned. "It's impossible to keep any secrets here."

"Especially when you have me to tell all."

"Not if I fire you."

"My lips are sealed. She seems like a nice lady. I just can't understand why she didn't want Andrew arrested."

"Leave it alone, John. Only Barbara knows her reasons. And we've got bigger fish to fry."

He reached his car.

"Enjoy your date. Tell Barbara I said hi. And for God's sake, don't be cheap. Take a gift."

"Got that covered. You think you're dealing with a kid or something?"

"I know how your head gets wrapped up in a case and you forget the world around you."

* * *

Sam Lyon's gardening shop was closed, but Harper caught him at home. And since Sam's greenhouse was at his house, he made up a flower arrangement.

"I really appreciate this, man."

Sam rarely smiled, but Harper thought he saw a glimmer in his eyes. "John called. I was expecting you."

Harper smothered a groan. "Guess this is going to be all over the island."

"Guess so." Sam was dating Alyssa's cousin, who was working on her master's in nursing.

"Set that wedding date yet?"

"Regina wants to wait until she gets her degree."

"When will that happen?"

"May."

Sam was a guy of few words. But he worked quickly and Harper was soon headed to Barbara's place. First, he had to run by home for the wine he left chilling in the fridge. Women liked nice things. He had to do this right.

He pulled into her driveway at five. She must have had the fan on because the aroma from the food had drifted outside, making him remember he hadn't eaten anything since lunch.

Harper stood at his car, scanning the area. Barbara was pretty isolated out here. Her house was on the ocean side. So was his, and boats could pull up at night without her knowing. He wondered if that had happened with Sarah. Could someone have stopped the boat at the marsh and dumped her body? Was it someone she knew or some crazy serial killer like Stanley Kingsley? It wasn't unheard of. But this place was too small to have two serial killers in a year terrorizing the area. His better judgment told him Sarah's killing was deliberate, not some serial killer. It was up to his department to determine the motive and opportunity.

He climbed the stairs to the front door.

Barbara wore a flowing peach dress that extended to the floor. He could barely see the outline of her generous curves. It had a scooped neckline that ended at the top of her breasts, tantalizing him. Her smile nearly undid him. He forgot he had the flowers.

"You're just in time," she said.

He finally remembered he was holding flowers and wine. He extended his arms. "For you."

"Opus II." Any kind of Opus wine was expensive. They only produced two wines each year.

"What are we celebrating?" she asked, and moved aside for him to enter.

"The fact that I finally have a date with you. And a home-cooked meal." He leaned down and kissed her lightly, but she pulled back a bit.

He was moving things too quickly for Barbara's comfort.

"Something smells wonderful," he said.

"It's almost done." She smiled even prettier. "Thank you. I'll put the flowers in a vase. They'll make a nice centerpiece."

"Why don't I open this for you so we can enjoy a glass with dinner? I had it sitting on ice so it's the right temperature."

"Perfect."

He followed her into the kitchen. Food was on

the stove. While he opened the wine, she dished the food onto platters.

"Looks like you've been cooking all day."

"Not quite. So how was your day?"

"Busy. I had a speaking engagement at church."

Barbara paused. So that was the reason he was dressed in his suit. "Why didn't you tell me?"

He shrugged. "Half of my job is public relations."

Barbara debated candlelight, but she loved to cook and entertain, and she saw no reason to change her ways because she was having dinner with a handsome, charming, totally irresistible man. She placed the flowers between the candles. When she looked up, Harper regarded her closely.

"Is everything okay?" he asked.

"Of course."

"You've been crying."

She offered him a wry smile. "I thought I erased the traces."

He approached her. "What's wrong, honey?"

"I was just thinking of my grandmother."

"Come here, baby. Why didn't you call me? Why did you suffer in silence?" he asked, regarding her a moment before he pulled her tightly into his arms. Barbara felt like crying again, but she contained her emotions. She didn't feel quite alone anymore either and that was good. Sighing, she inhaled a light whiff of his soap but mostly the unique essence of him. His heart beat comfortably against her chest.

His lips brushed across her forehead, yet there was nothing remotely intimate about the contact, merely a human connection from a caring soul. Barbara liked that.

The timer dinged and Barbara leaned back enough to meet his gaze. It was then she realized her hand was on his chest.

"Thank you," she said. "I better get that."

"Anytime, babe."

He followed her to the kitchen and put the wine within easy reach. She put a dish of scallops on the counter before she sipped hers.

"Are you hungry, or would you like to relax for a while?" she asked.

Harper wanted to choose relaxing, but he was hungry. His pause was so long Barbara glanced at him with a smile.

"Why don't we eat now and relax later," she murmured.

"Sounds like a winner. Can I help with anything?" he asked.

She shook her head. "Just keep me company."

"I've got that covered." He leaned against the counter and watched her, the aroma of various flavors wafting around him. It was a roomy, immaculate kitchen with wooden floors, granite countertops, cherry cabinets, and stainless-steel appliances. The window shelf over the sink held several pots of herbs, and beyond was the fading view of the ocean, a few lights twinkling from boats. It all seemed designed to lull stress away.

"Your place is beautiful," he said.

"My grandmother and I planned the renovations together."

Harper didn't want to make her sad again. It was obvious her grandmother's loss was still fresh.

The image Barbara presented to the world was a self-contained woman, warm, but she kept a part of herself isolated. Had he not come at the right time, he would never have known how upset she was.

Harper sipped his wine and studied this woman who fascinated him.

Sonya placed the money back into the pillowcase. "This isn't all of it," she told Boyd. "Only half." Their housemates spent the day in Virginia Beach and hadn't returned, so they had the place to themselves.

"You think they spent the rest already?"

She shook her head. "Elliot's hiding it somewhere else. But I know it's in the house. He's such a control freak, he's not going to take it to a bank."

"You had a hard enough time getting in there the first time. It's going to be impossible to get in there again. He's going to be guarding that place something fierce."

Sonya looked smug. "There's always a way."

"I hope we get this over with quickly. I have to get back home, soon."

"How soon?"

"I can wait a few weeks. I've already made my excuses for Thanksgiving."

"If I know Elliot, things will be wrapped up by then." She wouldn't care if Boyd did go back to New York. Sometimes she wished she hadn't hooked up with him.

They met when she tried to run a con on his uncle and Boyd caught her at her game. He told her he knew someone vulnerable with a lot of money, only he wanted to work with her. That he really liked her and they could work well together— as a couple.

Okay, the sex was good. Boyd knew his way around a woman's body. But she'd always worked solo. She'd hooked up with Andrew because of the trust fund. Only she had to get him away from Elliot to take advantage of it. And she needed enough money to last the five years until that trust fund was available to him.

"It's our turn to help out in the dining room," Sonya said. They shared communal meals at the artist colony. Everybody had chores.

"I went fishing today," Boyd said. "I caught the food. I'm not cooking it, too."

No way was Sonya leaving her money in Boyd's reach. He could jump up and leave at any time. "I worked last night. Besides, you didn't fish *all* day long." She sidled up to him, slid her body over his. She immediately felt the response of his erection. "We're supposed to be madly in love. Would a man in love leave his wife for even fifteen minutes?" She unzipped his pants.

"Depends," Boyd said, his voice strangled.

Sonya licked his lips. "On what?"

"How good the wife is to me."

Sonya smothered a groan. He was so tired. "I'm better than good, baby." She turned on the music and started out with a slow strip, teasingly revealing her body with dancing steps until she was completely undressed. Then she undressed him, kissing him as she did so, driving him insane with need. Nobody could say she didn't know how to please a man. By the time she'd shed his briefs, he was begging for mercy.

"Not quite yet, baby. This is just the appetizer."

She proceeded to show him just how good she was.

A half hour later, Boyd left the cottage with her. Sonya would send him out later on some ridiculous errand and get her money to her pre-appointed hiding place. She'd worked too damn hard to let it get away from her.

CHAPTER 7

Elliot got Minerva to make her pineapple cake and take it to the Claxtons to thank them for offering them refuge when they were robbed. A good thing, too, because Naomi invited them to dinner and they were happy to accept.

Elliot selected one of his expensive bottles of wine. He hated to give it up, but if they got that bowl, it was worth it.

"Everything smells wonderful," he said as they sat.

"I'm glad you could join us," Naomi said. "It's just everyday stuff."

Minerva smiled like she was supposed to. "You've been such good neighbors. We're lucky to move next door to kind people."

Elliot could tell Naomi was melting already. He barely tasted the food as he suffered through small talk. They were on dessert before he broached the topic.

"I hear your family's been here hundreds of years," he said.

"Nearly four hundred to be exact."

"No kidding."

She started to tell the tale of how her female ancestor got kidnapped by pirates and then shipwrecked. And how the women poisoned the pirates and escaped to the island. It was a fascinating tale.

"How on earth did they make it? Women all alone? No provisions?"

"Oh, they had the stolen spices, cloths, and things the pirates had looted. Even a golden bowl, bullion, and coins."

He suffered through another tale of how fishermen came the next year and the women soon married. But Elliot was interested only in the goods.

"So they traded all those things for tobacco and supplies?" he asked.

"Some of it. The bowl, some bullion, and coins are still in the family, except some of it was stolen a while back."

"Stolen?" Minerva said.

"We're still trying to track it down."

"Any idea who stole it?"

"I don't have a clue. But my granddaughter Alyssa is working on it."

"She'll find it eventually," Hoyt Claxton, Naomi's husband, said.

"I hope you find it. To have it in the family for so many years and to lose it is just awful," Minerva said.

"Her sister, Anna, put it away somewhere, and when she died no one could find it. That's another explanation," Hoyt added.

"It's stolen. If it wasn't, we would have found it," Naomi insisted.

Elliot suffered through another half hour before he and Minerva could leave. So maybe the bowl wasn't stolen. But he was going to check into it anyway. As soon as he got home, he called Mouse.

"Got another job for you," Elliot said and explained what he wanted.

"Got a few contacts on the island. I'll see what I can find out," Mouse said. "Do I need to remind you of my ten percent finder's fee on the selling price?"

"Yeah, yeah, yeah," Elliot said. "Just find it."

While Elliot was talking to Mouse, Andrew was at a bar in Norfolk. He was depressed about the way his dad was treating him. He decided to call Sonya. His dad thought he had no sense, but he knew where his woman was. Sonya wouldn't betray him. She was always nice to him. He wished he could be with her right now.

He hoped she answered.

"Hey, baby," she answered, and Andrew felt better just hearing her voice.

"What's all that noise in back?"

"Give me a minute."

He could hear her moving around. A door squeaked open and closed, and there was silence.

"We were having dinner. His family is having a party. They're a loud group."

"How is it there?"

"Hot. I'm going to take a dip later on just to cool off."

Andrew frowned. "They got air conditioning, don't they?"

"Sure they do, but I like having my windows open to catch a breeze. Anyway, since they have a pool, I'm taking advantage of it."

"I miss you, baby."

"You know I miss you, too. I'm waiting for the

time your daddy lets us stay together. I hate when he sends me away from you. How're you holding up?"

"Not too good. Broke my arm."

"Poor thing. How did that happen?"

"Fell. Daddy's counting on you to bring in a good amount. Somebody robbed half the money we had."

"After all that work?" Sonya sounded as outraged as Andrew felt. "How could he let that happen? I thought he was so smart?"

"He's got some new plan to make up the difference. There's this golden bowl missing. Old as dirt. From a few hundred years ago. Daddy's got some man looking for it." He went into detail about the bowl.

"I hope your daddy finds that bowl 'cause we need that money."

"Yeah, me, too."

"Honey, I wish I could talk longer, but I better get back to the party. I'll call you later on, okay?"

"Yeah, sure. I love you, Sonya."

"Love you, too, baby." She gave him those kisses through the phone and he smiled. "I'm gonna take good care of you when I see you again. And, baby, you know I can."

Andrew felt himself growing hard. Nobody made him feel as good as Sonya. He felt a whole lot better when he hung up. The only reason he went out with Barbara in the first place was because of his dad. She started coming on to him, and his dad told him he had to go out with her. Anybody who retired at forty-five had to have some money somewhere.

Andrew looked at his cast. And look how that turned out. His dad thought he knew everything, but there was a lot he didn't know. Sonya was a good woman. She loved him.

"You gone play or look at the wall all night?" the guy said, racking up the balls for another game of pool.

"One more game and I'm outta here. Lemme get a drink first." As he went to the bar he was still smiling about Sonya.

· Sonya was thinking about the golden bowl. She was going to have to dig up some information.

"What're you doing out here?" Boyd asked.

Sonya clutched her chest. "You're going to get hurt coming up on me like that."

"Why are you out here?"

"Andrew called. He missed me."

He grabbed her around the waist, then nuzzled her neck. "You don't belong to him anymore. You're mine." His kiss was long and slow. "All mine."

In your dreams, buddy. No man owned her, and he was going to find out just how much she was her own person before too long.

"You know I am, sweetie."

Trent drove slowly around the island and noticed the sheriff's car parked in Barbara's yard. If Barbara had been dating Andrew for a while and she followed him all the way to Paradise Island, why had she broken the guy's arm and held him for the sheriff? Something didn't add up.

Most of all, who broke into the Stones' home? Someone had to be watching them. Someone was there most of the time, which was why he hadn't broken in yet. Was someone else tracking them?

Trent didn't like too many oars in the water, not when it hampered his plans.

Was Barbara putting on an act? Was she dating the sheriff to keep him away from the Stones? Using sex to keep him off balance? Spreading her stuff around, was she?

Trent shook his head. A woman could turn a man's head. It was a lesson he'd learned years ago, never to mix business with pleasure. The sheriff was old enough to know better. It wasn't that Barbara was that much of a honey for the man to lose his head over. But then, the sheriff was old, too. He'd probably go after whatever he could get. To each his own. Heck, he remembered another old saying: "There's no fool like an old fool."

Barbara had some redeeming factors. He was sure she was a good cook. And the sheriff looked like he enjoyed good food. Today, many sistas couldn't cook and others wouldn't. Maybe food was the sheriff's inducement.

Maybe he had something on the side for an arm piece. Not on the island, though, or else the sheriff would be the one walking around with the broken arm. Barbara didn't take crap. And she could certainly handle herself. She'd put the sheriff in his place the other night.

Trent didn't like the idea of having to cross Barbara. He hoped it didn't come down to that, but if it was the only way to get his mother's money back, he was up to taking care of business.

There were a lot of fine single sistas on the island. Of course, *he* wasn't sampling any. Although if he had to stay too long, he might get desperate and have to trek to Norfolk. A man couldn't go but so long without hitting something.

* * *

Barbara set the table with fine china. Candles flickered around the flowers. The aroma of mouth-watering food added to the setting. Barbara asked Harper to say grace and afterward he dug in.

"It's all delicious," he said after sampling each item. "I've never tasted scallops cooked this way before."

After dinner, Harper helped Barbara clean up the kitchen.

"I'll pack some of the leftovers for you," she murmured.

"I won't turn it down," Harper said on their way to the living room. He tried to put the case on the back burner in his mind. He would drive by the Stones' house after he left.

There was a Russian samovar on a side table, along with figurines of a large bird. It was a formal room, yet comfortable, too, with Persian rugs and oversized furniture. Sitting side by side on the burgundy couch, they listened to music and Harper felt a warm glow of contentment.

"They're from Italy," she said, referring to the birds. "We got them when my grandmother and I traveled there fifteen years ago. The trip was my reward for my divorce."

"Is that what women do now? Instead of the honeymoon, they do the celebrating after the divorce?"

"I did."

Harper chuckled. "I still can't figure out how a woman with a thriving career in New York ended up on our little island."

"New York is too busy. I'm trying to decide whether I can live here for the rest of my life."

"Have you ever lived in a rural area?"

She shook her head.

"When I moved back here from Baltimore, it was hard leaving all the conveniences behind. Mostly pizza delivery and a whole range of restaurants. I'm not a shopper, but I imagine you miss having stores nearby."

"Tell me about it."

"But you'll acclimate. I did. And it's not like you can't visit New York."

"True. But it's a good thing I love to cook. Some of the foods I could buy at the corner store aren't available here. Not even in the grocery stores in Virginia Beach."

"I bet if you asked Cornell for a special item, he'd make it for you, or order it."

"That's a thought."

And so their night went. Talking about inconsequential topics, with Barbara enjoying Harper's company.

"My friend is bringing my favorite cheeses with her when she visits at Thanksgiving," she said later.

"Your friend is from New York, too?"

"Connecticut. She moved to New York the same time I did. She hasn't decided where she'll retire."

For a moment, something flashed in his eyes. If Barbara hadn't been watching him closely she would have missed it completely. Did she say something she shouldn't have? Then a mischievous smile softened his lips as he stretched his arm over the back of her seat. Barbara relaxed. She was just being paranoid.

"So do you think I'll get some insight into you when I meet your friend?"

Barbara hadn't thought about that. "I'm an open book. What you see is what you get."

Amusement flickered in his eyes. "I doubt that. Is she a hairdresser, too?"

"She's my stockbroker." That was true enough.

"Interesting. Think she'd take a look at my portfolio?"

"I'm sure she would."

Although the curtains were open, it was dark outside. The CDs continued to play, and as they talked, the soft music penetrated the intimate setting.

"Any progress on Sarah's murder?" Barbara asked, changing the mood.

"We've done quite a few interviews, and the Norfolk PD interrogated the old boyfriend there."

"Do you really think one of them killed her?"

"We can't rule out any suspects yet."

"Well, I don't know her, but I wonder what the real motive is? Who gained by her death? Did the boyfriend take out an insurance policy on her?"

"You're thinking like a detective," Harper said. "Pretty soon you'll be doing my job for me."

"The murder happened so close to me, I've been thinking a lot about it. I imagine she didn't make a fortune working for Mr. Hughes as a companion. Doesn't Minerva work for him now?"

"Yes, she does," Harper said, wondering where Barbara was going with this. "But you know, I really don't want to talk shop tonight unless you know something about this murder?"

"Who, me? I don't know a thing."

He shifted. "So tell me, Barbara, did you own a hair salon in New York?"

"No, but I've always worked with hair. I got my beautician's license when I was in high school. My grandmother insisted that a woman always needed something to fall back on."

"Smart woman." He leaned forward to kiss her, but she pressed a hand to his chest.

"Harper, we need to talk first. I can't promise you anything."

He brushed her hair from her face and tilted her chin so that he could look in her eyes. "What are you afraid of?"

"It's not fear. It's just . . . I don't know what the future holds. I don't know if I'm going to even stay here," she said. "I just don't want you to get your hopes up for something that might never happen."

"I'm just going with what I feel. And that'll have to do."

"You don't know me," Barbara said softly.

Harper stroked his hand over her chin. "That'll change."

"But I just don't want you to be disappointed."

He regarded her closely. "Again, what are you afraid of?"

"Expectations."

"Tell me about your ex."

"That was so long ago. And what's happening now has nothing to do with him."

"Did you see him when you were in New York?"

"We both worked in Manhattan, so we crossed paths now and then. I think he even remarried a couple times."

"But you've never trusted yourself enough to take that step."

She glanced at him. "We have something in common, then, don't we?"

"You know, by the time I caught my wife with that SOB, my marriage was already disintegrating. It hurt, but deep down I knew it was over long before we actually said the words. We were just prolonging something that needed to end. And I'm philosophical about it. In that atmosphere I probably wasn't the best husband. The divorce rate's pretty high in law enforcement—especially in big cities."

"But to end in that way . . ."

"Yeah, well. Life isn't perfect, Barbara. But I'll always be truthful with you and I expect the same from you."

Barbara nodded, knowing she'd already failed that test by lying by omission.

He took a long finger and turned her head toward him. "You're special."

From the beginning this thing had started on the wrong foot. It was doomed to disaster, but how could she get rid of any suspicions Harper had? How could she make him back off? And did she really want to? She felt something for him, too. The spark was getting too strong. Definitely a small blaze now. *If only.* She sighed. *If only.*

He was going to kiss her. She swallowed tightly as he closed the distance between them. One hand caressed the side of her face, then cupped her chin, stroking her gently.

She ached for his touch and leaned into him, the muscles in her stomach tightening in anticipation. Her heartbeat throbbed in her chest as their lips touched.

He nibbled at the corner of her mouth before his lips brushed softly across hers. When his tongue ran in a leisurely crawl over her mouth, Barbara moaned and opened fully to him. He covered her mouth completely and greedily, delving his tongue deep within her, tasting her. He drew her tightly against him, sucking every bit of the air from the room and from her lungs. Barbara's stomach undulated like waves on the ocean.

She felt burning need consuming her as he co-cooned her in his embrace. His heartbeat thudded against her chest.

Suddenly, he pulled back and Barbara felt bereft, lost. She reached out to draw him back, but he clasped her arms, holding her still.

"I have to go," he whispered, knowing if he didn't leave now it would be too difficult for him to do so later. He dragged in a breath. "You're just too enticing, woman."

He wanted to stay. *She* wanted him to stay. He could see it in her eyes. But he wasn't going to drag her to bed when in the space of a breath she told him their time was limited. He wanted her to need him as much as he needed her.

And was it a slip of the tongue when she said she'd moved to Manhattan at the same time her friend moved there? They had a lot to resolve before they moved on.

This relationship was progressing too damn slowly for him. There was nothing easy about slow and easy, Harper thought. As difficult as it was to leave her after one brief kiss, he did.

This could develop into something special and he didn't want to rush her. He hadn't dated another woman since Barbara came to town. And she could cook. My God. He rubbed his stomach. She'd even sent some leftovers home with him.

When he drove away, he veered from his regular route and drove slowly through the Stones' neighborhood. Everything seemed quiet.

When Harper made it home, he called Barbara,

but she didn't answer her phone. Must have gone to bed right after he left. He sighed, imagining her doing that, undressing slowly, showering, donning a seductive negligee.

He showered, got beneath the covers, and closed his eyes on another sigh. He didn't know how long he'd slept when the phone woke him. He glanced at the clock. It had been only half an hour.

"Yeah?" he asked.

"Somebody shot Andrew Stone tonight," the night duty officer announced.

Harper sat up in bed. "What?"

"He's at the clinic. Don't think's it's life threatening, but I'm on my way there. He was on his way home from the ferry. Happened when he was going into the house. And, Harper, it didn't wake anyone up. Whoever shot him must have used a silencer."

"I'll meet you at the clinic," Harper said, getting out of bed. As he pulled on his clothes, he remembered that Barbara hadn't answered her phone when he'd called.

The wind had picked up and he felt the gusts against the car as he drove the short distance to the clinic.

Andrew was moaning. A broken arm, cracked ribs, and now someone had shot him—all within the space of a week. Was he that unlucky or was something else going on? He remembered the night he tried to get money from Barbara. Andrew had said she'd come after him like a woman gone crazy.

Frowning, Doc scowled and glanced up with a don't-mess-with-me expression,

"How is he?" Harper asked.

"He'll live if he stops squirming long enough." Rudely yanked from her bed, she was understandably out of sorts. Looked as if she'd stepped into the first thing she found—a pair of jeans and sneakers. She'd never win a fashion contest. "You can have the bullet as soon as I get it out. For now, just go in the other room."

"It was Barbara. You know it was. You've got to arrest her this time, Sheriff."

"You saw her?"

"No, but I don't have any other enemies. I told you that woman was vindictive. She's not going to be satisfied until I'm dead."

"She's already gotten her revenge. What makes you think she's still after you? You didn't get her money."

"Women are like that. Especially her," he said. "She's not going to be satisfied until I'm dead and buried. She holds grudges."

"For God's sake, Harper. Do the interview after I'm through, else he's going to end up with a slashed vein," Doc said. "Get out until I'm done with him."

In the waiting room, Harper fixed himself a cup of coffee.

A while later, a drugged-up Andrew appeared.

With the bullet in an evidence bag, Harper helped Andrew to the car and drove him home.

"Have you spoken to Barbara since the attempted robbery?"

"Well, no. She spoke to my parents at the Greasy Spoon today, but not one word to me."

"You mean your dad and aunt?"

Andrew nodded, his gaze darting away. "Yeah, that's what I mean."

Harper shot him a hard glare. Was it a slip of the

tongue that he called them his parents? Or had his aunt been the mother figure in his life?

"Where were you coming from tonight?" Harper asked.

"I was in Norfolk."

"Did you have an altercation with anyone there?"

"No, just went drinking and playing pool. No big deal." Then he looked down.

Harper frowned. He played pool with a cast? "Any chance someone followed you?"

"I woulda known."

If he was sober enough, Harper thought. But the effects of the alcohol still hadn't worn off, and with the meds, Andrew was zoning out fast. "Are you telling me everything?"

"Sure. I didn't get in a fight with anybody. No words, either."

Harper parked in front of the house and helped Andrew out. "The deputy will take your statement after he finishes with the crime scene."

Suddenly, Andrew leaned heavily on Harper and he almost dropped him. The guy was barely conscious as Harper dragged him up the front steps into the house.

That statement would have to wait.

Monday morning, Harper stopped by Barbara's house just as she came outside for her walk.

"Need to change that schedule. I can time your walks to the minute."

"I'm not as paranoid as you."

She wore another cute jogging suit, black this time, with a zip-up sweatshirt, the hood pulled over her head. She stopped in front of him.

"You look tired."

"Long night," he said, leaning against the car. "I tried to call you when I got home."

"I took a long shower after you left, then went to bed. Why didn't you leave a message or call me back?"

He shrugged. "Went to bed after I called you," he said, regarding her closely. "Andrew was shot last night."

She appeared genuinely shocked. "Is he going to be okay? Who shot him and why?"

"The bullet went into his upper arm. And we don't know who shot him. He claims you did."

"Me? Why on earth would he say such a thing? I've never held a gun in my life. Why would he think I'd try to shoot him over one night's earnings?"

"Because you broke his arm."

"What do you think, Harper? Do you think I shot him?"

"What I believe isn't the issue."

"To me, it is."

"The truth is, all I can go on is instinct and the fact that I like you. A dangerous combination. It could be said I've lost my objectivity."

"But what does thirty years of experience tell you?"

"You don't want me to answer that." One hand cupped her cheek. As his mouth descended to hers, she moved a fraction and his lips grazed her cheek instead. Then she glared at him and her tongue swiped her lips.

He pulled her close, and this time he pressed his lips to hers. For a second, her body tensed; then she relaxed and her arms circled his waist. He tightened his hold on her, bringing her tight against him, feeling her delicious softness. His tongue burrowed deep into her mouth, tasting her.

His heart pounded in his chest. God, this woman got under his skin like no other. Harper pulled away from her, his breathing hard.

"What thirty years of experience has taught me," he said, his body raging with need, "is that I can't be objective when desire is ruling my head."

He let her go, got in his car, and pulled away with her still regarding him.

Barbara watched him leave with a mixture of emotions. She pressed a hand to her mouth. Desire and need raced through her with equal strength. And they hadn't gone to bed yet. She wondered why he was waiting. She was beginning to have emotions for this man that she hadn't felt for a very long time, and for him to think she'd shoot someone hurt. It shouldn't. It wasn't as if she wasn't being deceptive. Or that she'd told him the truth about anything, starting with Sarah Rhodes.

No, she didn't shoot Andrew, but her other secrets were just as bad. For the first time, she wondered if what she was doing was worth damaging her relationship with Harper, or what it could develop into.

Wednesday morning, Barbara stood at the edge of the marsh watching the Hughes's home through her binoculars. Another woman, younger than Minerva, was with him. Must be his daughter. Barbara smiled. If only she were a fly on the wall.

Barbara walked home and dressed for work. When she arrived at her shop, Trent was outside smoking a cigarette.

"You understand there's no smoking in the shop," she warned. Something she forgot to check when she hired him. She hoped he wasn't one of those smokers who needed a cigarette break every half hour. At least his clothes didn't stink of cigarette smoke.

"Yes, ma'am." He crushed the butt beneath his boot.

What was it with the "ma'am"? He made her feel eighty. "This is not going to work with you calling me ma'am."

"Okay."

"There's an ashtray inside. I don't want butts on my sidewalk. Doesn't look good."

"Yes . . . um . . . Barbara."

"Your references checked out." She had a full day of back-to-back appointments. She'd tried to come up with another plan for the Stones, but she was at an impasse. Maybe she would have to go to Harper, after all, and ask for help. But then the seniors would never get their money.

Barbara was wondering whether Minerva would show up for her ten o'clock hair appointment when her cell phone rang. She glanced at the number and recognized it belonged to Ivy Russell, one of the women the Stones had scammed.

"Trent, can you excuse me a minute?" she asked, and stepped outside to answer.

"Barbara?" Ivy asked.

"I'm here."

"I was wondering if you've had any success in getting my money?"

"I'm sorry I haven't, but don't give up. I'm still working on it."

"I can't even afford all my medicine any longer. The bill is nearly six hundred a month out of pocket. So far I've been able to borrow from the family, but I can't keep doing that."

Barbara felt the weight of this woman's distress on her shoulders. She had to come up with another plan.

"I'm working on it, okay? I'll call you soon," she said, ending the call.

As much as she'd like to leave this at Harper's door, she couldn't. He had to work within the law. He couldn't just get the money and give it to the victims. It would take years for a court to sort it out. And all the victims were seniors, and all of them desperately needed their money. She had to do this.

Even if it destroyed their relationship.

Harper wished he could have run with Barbara before coming to work. When he'd mentioned running at six, she nixed it quickly. She'd said she got up before five most of her working life, but don't even think of bothering her before eight.

What hairdresser got up at five in the morning? She didn't have children to cook breakfast for before school, and she didn't have any dogs to walk. Customers certainly didn't show up at the hair salon that early—at least not the women he knew.

He'd found a fresh size 9 men's running shoe print near the Stones' place. It looked as if someone had been waiting for Andrew to return home. Men's shoes ran a size smaller than women's. A women's 10 was a man's 9. So either the intruder was a man or a woman wearing men's shoes.

Which did not eliminate Barbara, especially with her failure to answer the phone when he called her.

When Harper entered his office, his secretary

and deputy, John Aldridge, were laughing. There wasn't a damn thing funny about this situation. Not after the crime spree they'd had the last few months.

"Coffee ready?" he asked, just in case he'd have to fix his own.

"John started a pot," his secretary said.

Harper opened his office door, and scowled. Who was in his . . . He sighed.

A Kevlar vest perched on his chair as if it were a living, breathing person.

John approached him, grinning. "Thought you needed some protection, Sheriff, now that you're dating."

"Do I look like I can't handle my woman?" Harper asked. He was twice the size of John. A heck of a lot brawnier, too.

"Ah, no, Sheriff." Still grinning, John retrieved the vest and carried it to storage.

Harper sighed. The holiday season was coming up fast and the last thing Harper needed was folks afraid to go outside because of some hotshot roaming the island.

Many islanders owned guns. It wasn't like the city with the no-gun push. Before you knew it, islanders would be shooting at each other or at some kid sneaking home through the neighborhood after his parents' curfew.

He thought back, reviewing any new people on the island—Trent, in particular. The cabin owner's brother-in-law had reported gunshots at the outhouse days before Trent arrived. Trent lived near the marsh where Sarah's body was recovered. Could these crimes be connected?

The outhouse had been shot up with a Glock.

Andrew had been shot with a .45. The outhouse shooting occurred before Trent arrived.

Harper rubbed his forehead. Two crimes had occurred at the Stones'. First the robbery and now the shooting. Who were these almost invisible people to attract this negative attention?

Robberies didn't occur often on the island. Shootings were rare. Naomi Claxton was known to keep a "little spare change" in the house for emergencies, yet no one had ever robbed her. Of course they'd have Alyssa on their case, and who on the island wanted her breathing down his neck? And Naomi had sons, practically all of whom rose to six five. Then you throw in the countless grandsons and granddaughters. And the fact that everyone knew her husband, Hoyt, owned a shotgun and that Naomi wasn't afraid to shoot it. A thief would reason that she wasn't worth the trouble.

He called John into his office. He wanted him to interview the Stones again. Find out their histories. What kind of work did the old man do? And the son and aunt? What did she do before she became Hughes's caretaker? But he wanted to know where each of them worked before they came to the island. He wanted to know everything.

Usually Harper didn't go after the victims. But the son had robbed, correction, *tried* to take money from Barbara. More than likely this wasn't his first offense. Obviously he'd gotten away with it before. Perhaps the incident with Barbara would convince him to change his ways.

His secretary set a cup of coffee on his desk. Harper waved his thanks.

* * *

Minerva arrived late for her hair appointment. Had Trent not been there, it would have thrown Barbara's entire day off. He washed hair like a pro. It was obvious he'd worked in a salon for a while, and her customers were pleased with the washes—and him. He'd even had time to do nails.

By the time Harper entered the shop for lunch, heads were under the dryer and Barbara could actually stop for a few minutes. Knowing his appetite and that for some reason he'd stop by, she'd packed an extra chicken salad sandwich with multigrain bread. She'd even added cut-up fruit with a dollop of whipped cream.

"Oh, baby. This is good," was all Harper said.

Trent talked someone into a manicure and they enjoyed a few minutes of privacy.

Harper sipped bottled water. "You're making me seem cheap, you know?"

Barbara swallowed her food. "How is that?"

"I'm always eating your home-cooked meals. Why don't I bring something by tonight on my way home? Make me feel better? I know you're a fabulous cook and it'll take a lot to even match."

"The Greasy Spoon isn't the best place for dinner, Harper."

"I can do better than that."

"I'm going to be late."

He glanced in toward the main room, in Trent's direction. "How late?"

Barbara leaned so she wouldn't be overheard. "The news about Trent has spread. I'm getting calls left and right."

Harper scoffed. "If men only knew," he muttered, shaking his head.

"Don't be ridiculous. Women don't come here to

get their groove on. We fix hair and nails here, period."

"But the men don't know you got some guy feeling up on their wives' and girlfriends' legs."

"We will not discuss this again. You just never noticed before."

"I never came in here before, except for interviews."

"Am I going to have a problem with you?"

Barbara had that no-nonsense look on her face. Harper knew he had better keep his feelings to himself. After all, she already knew how he felt about that guy feeling *her* legs.

"No problem."

"I don't plan to stop getting pedicures because of your ridiculous bias."

"That's from your point of view. I don't consider it bias."

"My point of view is the one that counts."

"I'm a man protecting his space." Harper decided reasoning with Barbara would do no good. He'd have a little talk with Trent the next time he saw him. Satisfied, he smiled at Barbara.

Barbara pushed a finger into his chest. "And you had better not approach Trent about my business. If you do, you're toast. Got it?"

Harper held up his hands. "I said I didn't have a problem with him."

She regarded him suspiciously.

Okay, so this little petty thing with Trent wasn't worth disturbing the waters. Obviously she wasn't romantically interested in the younger man.

"You never told me what time you'll be home."

"Around seven-thirty."

"I'll pick up the food and close up with you. How does that sound?"

"Trent will be here."

"But I'm the sheriff. I'll feel better if you have my protection."

"Whatever pleases you."

"I like the sound of that. Wish you would say it more often." Harper could only manage a small smile, because Barbara didn't go out of her way to please him. She must have been a hell of a business-woman. She let nothing interfere with it.

But there was softness, too. She'd been alone so long, she was accustomed to taking care of business by herself. Keeping her own counsel. It wasn't going to be easy fitting another person in her schedule. He should know. He had that same problem. But most of the women he dated didn't mind his inter-ference.

When he was ready to leave, he leaned over and kissed her.

CHAPTER 8

Elliot sat at the table in IHOP, nursing a cup of coffee. Although he was known for punctuality, Mouse didn't show up for their six-thirty meeting that morning. It wasn't like him not to show and not call either. Elliot had called him several times, but he didn't answer his cell phone. Elliot couldn't wait around too long, since he had to get the car back in time for Minerva to go to work.

It was now almost time for her to get off work and Elliot had beef stew simmering in the oven. He finally had time to read the newspaper. Spreading it out, he started with the first page. When he got to the local news, his eyes widened. Mouse had been in an accident.

"What the hell?"

Andrew appeared from the living room. "What is it?"

"Mouse is dead."

Puzzled, he asked, "Who's Mouse?"

Mouse had been killed in a car crash the previous day. Hit-and-run with a stolen car. Elliot laid the paper down. He couldn't believe it. Mouse was dead.

Andrew shifted uneasily. "Who's Mouse?" he repeated.

"The guy I hired to find our money."

"And he's dead?"

"We were supposed to meet this morning and he never showed up. Said yesterday he'd found something."

"You think that's why he's dead? That the person who stole our money killed him?"

Wearily, Elliot swiped his hand across his face. "I don't know." But he didn't like this one bit.

When Elliot heard Minerva's tires squeal in the driveway and a rush of footsteps, he wondered if something else had happened. He yanked the door open and she rushed inside like her coattail was on fire.

"What's wrong?"

"Elliot . . ." Her mouth worked, but words didn't come out. She dropped her purse on the floor.

"Calm down. What's going on?" he asked, hearing Andrew moving beside him as he moved to the table and settled Minerva on a chair. She usually kept her head during a crisis, but with everything going on . . .

"I almost got fired today," she finally said.

"Fired? What the hell did you do? All you gotta do is sit with the guy and fix his food," he blasted. "Damn it, any nitwit can do that."

Her eyes snapped daggers. "I'm not a nitwit, Elliot. Stop talking to me like that. I didn't do nothing! Lambert's daughter showed up out of the blue and tried to fire me on the spot."

"You talk to her three, four times a week. I thought she liked you."

"So did I. I don't understand it."

Tiredly, Elliot rubbed the back of his neck. Mouse was dead. And now this. "So you're out of a job?"

"Lambert wouldn't let her. He said he was very pleased with my services and didn't want anyone else. But his daughter said her brother is arriving soon and he's got to move to California with her." Minerva wilted in her chair. "Elliot, what's going on? First, we're robbed. Then Andrew's shot. Now I'm on the verge of losing my job for no good reason."

"The man Daddy hired to find our money died, too."

Minerva's eyes widened. "What?"

"Don't get your panties in a twist. He died in an accident." He couldn't deal with Minerva's hysterics. He had enough worry for the two of them.

She squinted. "Do you think someone from our past is hunting us down?"

"These people have nothing to do with our past. Somebody's been running his mouth." He glared at Andrew. "Did you tell anybody we were moving here? One of your friends back in Philly?"

"Not me," Andrew said, shaking his head.

Elliot leveled a glare at Minerva.

Minerva threw him a glance. "Who would I tell, Elliot? Don't be ridiculous. Nobody even knew we were moving here."

"This whole damn thing is falling apart." He wondered what information Mouse had gathered. And if he'd actually retrieved the money.

"Maybe we should leave," Minerva suggested. "I've got a bad feeling about this place. Especially after what happened with that old woman Dorsey. She was spying on us that day. Do you think she told anybody?"

"She didn't get a chance to. I followed her home. Caught up to her and tailed her without her even knowing it. And I know she didn't get to talk to anybody once she got there."

Minerva twisted her hands in her lap. "We never had this much trouble before. This place is small. It should have been a piece of cake."

"That's why it'll work out. Their police department is nearly nonexistent."

"I don't know," Minerva said slowly. "The sheriff is snooping, although he likes to make us believe he's slow, he's got something up his sleeve. That's why I want to retire from this business. I don't want to end up in jail at my age."

"Be serious. If we can get away with it in Philly where they got a real police force, you really think they can do anything in this cowpoke town?"

"They don't have as much crime here," Minerva said. "They got time to concentrate on just one case. Philly is riddled with crime."

"Our names are clean." He leveled a look at Andrew. "You talk to Sonya lately, boy?"

"Over the weekend, when the old man she's taking care of went to dinner with his family. She still says she can't do nothing 'til close to Christmas. Too many kinfolks nosing around. But they trust her and he likes her." He shrugged. "Things there should turn out okay."

Elliot scratched his head. Minerva had a point. If he hadn't put down six months' deposit when they'd arrived, he'd pack their bags and leave right now. But the old man was loaded. They'd lost half their money. Lambert, alone, could make up most of the difference. And Elliot could never get Minerva to work another job. Talking her into doing this one was hard enough. And he was tired of doing them himself. They were getting too dangerous. He'd promised Minerva this would be their last one.

"Andrew, I want to know what's going on."

"Nothing, Daddy."

"Boy, if I find out you're lying to me, I'll knock you into next year."

"Daddy, all I do is hang out at the bar playing pool."

"You been meeting with Sonya?"

"Sonya? She's not here."

"Tell the truth. She's the only one who coulda known about that money."

"I'm telling the truth. She's not here. I woulda told you if she was. I'm part of this family, too."

"Then she's here on her own."

"That's not true."

"It's got to be her. There's no other explanation. No one else woulda thought to look under all that junk."

"I've been thinking that, too," Minerva said.

"We can get Barbara to invest the money we have left," Elliot said. "I don't see any other alternative. She said we could double, even triple our profits."

"How can you even think of doing business with that woman?" Andrew cried. "After what she did to me?"

"Quiet," Elliot snapped. "This is business. We can't afford to let personal grievances interfere. We're between a rock and a hard place here. We've got to come up with something. I'm ready to leave the country. Too much mess is happening here. And now that Mouse is dead, we can't count on getting our money back."

"We left some places just in the nick of time. A few of the families tried to threaten us." Minerva scrunched up her face. "You think somebody hired someone? Or decided to come after us?" she asked. "Maybe that's why Andrew was shot. Sonya wouldn't have shot him."

Elliot paced from the fridge to the stove. "I don't think so. We've changed our names too many times. But who can tell? But Barbara is dating the sheriff. He looks like a straight shooter. If she had something to hide, she'd stay clear of him."

"So you really think we can trust her?" Minerva asked skeptically.

"Yeah, but in the meantime, you keep going to your job and putting on a good face. I'll call Barbara at the shop about a write-up on this stock she's talking about. At least we can do some Internet research to see if it's legit and if this company is really going to buy the other one out."

"She's got some guy working for her now," Minerva said. "He washes hair and does nails. Does a good job, too."

Elliot shook his head. "Like I said a dozen times, that woman's making money hand over fist," he said, throwing a narrowed glance toward his son. "You could've been working there, Andrew. At least washing the hair if nothing else."

"I never worked in a beauty parlor," Andrew said.

"You act like you can't learn. She coulda taught you how to wash hair. You wash your own. How hard can it be?" Elliot shook his head. "Boy, you just won't do right. Ya couldn't see a good thing if it hit you in the face." He sighed. "Let's keep our eyes peeled for Sonya. I've got a feeling she's right under our noses, or else she hired someone. She knows too much about us."

Barbara's last customer was Vanetta. Lisa had scheduled an appointment for her after everyone else had left. Barbara had even sent Trent home for the evening.

"How have you been, Vanetta?"

"Fine. Thank you for taking me so late."

"Anytime. And, Miss Lisa, how is your business plan coming?"

"I don't know. I haven't done much with it."

"She's been nagging me so much about doing things and to have my hair done, she doesn't have time to take care of herself," Vanetta said. "I told her she should get busy on it."

"You need to get out of the house. And you know if your hair isn't fixed properly you'd use it as an excuse not to mix among folks," Lisa said. "There's a function in Virginia Beach this weekend. The two of us can go. I know you like going there. At least you used to."

"I haven't been in the mood lately," Vanetta said.

"You don't have to be in the mood to go."

"You'll feel better if you get out," Barbara said softly. "Staying in the house can be depressing. I know it's difficult in the beginning, but as time passes, and I know it's disturbing to hear people say this, but time does heal."

"See, Vanetta?" Lisa said with a smug nod. "That's the same thing I've been telling you. If you don't believe me, you can believe Barbara."

Vanetta sniffed. "I appreciate you sticking by me,

Lisa. You've got better things to do than waste your
time on me."

"That's not true, Van. I love you. You're my sister."

Barbara's heart saddened. People could deride
Lisa, but she was really sticking by Vanetta. It was
nice to have family, somebody to be there when the
going got too tough to bear. Money didn't begin to
make up the difference. Vanetta had money. The
good thing was she had family, too.

Barbara patted Vanetta's shoulder and continued
working with her hair. Vanetta was another example
of the havoc men caused in women's lives.

So why did she look forward to seeing Harper
every day when she got off work? He'd been showing up on a regular basis, and her heart gladdened
every time she saw him.

Vanetta and Lisa were talking again about Lisa
starting her business and Barbara tuned in on the
conversation.

Her house needed a good cleaning, and even
though Lisa was a little over the top, everyone said
she did a wonderful job of cleaning and stayed out
of your business. In New York, Barbara had a regular cleaning lady who came by every two weeks.
She'd been doing it herself since she arrived on the
island. There really wasn't a cleaning service, although people hired by word of mouth.

"Lisa, I've been wondering if you can clean my
house before Thanksgiving. Do you take outside
jobs?"

"Sometimes on my days off."

"See, Lisa? I told you people needed your services, but would you listen to me?" Vanetta said.
"Jordan will be moving to the island as soon as that
huge house is finished. He's going to need a clean-

ing crew. Not just one person. And there are others, too, who would like to hire someone on a regular basis. There are the summer people who'd like their place dusted once a month. All of it can add up to a thriving business."

"Vanetta," Lisa said with a sigh. "I told you I don't know a thing about business."

"And I told you, you can learn, and I'll help you."

"We're back to the money again."

"You know I'll help you financially. If Matthew did nothing else, he left enough money for me to more than survive for the rest of my life."

"But Jordan wants you to work in his office while he's away building those hotels."

"He already has a manager at the one in Virginia Beach."

"I don't know."

Barbara had heard disparaging talk about Lisa. But Lisa had probably been knocked down so many times, it was hard to get back up and fight. She didn't trust herself anymore.

"I could teach you everything you need to know. I had a double major and one of them was business," Vanetta said.

"We'll see."

Barbara finished working the perm in Vanetta's hair and guided her to the shampoo bowl. She washed the perm out and deep conditioned her hair, putting Vanetta under the dryer hood for a few minutes for treatment.

Lisa went outside to take a smoke.

Barbara was in the process of looking at tomorrow's schedule when Elliot called, asking about information on the stock she'd mentioned before the drama with Andrew. Just in case Lisa returned before she finished the conversation, she went to the kitchen and closed the door behind her. Her heart pounded in her chest. She took deep breaths to calm herself before going on with the conversation.

"Elliot, I gave you that information because Andrew and I were dating and I thought I could trust you. I wasn't supposed to. I can't even talk about this over the phone," she informed him in hushed tones.

"I understand. I know things didn't work out with you and Andrew, and I can't tell you how sorry I am about that, but I just wanted a little more information about that stock."

"Elliot, I have a customer right now. Why don't we talk later?"

"I can run by your house after work."

"Oh, no. Tonight won't work." Barbara sighed. "Why don't you come by my shop at nine-thirty tomorrow morning before any of my customers arrive? Then we'll have a few minutes to ourselves. But I'm warning you . . ." She paused, counted to ten. "Anyway, we'll talk tomorrow," she finished and hung up.

Barbara all but screamed "Yes!" beneath her breath so Lisa and Vanetta didn't hear her.

When she returned to the room, she washed the conditioner out of Vanetta's hair and rolled it, tucking her head once again under the dryer.

Instead of cleaning, she sat beside Lisa who was glancing through magazines while she patiently waited for her sister. Lisa glanced up. "You know if you really want to run your own business," Barbara said, "helping you might give Vanetta purpose right now. She needs something to focus on other than herself and her tragedy. Don't get me wrong. I'm not telling you to start a business. Only that if you wanted to begin one, she could help you."

Lisa sighed, dropping the magazine on her lap. "I'm worried about her. She's not pulling out of this as quickly as I thought she would. She seems to be getting worse. I try planning things, but when I get off work and go to her house, she's still in bed sometimes. Mama tries to help, but Mama drives her crazy."

"She did well on the art show at the artist colony. Pulled it together quickly, too."

"But she gave up after that was over. It was as if she used all her remaining energy to get through it."

"Healing takes time. And having family to help her through helps."

Unlike herself, she thought again, it was good that Vanetta had close family. If Liane hadn't stood by Barbara after Dorsey died, she didn't know how she would have managed her grief. But Vanetta was surrounded by the loving arms of a huge family, from parents to grandparents to siblings and cousins. Although the grief was sharp, at least she didn't have to wallow in it alone. Barbara shook her head with a touch of envy. How nice to be surrounded by family that way. To have people who cared about you and loved you no matter what.

By the time Harper arrived at the beauty salon, freshly showered, Barbara had cleaned the shop and was ready to leave. After dropping the day's money off in the night deposit box, they drove to her house. Barbara was starving.

She saw the containers of food and smiled. "You stopped by Cornell's?"

"When I'm dating a woman like you, I have to go for the best."

She quirked an eyebrow. "Do you think you can wait long enough for me to shower?"

"Sure. He tucked in a few things to nibble on. Told him I didn't know how long I'd have to wait."

"I won't be long." Barbara showered quickly and donned a long green dress before joining Harper. He was watching the sports report, but the food was on the coffee table already heated. The aroma drifted in the air, making her even hungrier.

Barbara had expected steak, but he'd ordered grilled chicken with Arborio rice and string beans. And it was delicious.

"You can be trusted selecting food, after all," she said after the first bite.

"I've been single a long time."

Dessert was fresh strawberries and whipped cream.

After their meal, they discarded the containers and relaxed on the couch. Harper lifted her feet to his lap and began to massage them, his magical fingers both firm and gentle. He eased up her ankle, then her calf. He was watching a game, and not being a huge sports fan, Barbara leaned back and closed her eyes—and enjoyed the warmth of his strong hands stroking her. But his touch soon veered from magical to erotic.

"What did you do before you became a hair stylist?" he asked softly.

"I worked on Wall Street," Barbara said. If he ever got suspicious about her, that information was easily accessible. He probably already knew.

Harper's eyebrows rose. "And you have a stock-broker for your personal use?"

"Sure. Even though I make my own selections."

Stocks had gone bust and so many brokers were out of jobs. Harper considered that, as a broker, she would have had most of her assets tied up in the market and probably lost a mint when it spiraled down.

"Do your feet hurt from standing all day?" he asked.

"My back bothers me more." She smiled. "But your massage feels wonderful."

"Guess I'm going to have to massage your back, then."

Barbara's gaze touched his. Harper was leaning close, and came closer still, narrowing the distance between them. Barbara saw the desire in his eyes just before he kissed her briefly on her lips.

"You taste like strawberries."

"Umm."

He tilted her chin with his finger and brushed his lips over her forehead, her cheeks, her chin with affectionate, playful strokes, teasing her.

She moved to kiss the edge of his mouth before she swept her tongue there. He moved his head just enough to brush his tongue with hers.

A playful interchange quickly moved to erotic and desire began to pool inside her. He deepened the kiss, his tongue rolling languidly over her mouth's interior. They kissed in an intimate sexual rhythm.

Barbara worked her hand beneath his sweater, feeling the corded muscles beneath smooth skin.

He shifted to lie fully on her, rocking his hips slowly, intimately against her.

It had been a long time for Barbara, and this slow

meeting of mouths and bodies was driving her insane with need.

"I've been ready for you forever," Harper whispered. "Barbara, I want to make love with you. But I'm too old to snatch a feel on the couch."

She nodded toward the hallway. "My bed is that way."

"Are you sure you want this?" he asked, holding his breath. Harper wanted to be sure she was as ready for him as he was for her.

She smiled, her eyes glazed with desire. "I'm sure."

"I guess we should get the preliminaries out of the way. I have no STDs. If you need the papers to prove it, I'll get them from my doctor."

She was suddenly shy. "I'm clean, too. It's been a long time for me, Harper."

"Just hearing you say you've saved yourself for me is driving me crazy."

He sat up, pulled her up from the couch, and kissed her again as he backed her down the hallway. She turned on the bedside lamp and he got his first view of her bedroom, but only a brief one. It was a very feminine room, just the opposite of the "take no prisoners" woman who put him in his place, without being fussy and with green being the predominant color, dotted with splashes of rose and cream.

"This is you," Harper said. But Barbara was consuming his mind, not the bedspread. He tugged her into his arms and kissed her again before they fell on the bed in a tangle of arms, legs, and bodies.

He brushed her dress aside, caressing her smooth legs as he strung kisses across her breasts. He touched her full hips, her stomach, then parted her legs to stroke her intimately.

Barbara moaned.

"Like that? You've got to tell me what you're feeling, babe. I want to make this great for you."

"It is," she said, pulling his sweater over his head and tossing it aside.

For the first time, she gazed at him, then stroked his firm chest splattered with crisp hair. "I'm burning up here, baby."

"So am I. For a completely different reason. I want you completely on fire."

Barbara moaned. "This can't be one sided," she said with a quick indrawn breath as he began to stroke her.

She unsnapped his pants and reached for him. He moaned deeply and gently used his teeth to tug on her nipple through her dress, dragging the very breath from her lungs.

"You've got to slow down, babe, so you can catch up with me."

"I'm with you all the way."

He dragged her dress over her hips to reveal cute black panties and took a moment to draw his fingers around, over, and beneath them. He dragged the dress up a few more inches over her breasts covered with a matching lace bra and stopped.

"Pretty undies."

She blushed.

"Beautiful woman."

She laughed.

He bent, nibbled at her breasts, then stroked the tops with his tongue before he pulled the dress completely off her. Unsnapping the bra hooks, he got his first view of her generous breasts and buried his face there before he stroked her until she cried out her desire.

She pushed him on his back and pulled off his pants and his briefs, and stroked the corded muscles of his thighs.

They touched, they caressed, they tasted, they stroked, and loved each other. He whispered his love for every part of her body until her desire and impatience to have him grew to explosive proportions.

Then he donned a condom and entered her. She cried out in pleasure. She held her thighs tightly against him with him imbedded deep inside her, several seconds ticked by as they gazed at each other, each revealing desire and vulnerability.

He brushed her hair aside. "I'll remember this moment forever." And they began to move.

It had been so long for Barbara that her body seemed to vibrate with liquid fire as his body moved sinuously against her.

She tightened her arms around him. Felt the length of the muscles in his back, and his hips as her fingers trailed over him. Slowly and surely, she was drawn to a height of passion she'd never known before. Never even thought possible—until now.

Tremors inside soared to awesome heights, and she abandoned herself to the whirl of sensations until suddenly, electricity seemed to arc through her. Her thoughts fragmented when she climaxed and screamed out her pleasure.

Harper pumped one last time, the muscles in his entire body tightening. His moan was deep and guttural when he spilled his seed.

She was filled with too many emotions to speak, and for moments time seemed to stand still as they pondered their moments of joy.

Finally, Harper shifted beside her, gathering her

into his arms as they waited for their heartbeats to slow to normal.

He kissed her softly on the neck. "You were worth the wait."

She smiled up at him. "And so were you."

"Worth every agonizing moment." He stroked her arm. Her head rested on his shoulder as the sounds of the night blended with the peaceful moment and they drifted off to sleep.

CHAPTER 9

Barbara and Harper made love an hour before she hopped out of bed and showered. He was still sleeping when she headed to the kitchen. She had to get him up and out so that she'd have time to look over the package of information for Elliot. She made coffee and brought a cup to the bedroom. He was still sleeping.

Barbara really liked Harper. Although they hadn't formally dated, Naomi Claxton had thrown them together on various committees, and Barbara knew he was kind and generous. In the end, someone was going to be hurt, Barbara thought, and that might be the both of them. She didn't want to hurt Harper. She closed her eyes briefly and approached the bed, sitting beside him.

"Hey, sleepyhead." She rubbed her hand down his arm.

His eyes opened and he smiled at her. "I can get used to this," he said as he sat up against the pillows and took the coffee from her.

Barbara admired his amazing chest—wanted to crawl back in bed with him.

"Perfect."

"Breakfast will be ready soon," she said, preparing to stand, but he pulled her to him.

"I wish I could jog with you, but I'm in court all morning."

"Oh, that's too bad." She contained a groan of relief. As much as she enjoyed their lovemaking, she needed him up and out. She ran a finger down his chest and kissed his morning stubble. "You can use one of my razors. I don't know if it'll do for you."

"It'll have to."

She pushed up from the bed. "I put two on the countertop. I'll fix breakfast while you shower."

Barbara had breakfast spread out when Harper entered the kitchen.

"Smells delicious," he said.

"Go ahead and sit. It's all ready."

Harper filled his cup with coffee and Barbara carried two bowls of brown sugar topped cinnamon-banana oatmeal to the table along with a platter with pieces of Canadian bacon. A large bowl of cut-up fruit was already there, along with orange juice.

It had been years since Harper had eaten oatmeal and he hadn't liked it that much. Maybe the eggs would be the second course.

Barbara stabbed a slice of the bacon and slipped it onto his plate, then placed one on hers and picked up her fork. For some reason, she seemed to be in a hurry.

"Got plans this morning?" he asked.

"I was going to try to get a walk in before work, but that's it."

Harper nodded, regarding the table. She must be out of eggs, he thought. After all, she hadn't expected him to spend the night. He lifted a spoonful of the oatmeal. He could get through this, he thought reluctantly. But the unexpectedly delicious taste exploded on his tongue. He tasted the banana, the cinnamon, and the brown sugar.

"My God, you can make a feast out of anything," he said, digging in with enthusiasm.

She smiled.

Just before he left, Harper held Barbara in his arms. "You trying to tell me something?"

"What?" She looked puzzled.

"That I'm gaining too much weight or something."

"Are you fishing for compliments? You're perfect the way you are," she said shyly. "We can't eat eggs and pancakes every day. Too rich. We save that for special occasions."

"Oh." He kissed her fully, feeling her wonderful curves pressed against him. His body responded instantly, making him want to drag her back to bed before she pushed him out the door and closed it firmly.

Barbara immediately went to the bedroom-turned-den, unlocked the drawer to the credenza, and pulled the folder on the stock she'd dangled before Elliot. She flipped through it to make sure all the colorful pages were in place. Everything was there. She shoved it back into the credenza and locked the drawer. She noticed her grandmother's picture was out of place and puzzled, she moved it to its regular spot.

Had she moved it there? Barbara couldn't remember.

"It's finally shaping up, Grandma," she whispered, looking fondly at the picture. As much as Barbara hated to take pictures, her grandmother loved them.

Dorsey was wearing one of her famous hats, and her smile was warm and radiant as she peered into the camera.

Tears gathered in Barbara's eyes. It was going to take a long time to get over Dorsey's passing. Eyeing the picture critically, Barbara left the room.

Because of Harper, she was getting a late start today, but she didn't mind. Dorsey would approve of him. She loved a good-looking man.

Harper questioned everything. The downside to dating a man in law enforcement was the information he had access to. She was a licensed stockbroker, information he had easy access to. He'd already known about her background when he asked her, the slick devil.

What concerned her was why he felt it necessary to check up on her. What did she do to cause his suspicion? Did he really think *she* shot Andrew, or was he following up on Andrew's babble? She didn't even own a gun, for heaven's sake. The last thing she needed was to draw Harper's suspicion. He hardly gave her room to breathe as it was. He was in her shop every day for lunch. At her house for dinner. Of course, she was exaggerating. He was working a major case, and she had plenty of time to do the things she needed to, like this morning.

But Lord have mercy, he was pure dynamite between the sheets. And he had stamina. She felt twinges in muscles that hadn't been used in years.

She changed into her walking clothes and smiled as she locked the door behind her. She'd already gotten a workout that morning and last night, but she hadn't been by Lambert Hughes's house lately.

The wind from the ocean hit her hard, whipping through her sweats. But the waves lapping at the shore had a calming effect. She walked briskly for the two miles to Lambert's place. Once there, she stood hidden behind the bushes to see if Minerva would bring him out with his family there, or if they'd been able to fire her.

Minerva and he were sitting on the glider. Minerva appeared to be upset and Lambert was consoling her. She could see the daughter watching them from the window. Although Barbara couldn't see the younger woman's expression, she knew she must be frustrated.

Lambert gathered Minerva in his arms and held her tightly. He seemed to be saying he wouldn't believe a word his daughter said about Minerva. So, Lambert's daughter had been unable to move him concerning Minerva. She would only isolate him further if she pushed too hard.

Shaking her head, Barbara started to head for home, but she heard someone approaching. She backed away from the bushes just as Trent reached her.

Why the hell would he be jogging in the marsh when he could jog on the beach or the road? His shoes were caked with mud. Of course, he must be asking the same of her.

"Hey, Barbara." He came to a stop near her and stretched his muscles.

"Nice day for a walk."

Trent glanced toward the sky. "I thought so. Have to keep in shape."

She wouldn't dignify that with a response. "Yeah, well, the bad thing about coming this far is I have to hike back home."

"Not so bad. I like it here where it's safe to jog outside."

She couldn't imagine him being afraid to jog anywhere.

"You live near here?"

She nodded in the direction of her house. "Just a couple of miles that way."

"I'll walk with you. I'm renting the cottage up the road."

"The place where the woman was found?"

"Yeah, sheriff stopped by to give me a heads up. They found the body just before I got there. I tell you, I've been keeping my eyes open."

He paced his steps to hers.

"This is a nice place, though. I never thought I'd like the country so much," Trent said.

"It grows on you."

Trent walked her all the way home, for the most part, keeping up a one-sided conversation.

Barbara was glad to be home. "Would you like a drink of water before you head back? You must have over three miles to go, at least. Sure you don't want me to drive you?"

"Oh, no. This is nothing. But I will take that water."

Inside, Barbara gave him a bottle of water and sent him on his way. Only he didn't walk this time, he jogged. Nearly seven miles. Barbara couldn't fathom even walking that far.

Barbara watched Trent for a moment and got herself a bottle of water; then she showered and dressed.

On her way out, she stopped in her office to re-trieve the folder. As she bent over, she noticed her grandmother's picture had been shifted. She knew because she'd moved it back in place when she was in there earlier.

Barbara began to check the credenza. It had been rifled through, too. Not noticeably, but Barbara kept her desk drawer neat. She could tell the person who'd been there wasn't as neat.

How did someone get in her house, and why? She grabbed a knife and went through her entire house.

Someone had looked through her drawers. Was it Elliot? Did he now know who she was? Was he going to try to kill her now? Should she call the police?

What if Elliot broke in and saw the photo on the desk? It would give her away. Barbara unlocked the credenza and slipped the picture into a folder in the back.

But what if it wasn't Elliot? Then who could it be? And what was the person looking for? Money? She checked her purse. All her money and credit cards were there.

She glanced at the clock. She had to leave now if she was going to meet Elliot in time.

Elliot arrived at Barbara's shop at nine-thirty sharp. The furnace had already started to warm the building. "Can I get you some coffee?" she asked. "I just put on a pot."

"Sure."

"Sugar or cream?"

"Couple spoons of sugar and cream."

While they got through the pleasantries, Barbara looked for any sign that Elliot knew her identity, but he seemed oblivious. She was cautious about meeting him alone, knowing he'd killed her grandmother and Sarah. He'd have no compunction about killing her, too. She had a sharp knife tucked into her jacket pocket. For the first time, she wished she owned a gun.

While she prepared the coffee, she put muffins and cinnamon rolls on the tray. "It's good to see you, Elliot. How are Minerva and Andrew? I was so sorry to hear about Andrew's shooting."

"Luckily, the bullet didn't hit anything major."

"And Minerva? I miss seeing her."

"She misses you, too. Thought of you almost as a daughter. How've you been?"

She bet they did. "Good. Business is so brisk, I've hired on help."

"Minerva told me. She liked the wash he gave her. Said something about magic fingers."

"Maybe next time she'll let him give her a manicure and pedicure."

"Maybe. But I want to talk to you about that stock."

Barbara carried the tray to a sofa table and handed him his coffee.

Elliot sipped and frowned. "This is some good coffee."

"Only the best."

"Now about that stock."

He's getting desperate, Barbara thought, and wondered why. "As I said yesterday, I wasn't even supposed to talk to you about it. I only did because it was like talking to family. And now . . ."

Elliot shifted in his seat. "Minerva and I always liked you, Barbara. You know that. We were hoping . . ." He glanced away, embarrassed. "Well, children don't always do what you want them to do."

Barbara patted his hand in commiseration. "I understand."

"Minerva and I are getting up in years, and with

the stock market crash, we've lost half of our savings. You know how tough it is."

It took everything in Barbara to keep from exploding. Was that what the robbery was about? Had someone stolen half their money? Who and why?

"It's a tough pill for seniors," she said. "Living on fixed incomes, they suffer most."

He nodded. "So you see I'm between a rock and a hard place. Minerva needs to retire," he said. "Her back's acting up. She's a health care assistant for seniors and has to do heavy lifting sometimes. This job is good for her because Mr. Hughes is still pretty healthy. But who knows how long that'll last or how long we'll be here?"

All the lifting Minerva did was a cup of tea, Barbara thought, or to stroke Lambert or whoever she was bilking at the time.

"I've already retired, but Social Security just isn't enough for folks to live off. The cost of medicine alone is sky high. Rent isn't getting cheaper either. Food's going up. Not to mention gas."

Barbara patted his hand. "I'm so sorry, Elliot. I'm not that far from retirement myself, and believe me, I worry."

He gazed at her appealingly. "So you understand where I'm coming from."

"Of course I do. It's just . . . you know after the feds have come down on insider trading, my broker just won't take the chance. She doesn't want to end up in jail, and if someone as wealthy as Martha Stewart can get caught, well . . ." She left the rest unsaid.

"But you said she was going to invest for you."

"She's my friend. She trusts me. If she gets caught, I'm not going to talk."

Elliot frowned, thinking.

Barbara sipped her coffee.

"She doesn't have to know it's us, does she? I mean I could give you the money and you can let her think it's from you."

This man was so accustomed to dealing with his money illegally, he didn't even see the tax consequences.

"I don't know," Barbara said slowly.

Elliot's hand gripped hers. "We need this, Barbara. I know what Andrew did was wrong. But we always loved you like a daughter. Could you find it in yourself to help us out?" he asked with desperate appeal.

Barbara regarded him, biting her lip. Suddenly, she sighed. "You're a good man, Elliot. And for that reason alone, I'll help you." For some reason, after all she'd been through, after all the scams they'd pulled, this seemed too easy.

Pleased, he settled back in his seat and exhaled audibly. "Do you have some information on that stock?"

"Sure." Setting down her coffee, Barbara went into the kitchen and pulled out the slick looking packet. "They've just got FDA approval for one of their drugs," Barbara said, returning to the room. "A Swiss company is in the process of buying some of their patents. It's a pharmaceutical and the stock isn't doing that great at the moment. But that patent has changed everything."

"How long do you think this will take?"

"About two months, three at the most. They're in quiet negotiations as we speak. So the sooner you invest the better. Once word leaks, their stock is going to shoot up immediately," she assured him.

"I guess we can stay that long."

"You're planning on leaving?" she asked, innocently,

knowing very well they weren't going to stay. "I like it here. I thought you were planning on settling here."

"The damp weather isn't good for Minerva's arthritis. She wants to settle in a warm, dry climate. We're considering Arizona."

"Do you know anyone there?"

He shrugged. "We make friends easily."

"Well, they say you should rent for a year or so just in case the place doesn't suit you," Barbara suggested.

"Yeah, that's what we did here," he said, nodding his head. "And it's not working out."

"Well, let's see what we can do about that. How much were you thinking of investing?" she asked.

He named a sum far above what Barbara expected. How many people had this family bilked?

He stood, gripping the folder in his hand. "I know you have customers coming soon. I'll get out of your way. I'll look this over," he said, "and meet you again in a couple of days to discuss delivering the money."

Barbara nodded.

As Elliot left the building, Trent was coming in.

"He was here for a haircut?" he asked, nodding toward Elliot.

"No." Barbara didn't see the need to explain her business to an employee and left it at that. She was already pissed off at Elliot. Good thing Trent had the good sense to drop the subject.

The nerve of some people. Elliot was concerned about *his* retirement when he'd systematically stolen the retirements of countless others. What about *those* seniors?

"You okay, Barbara?" Trent asked, staring at her.

"What?" Barbara snapped.

Trent all but jumped back. Holding up his hands, he said, "All I asked was if you were okay."

She had better calm down or he'd get suspicious. "I'm fine," she muttered in a calmer voice, and even managed a small smile. "Thank you for asking."

He nodded and walked away.

Barbara needed to rant. Liane was her ranting partner. Her first customer wouldn't be there for another ten minutes. She grabbed her cell phone and went outside without even donning a coat.

"Liane, do you have a minute?"

"Sure, what's up?"

"That sonofabitch came by wanting to invest money for his retirement. He needed to have enough for him and Minerva to live off of. Can you believe him? He's thinking of retirement and he stole the livelihoods of others already in retirement. If I had a gun, I'd shoot him myself."

"Now he's right where you want him, isn't he?" her friend pointed out.

"Yes, but . . . God, I am so angry." Barbara must have looked like a crazy person marching up and down the sidewalk. If she didn't get a grip, somebody was going to call Harper and he'd wonder what was going on.

"Calm down," Liane said in a soothing voice, just the way they calmed each other in the bathroom at work when one of the guys pissed them off. "Your plan, as crazy as it is, is working out just the way you want it."

"I know. But it's just that some people have no conscience or heart, and that's hard for me to swallow."

"You loved your grandmother, and Elliot carelessly and uncaringly stole from her, then took her life," Liane said softly. "Of course you're upset. But you're going to get her money back."

"And then some. He's paying me in cash," she said. "But, Liane, I can't get Dorsey back."

Suddenly, Barbara felt devastated.

"Remember, your grandmother lived her life to the fullest. She didn't waste a second of it. She was a feisty woman and she went down fighting. What better legacy could she have? She wouldn't have wanted to go out any other way."

Barbara began to calm. "There's something else. Someone searched my house when I was out walking this morning."

"Barbara, this is getting dangerous. You have to talk to the sheriff."

"And tell him what? That I'm about to break the law? He'd pull Elliot in and I'd never get the money."

"But Bar—"

"I can't, Liane. I got a call the other day. One woman they scammed is borrowing money to pay for her medication. These people need their money. They can't afford to have it tied up in the courts for years. By the time the attorneys are through, they'd be dead and the attorneys will have most of the money. This way the money, all of it, will go to the people who lost it."

"Barbara, I'm afraid for you."

"Harper meets me here each evening after work and he goes home with me."

"But he can't always be with you."

"Even if I told him, he wouldn't always be with me." A car sped into the lot and bounced to a stop. Her first customer had arrived. "I have to go."

"Promise me you'll talk to Harper if anything else happens."

"I promise."

Liane sighed. "Maybe one day you can trust him with your secrets."

Trent watched Barbara talking on the phone and wondered what was up. Elliot, at least that was the name he was using now, left happy, and Barbara was smiling as he left, but as soon as the door shut behind him, she was roaring mad. Almost snapped his head off. And she was spying on Elliot's wife earlier. The same as he was going to do. What was up with that?

Trent was feeling a little stiff. He usually jogged five or six miles, but never eight. That morning he'd gotten a workout and then some.

He kept wondering why Barbara was working a regular job when the others weren't. Did the old man come for her money? She beat the heck out of Andrew when he tried to steal from her. The tale was still circulating around town, especially at the bar. Trent couldn't see her getting up off anything if she didn't want to. So what the heck was going on? She didn't need them, not the way they needed her. He couldn't figure it out.

Barbara had called a security company to have their best alarm system installed. She'd first asked Harper which system was the best, of course. He was curious as to why she felt she needed one. She used the excuse of the woman's murder, and that she often came home late and alone. Whether he bought her story she wasn't sure, but he recommended one, even pulled some strings to get it installed quickly.

* * *

The Tyler Perry play was wonderful Saturday night. Afterward, Barbara and Harper went to a jazz club and listened to music. They sat back in comfortable club chairs. Harper drank a club soda and Barbara a margarita.

"Are you ready to tell me why you need the security system?" he asked, surprising Barbara with the question.

"I already told you. I'm alone so much. And anything can happen when I'm gone," she said. "The thing with Sarah has spooked me. There was the break-in at the Stones'. What's going on?" She put the ball back in his court. It was his island and he hadn't solved the crimes.

He stared at her so long she thought he was going to pursue it further. Then a Coltrane song played and Barbara closed her eyes with a smile.

"I just love this song," she said.

"Want to dance?"

"Yes."

On the dance floor, he gathered her into his arms. He had to have a million questions about her actions, but he didn't broach any of them. Pulled into his close embrace, Barbara felt the steady rhythm of his heartbeat and the heat from his body.

At first she was tense. Her feelings were growing for Harper and although she wanted to step back and take a breath, for once she was going to live in the moment. She hated the lies. She hated the misconceptions. But what could she do?

Right now, she was going to enjoy this. Her experience with Harper was something she could put in her memory book when she was back in Philly or New York.

Barbara sighed heavily, feeling his pleasant strength against her. She ran her hands slowly and seductively over his back. She was going to enjoy this, she thought, as she felt more than heard a moan from deep in his throat. His lips found hers and he kissed her tenderly. She sighed and all but melted into him.

They took the last ferry back to the island. It was cold and brisk outside, but Harper got out after he'd parked. The captain was on deck.

"It's been a windy one tonight," the captain said.

Harper tugged up the collar of his coat. "You got that right."

"Hey, you ever find out who killed Sarah?"

Harper shook his head. "Still looking."

"Say, I've been seeing a couple of newcomers ride the ferry two, three times a week. Thought they were staying at Gabrielle's place, but they don't look like they could afford it."

"Do you know their names?"

"Naw, usually stay to themselves."

"And how long have they been visiting?"

"Couple months now. Maybe they have relatives or something. Never see the girl with anyone, but I see the guy with this dude named Andrew. Andrew always walks and sometimes this guy gives him a ride home."

Harper zeroed-in on Andrew. "What do they drive?"

"Old beat-up Ford Taurus. I thought maybe they

had jobs in Norfolk or the Beach," he said, referring to Virginia Beach.

"Thanks for the update," Harper said, noticing that it was time for them to leave.

"Anytime. Time for me to earn my pay."

As the captain walked off, Harper returned to the car.

He'd left the engine idling so Barbara would stay warm. A burst of cold air came in with him. He glanced at Barbara.

"Stay with me tonight?" He'd spent several nights with her, but she hadn't been to his place once. He wanted her to see where he lived.

When she didn't respond, he said, "We can stop by your place for clothes."

"Okay."

Barbara had only seen Harper's house from the road. He activated the garage door opener and drove into the two-car garage. There was a third door large enough for storage or a motorcycle, but nothing was stored there.

Harper grabbed her small suitcase from the backseat. "In anticipating your visit, I got Lisa to clean so you wouldn't have any complaints about my underwear on the bathroom floor."

"I should hope not. You're old enough to pick up after yourself."

"Duly noted," he said, giving her a salute.

They entered the kitchen from the garage and he popped on the light. Barbara stopped.

"Oh, Harper, this is beautiful." The granite countertop was a mixture of brown, black, and beige. The beige matched beige cabinets, and the brown matched the walnut island. He had stainless-steel appliances.

"So what special features do you have?"

"To tell you the truth, I don't really use most of them. My mom and sister-in-law had their way with the kitchen and bathrooms."

"I love it. Everything's stored." There were a few glass cabinets that showcased china and figurines.

And the breakfast room showcased a lovely bay window. In front of it was a low table with two chairs. The other matching chairs were moved to a sitting area in the great room.

"Do you have a living room?"

"I do, but I use it for an office since I don't need a formal living room. But that can be changed. I'm flexible."

The great room was huge—at least twenty by sixteen with a two-story ceiling.

"Master bedroom's on the other side of the great room," he said, and led her to a huge room almost as large as the great room. "There's an empty closet for you. I had Lisa store my overflow junk upstairs."

His bedroom was twice the size of hers, not to mention the huge closet outfitted with drawers and shelves for storing clothes and shoes.

The master bedroom was more masculine than the living area, with a brown and beige comforter.

In the master bath, there were two sinks on opposite walls and a separate water closet. A large shower was in one corner, and a sunken tub was set at the very end under a window.

"I rarely use that tub. I use the hot tub outside," he said.

Lisa had laid out fluffy towels and washcloths on the towel bar.

"When did you build this?"

"About six years ago. I bought a small cottage when I first moved here. But it was time for a larger living space. And when you moved here, I was glad I had someplace to bring you."

"This is amazing."

"I'll show you upstairs tomorrow. That's where the game room is, with the pool table and pinball machine."

"Your nephews and nieces must love to visit you."

"They do. You'll meet them at Christmas. They're going to spend it here this year."

Barbara nodded, a little nervous about meeting his family. They weren't that serious yet.

"I'll give you time to change." He approached and cupped her chin. "I want you to feel comfortable, Barbara, as if you were home." He kissed her lightly and stepped back.

Barbara nodded.

"Do you want to take tomorrow off, or are we going to church?"

Barbara couldn't remember a Sunday when she didn't go to church. Dorsey had dragged her there every Sunday and she continued to go when she visited Dorsey in Philly.

"Church," she said.

He nodded. "Guess we better get ready for bed, then. I'll give you some privacy."

CHAPTER 10

Sonya got up early the next morning and brought breakfast back to the cottage for their roommate, shocking the woman. She was still asleep when Sonya knocked on the door.

She hadn't mentioned the bowl to Boyd—and didn't plan to. But she had a funny feeling that bowl her roommate's friend was making was a replica of the original golden bowl. It was too much of a co-incidence that another ancient bowl was floating around. Which meant the friend knew where the valuable bowl was, and Sonya planned to find out.

"How're your projects going?" Sonya asked as the woman sat up in bed to eat.

"It's going fine," she said. "I haven't had breakfast in bed in years. They certainly don't give you the star treatment here."

"Everyone needs to be pampered. But we can't complain. The room and board's cheap."

"I don't know how cheap it is. They get a fraction of our profits on top of rent."

Sonya shrugged. "What can you say? Nothing's free."

"That's for sure."

"You were saying your friend was having some problems with her project. If she needs help, just let me know," Sonya said breezily. "Boyd and I are leaving for Thanksgiving, but I'll be happy to help when we get back."

"I've never seen you sculpt. You do beautiful paintings."

"I work both mediums," Sonya said.

"I'll tell her. You have a great holiday."

"Are you visiting your family?"

"I'll be here."

"I've got to pack."

"And I have to get ready to work in the gallery," her roommate said.

"Check you later." Sonya didn't want to appear too eager. Her roommate would get suspicious. She and Boyd weren't going anywhere for the holidays. She wanted it said that they weren't around when things happened on the island.

Barbara went to services at Harper's church, but afterward he dropped her off at her house so she could get her car and drive to his.

Harper headed home to change and called John to discuss his conversation with the ferry captain.

"Talk to Gabrielle about it. They're driving an old Taurus. But I can't see how they can afford the B and B's prices if they can't afford a newer car. But we're going to cover all the bases."

"I'll go by Gabby's place now. I've seen a Taurus lately. A 2001 model."

"Who was driving it? Man or woman?"

"Some guy. A stranger."

"I'm headed to the artist colony to question the owner," Harper said.

"Artists are always coming and going from that place."

As soon as he changed, Harper left for the artist colony. Located on the other side of the island, it consisted of a collection of old cottages with a huge white barn in the center divided into rooms for painting. The sculpturing and glass blowing took place in separate buildings.

The cottages and barns were all freshly painted. The grounds were well maintained. In the spring and summer, flowers would flourish.

Several cars were parked in front of the gallery, which, like most of the other buildings, was a white one-floor cottage.

It was run by the daughter of the woman who'd started it. Nancy's mother had formed the colony five years before she died, buying up the surrounding summer cottages from a family who rented them out. Nancy married and kept the colony going with the help of her husband, but Nancy did not have her mother's immense artistic talent, although she was an amateur sculptor.

One of the conditions for living there was that each person had to participate in the upkeep of the buildings. A portion of their sales went to maintain the colony.

The colony also planted a huge vegetable garden each year, and they usually ate their meals together in a second building smaller than the studio.

Harper climbed out of his car and headed to the gallery.

Nancy was showing a painting to a customer. Harper indicated he wanted to speak to her when she finished. He studied the surroundings while he waited. A woman in a long, flowing, vividly colored patchwork skirt with a peasant blouse manned the cash register.

One of the artists was discussing a seascape with another couple. Harper wondered if she'd painted it.

Harper was studying a painting of the colony when Nancy approached him. She was thin and had a café au lait complexion. She wore a jean skirt with beadwork with a colorful red blouse. Her hair was done in a French twist.

"What brings you here, Sheriff?"

"I see business is brisk," Harper said, nodding toward the crowd.

"Weekends are the busiest times for sales with people from the mainland."

"We're still looking for Sarah Rhodes's murderer."

"Oh, that poor child. She used to come here to look at the paintings. She couldn't afford them, of course, but she certainly enjoyed art."

Harper jotted that down. "Did she mingle with any of the artists?"

"Oh, no. She was friendly, though."

"In the last month have any of your artists had a sudden cash input? Maybe from an uncle or parent?"

"Not as far as I know. Everyone here is living on a shoestring. None of them have wealthy families. From time to time, we do get those who have an independent income, but that hasn't happened in the last few years."

"Any new arrivals in the last two months?"

"One couple arrived the middle of September. The woman is the artist. Actually, she painted the picture of the grounds you were looking at. She has a very promising career ahead of her."

"They wouldn't by any chance drive a brown Ford Taurus, would they?"

"Actually, they do. Her boyfriend works in Norfolk. She works there part-time for living expenses."

"Are they here now? I'd like to meet them."

She shook her head. "Both of them are off-island right now. They're leaving to visit their families for two weeks. They won't return until after Thanksgiving. I can call you when they're here if you'd like to talk to them."

"I would." Harper handed her a card with his cell number and office number. "As soon as they return," he said.

"Do you know where they work?"

"I'm sorry, I don't."

On his way home, John called Harper. "I talked to Gabrielle. She hasn't had anyone staying there for that length of time."

"I lucked out at the artist colony. But they weren't there. Nancy will call me when they're in."

"So are you on your way to the office?"

"I'm going home."

When Harper disconnected, he smiled. He was going home, to Barbara. For so long he'd wanted someone to welcome him home, and finally he had her.

Barbara absolutely loved Harper's kitchen—his entire house, actually. Before church, he'd taken two steaks out of the freezer to thaw. She was marinating them in a little red wine and olive oil. He'd promised to grill them outside.

She was going to keep it simple. She'd washed and put foil on the sweet potatoes, the salad was in the fridge, and the homemade dressing on the counter.

Barbara sat at the bay window and regarded the ocean. What a lovely view. She watched snow birds frolic near the water. Farther down she saw a couple walking. She was still a little nervous about whether Elliot would actually go through with the stock deal. She couldn't consider it a done deal until she had the money in hand.

She heard the garage door activate. Harper was home. A minute later, he came through the door.

"If you start the grill I can put the sweet potatoes on," she said.

"Get your jacket. I'm going to show you where everything is."

"How did things go today?" she asked, donning her coat.

"They weren't there. But they haven't come into any money either."

She grabbed the potatoes and they went out the sliding door. There was a huge outdoor fireplace on the porch.

"Is that another fire pit in the yard?"

He nodded. "Near the hot tub. You and I can get in later. You're going to love spending time out here." He lit the grill.

"In the summer."

"In the snow and ice, too."

"Keep dreaming." Barbara placed the potatoes on the rack and closed the hood.

Harper put his arm around her as they walked back inside. "I'm going to turn you into an outdoors girl yet," he said, and Barbara believed he might at that.

"Harper, do you really think Sarah's death was the result of a robbery?"

He nodded. "She had five grand on her, but we haven't given out that information."

"In cash?"

"Yes, it was a gift from Hughes so that she could buy a used car. Hers had broken down and she needed transportation."

Maybe Elliot didn't kill Sarah, Barbara thought. But he definitely killed Dorsey. She believed that even though Dorsey's neighbors had tried to dissuade her.

Harper showered while Barbara finished dinner. Now he was watching the football game while Barbara enjoyed herself in the hot tub in his bathroom. The bubbles almost overflowed the lip. She'd lit candles around the tub. And she was enjoying a glass of wine. It was time for her to realize some of those fantasies she used to have.

"Harper?" she called out.

"Yeah?"

"Can you bring me a towel?"

"Aren't there towels in there?" he asked, clearly into his game.

"I can't reach it."

"In a minute."

It was five minutes before he actually opened the door.

"What the . . ."

Barbara held out a glass of wine. "Would you like to join me?"

She didn't have to ask him twice.

"What about your game?"

"I'll catch it later," he said as he slid into the tub behind her. She leaned back against his chest.

"Two months ago, I never would have dreamed . . ."

She rubbed the inside of his thigh. "Dreamed what?"

"Romantic nights like this with you." He cupped her breasts, caressing her nipples.

"Just so you know—I've had a few fantasies about you, too."

"Glad to hear it." He released her and leaned back himself, carrying her with him. "I still can't figure you out."

"What's bothering you?"

"What did you see in Andrew?"

Barbara nearly groaned. "I thought he was a nice guy."

"Come on, Barbara. I was trying to put the moves on you and you chose him."

"We never went out on a date."

"You were so quiet and standoffish. And always tense around me. I was trying to work my way up to a date. I thought if I moved slowly, you'd learn to relax around me."

"Andrew is in the past. Is he important now?"

"It just puzzles me that a woman like you would date someone with no more sense than Andrew. You're too smart for that."

"Nobody asks older men why they date younger women. But you're going to put me through the third degree about Andrew?"

"At least the women have something going for them."

"What? A nice body? Paid-for boobs? They're great at sucking dick when a guy's paycheck is high enough?"

Harper groaned. "I'm digging myself in with this one, aren't I?"

"Deeper and deeper."

"Baby, don't talk like that or we won't be relaxing in here much longer."

"Well, that was the plan until you pissed me off."

"Let me remedy that right now."

And for the next hour he put action to words, unrelenting in his need to satisfy his increasing desire for her. Barbara had never made love with such deep absorption that it left her gasping for breath and wanting more than ever to hold on to what she had.

It was hard getting away from Harper. They spent every spare minute together. But the next morning, Barbara told him she was going to the mainland to shop for groceries and for supplies for her shop.

She met Lambert's daughter for breakfast.

"Thank you so much for meeting with me," Cassandra Houston said. "I'm at my wit's end. Dad won't believe anything I tell him about Minerva. He thinks she's the best thing since the arrival of Jesus. He thinks of her as his girlfriend. Can you believe that?"

"It's their way of gaining trust. She's sweet to him. The one thing I learned a long time ago was that confidence women know how to treat men. And she's good at it. She's had years to hone her kills. And so has her husband."

Cassandra leaned back, shocked. "I never would have believed my father could have the wool pulled over his eyes this way. I'm going to the police."

"That's a good move, except, has she gotten any money from him yet?"

Cassandra sighed. "No."

"They won't do anything. But at least you can have it on record. And since it's a small town . . . I don't know. I'm dating the sheriff. Our relationship is rather new, and I haven't mentioned my reason for being here. He cares about the people here, so I think he'll try to help you."

"Why won't you tell him?"

She told her about the legal process for returning the cash back to the owners and how she didn't actually have the money yet.

"How long before you think they'll give it to you?"

"Couple of days at most."

"Call me as soon as you get it. Then I'll go to the sheriff."

Barbara nodded. "They deal in cash, so there's no record that the money transfer transpired. They will deny it. And they don't keep their money in American banks. If they have an account at all, it's off-shore. That's easy to do," Barbara said. "You can try getting power of attorney, but by the time you have your father declared incompetent, it'll be too late. She has him in her grips now, and she'll move quickly. She knows his family is here."

Cassandra was clearly disturbed. "How can these people get away with this?"

"They hit fast and move on to a new location under another identity."

"She actually cried these big boo-hoo tears and had him angry with *me* for upsetting *her,*" Cassandra said in outrage. "Can you believe it?

"I don't know what to do. Both my parents worked very hard for their money. My mother died twenty years ago, and I don't want my father's retirement money for myself. I just want him to be comfortable for the rest of his life. I want him to be able to travel, to play golf, to enjoy the comforts he's worked so hard for. And most of all, I don't want him hurt." She sighed, a tear slipping down her cheeks. "But I'm afraid it's already too late for that. He's going to be heartbroken when this is over. And he doesn't deserve that."

There was nothing Barbara could say. It was all true. As she made her way back to the island, she felt as if someone was watching her. She often got that feeling lately and didn't understand where it was coming from. She'd turn, thinking someone was glaring at her, and everyone would be engaged in conversation. It had gotten to the point where she was nervous in her own home, even with the security system. She'd never been afraid before, even in New York, where crime was off the charts.

She shook her head. She was becoming paranoid. But she couldn't shake that feeling.

Tuesday morning, Elliot stored the backpack in the trunk of his car and then ran to the local gas station to fill up the tank. Minerva should be finished with her breakfast, he thought as he went inside and tossed the keys on the countertop.

"Elliot, I've changed my mind," Minerva said before he could get out of his coat. She was still at the breakfast table, and for a change Andrew was up in time to join her. She was leaving for work in a few minutes.

"About what?" Elliot asked, dropping into a chair and grabbing a sweet roll. He bit into it and grimaced. The ones Barbara had served were much better. Wonder where she got them from?

Minerva worried her bottom lip. "I've been thinking about that money. I'm getting a weird feeling about giving it to Barbara. I'm on pins and needles at work. Lambert's daughter watches me like a hawk and it's making me nervous. That money is all we have left. I'm feeling that a bird in the hand is better than two in the bush. You don't know what could happen with that stock she's talking about. I'm not willing to trust it."

"Minerva, we don't have enough to live off. We've already discussed this, and the paperwork Barbara gave us looks good. The company's legit."

"I know. But we'll have nothing if something goes wrong. What if Barbara gets in an accident or dies? There will be no proof that we ever gave that money to her. We'll never get it back."

"Minerva, what the hell's gonna happen here in this town? Barbara barely ever leaves the island."

"Look at our son and you can ask me that question?"

"I'm figuring Andrew got into something in Norfolk he's not telling us about, just like he messed up with Barbara."

"Daddy, that's not true . . ."

"Quiet, boy. I'm talking. Minerva, it's a safe investment and better than anything else I can come up with. If we set up another scam, it'll take time. We'll run the risk of getting caught."

Minerva crimped her mouth. "I don't care. Let's hold on to what we've got."

"Minerva . . ."

"I mean it, Elliot. I've always gone along with your plans, but not this time. If half of it hadn't been taken, I'd go along with it, but we can't afford to lose this on top of what we've already lost."

"You always were too cautious."

"I told you to put that money in an offshore bank. Then we would have it."

"The feds look at that stuff."

"Tell Barbara you changed your mind." She shoved her chair back. "I've got to get to work."

Minerva was a stubborn woman when she made her mind up about something. Frustrated, Elliot watched her disappear into the back room. He got up, gathered his keys from the counter, and stomped to the door. "Tell your mother I'll be waiting in the car."

"What you gonna do, Dad?" Andrew asked, watching him closely.

"Exactly what your mother said. I'm going to tell Barbara I changed my mind."

Outside, Mrs. Claxton waved and Elliot smiled and waved back. The old hag was blasting her husband. Elliot scoffed. It would be a cold day in hell before he let a woman tell him what to do. He was going to drive right up to Barbara's house after he dropped Minerva off at work and give her that money.

Elliot arrived at Barbara's house shortly after she got home from Harper's place. She and Harper had exercised on his equipment together that morning. And since Lambert's daughter was in residence, she decided not to walk past his place. It would be interesting if she met Trent on the path.

Elliot carried a backpack.

She hated to let scum into her house, but what

choice did she have? She managed to summon a smile as she opened the door. "Come on in."

Frowning, he exploded into the room with a desperate air. "I can't emphasize enough how much this money means to me and Minerva."

"I understand," Barbara said empathetically. It meant a lot to the people he stole it from, too.

She tried to tamp down her enthusiasm at getting hold of that money.

He patted the backpack. "That stock looked real good. I looked it up on the Internet and there were some good things about the parent company." He patted the backpack. "So you take real good care of this for us."

"Don't worry about that. I'll look after it as if it were my own," she said. "I'll have it transferred to my friend right away."

Barbara took the money out of the backpack, stored it in her briefcase, and handed his backpack back to him. Again, Elliot didn't respond to her as if he knew her true identity. She'd probably be as dead as Sarah by now if he knew. All the pictures Dorsey had stopped when she was a senior in high school with long hair and braces. She had no fear that he knew what she looked like.

"I'll call as soon as I have any information," she told Elliot, and showed him to the door. She thought about Harper. He and his officers were always driving all over the island. "And, Elliot, just in case someone saw your car in my driveway, why don't I just say that you were here to pay for Minerva's hair."

"That works for me," he said, and Barbara closed the door after him.

After he left, Barbara counted the money and

took stock. It was a rainy morning and no one was walking along the beach. She looked across the road to a partially wooded area. She shivered. She was so isolated. The next house was down the beach. She wished she had a garage instead of a carport. Assuring herself she was alone, she drove to the bank and placed the money in a safety deposit box she'd rented months ago.

Once that was done, Barbara released a long breath. The money was in her hands. Finally. She had at least enough to pay back the five people she knew, not the amount Elliot took, but enough for them to be comfortable. Much more than was stolen from her grandmother.

Dorsey's estate came to Barbara. She wouldn't keep her grandmother's share. Dorsey would forgive her. Barbara wasn't one to sneeze at money, but she'd earned enough that she really didn't need it as desperately as the seniors she'd encountered.

She felt like seeing Harper, but she didn't want to depend on him. She was with him every night as it was. She knew he sensed her unrest, that she was uneasy about something. She was surprised he hadn't pushed her for answers.

At home, it all felt anticlimactic. She'd accomplished her goal. She could leave, but where would she go? She didn't have a job to go to.

Barbara called Lambert's daughter's California number and left a message. Cassandra had said she retrieved her messages daily. She couldn't take the chance of leaving a message on a cell with Minerva in the house. She was sure the woman snooped. She could easily pick up a cell phone and toggle through the last numbers called.

The holidays. She and Harper hadn't talked about

what they were doing for the holidays. Thanksgiving was next week. He would probably visit his family in North Carolina.

Had her grandmother lived, they'd probably be traveling by now. Spending Christmas in Germany or England.

Barbara sighed. She never expected to meet a man like Harper. Her marriage had been so brief that she thought she'd never go for it again. But yet . . . Harper was everything she'd ever wanted in a man. He was considerate. He cared. That was what touched her heart most. That he was good to her. She didn't have to be skinny or put up pretenses except for the strictures she imposed on herself. He was satisfied with her and didn't expect her to change for him.

And she'd given him nothing but lies. He'd never forgive her when he found out what she'd done. Barbara didn't know what to do or where she belonged.

She gazed out toward the ocean. It was drizzling and the waves were peaceful. There was something special about watching the ocean from Harper's place. Sunday night he'd started a fire outside and they'd snuggled beneath the blankets.

I don't want to lose this, she thought.

Barbara sighed. At least Liane was arriving Saturday. It would be good to have her friend close by. Except Liane had made reservations to stay in the B&B and wouldn't let Barbara talk her out of it.

Tuesday morning, Harper drove to Trent's place. He opened the door before Harper knocked.

He looked surprised to see him. "Morning, Sheriff. What can I do for you?"

Harper nodded. "I just keep wondering why a young man would settle on an island with no entertainment. Especially one from D.C. where the partying is hard."

Trent seemed to relax a fraction. "Is there a law against a person getting a little R and R?"

Harper studied him. "I saw you running near the Stones' the other morning."

Trent shrugged. "I like to keep in shape. I met up with Barbara near the marsh the other day, too. I don't always run in the same place. It breaks the monotony. Are there specific places where I should and shouldn't run?"

"I'm curious about the shooting. Andrew Stone was shot a while back. They must talk about it in the beauty parlor."

Trent nodded. "Practically everybody who comes in."

"And I noticed you have a record." The record was sealed, and without a court order Harper couldn't get to it.

"Not lately. I was still in high school. I haven't gotten in trouble since then."

"You led me to believe you'd just gotten out of the military when, in fact, you got out seven years ago."

"Sheriff, I didn't shoot that man. Now, unless you have anything concrete . . ."

"I'll be around," Harper said, with the warning that he'd be watching him closely.

Trent tried to use all the D.C. cool he possessed as the sheriff watched him leave. Maybe it was time he left the area. Move to the mainland, as the locals call it, and keep a watch from there. But being here was a lot more convenient. And he couldn't leave without his mother's money.

Except for that high-school incident, Trent didn't have a record. He made sure of that.

Harper sat at his desk, tapping his pen against the blotter. Earlier, on his way back from Trent's, he considered dropping by Barbara's place to steal a kiss or something. He drove past. But the Stones' car was leaving as he slowed down to make the turn. It wasn't Minerva, but Elliot. What was he doing at Barbara's place? He let Elliot pull out in front of him but didn't turn into Barbara's drive. He followed Elliot until he turned off at his home, then drove back to the precinct.

Barbara had a lot of secrets, which made him uncomfortable. The Stones couldn't be into anything good. And they weren't the kind of people he wanted her mixed up with.

His intercom rang. "Harper, a Ms. Houston is here to see you."

"Houston?"

"She's Mr. Lambert Hughes's daughter."

"Send her in."

Harper stood as the woman entered the office. She was a pretty woman in her late fifties.

"Have a seat, Ms. Houston."

"Cassandra, please. I have a feeling we're going to be spending a lot of time together."

"Oh?"

"It's come to my attention that my father's caretaker, Minerva Stone, is a swindler."

Harper frowned. "You have proof of this?"

"No, but my source was good."

Harper frowned. "Who is your source, Cassandra?"

"I can't tell you that. But the person warned me to get rid of Minerva before she fleeces my father out of his life's savings, the way she has several other seniors."

"And have you fired her?"

Cassandra sighed, shaking with frustration and anger. "He won't let me." A tear rolled down her cheek.

Harper grabbed a box of tissues and set it on the edge of his desk. "Just take your time."

"I am so angry. He is in love with her," she said in outrage.

Harper wondered if it was a case of a daughter hating the fact that her father could fall for a woman who wasn't her mother.

"It's like she's his girlfriend instead of his companion. My God, I just don't understand it. It's like she has a spell on him. Is there anything I can do?"

"There isn't a law against falling in love. Do you have evidence that she's stolen money from him?"

"No, I finally talked him into giving me power of attorney, so he no longer has control over his money. This way she can't steal from him, but I'm worried about him emotionally. And I thought you needed to know about these people."

"I'm glad you came to me."

"And I also discovered she's married to Elliot, and she and my father are acting like married people. It's shameful. My God, if he could have sex at ninety, they would."

Harper straightened in his seat. "I need names. People who the Stones have robbed? Can you get them for me?"

"I'll try."

When Cassandra Houston left, Harper ran the Stones' names through other databases before he called the FBI's confidence unit.

It also gave him the connection to Sarah. Sarah had money on her. Five thousand wasn't anything to sneeze at.

The next day, after Barbara exercised on Harper's equipment, she drove home. When she got there, Naomi was sitting in her car waiting for her.

She opened her door and climbed out. "Can you get that bag out of the back seat for me and bring it inside?" the older woman asked.

"Of course."

Barbara retrieved the tote. Naomi was a little slower getting up the steps, but she climbed without assistance.

"Have you been waiting long?" Barbara asked.

"Not long," she said, breathing hard. "You've got a lovely view from here. I always loved this home."

"I love it, too. Can I get you something to drink or eat? I have coffee, tea. Even a coffee cake I made earlier."

"Coffee with cake will hit the spot."

Barbara set the items on the table and dished up the cake, handing it to Naomi.

"I haven't had coffee cake like this since your grandmother left here," Naomi said, taking a bite.

"My grandmother?" Barbara asked.

"Yes, I remember Dorsey well. She was closer friends with my sister, Anna, in school. I know she's passed away. She'd written me that she was eager to return here, and that you were going to bring her back to live here with her."

Barbara nodded.

Naomi laid a hand on hers. Her gentle, caring touch moved Barbara. "I'm glad you decided to move here. You're family and you should be here."

"I don't have any family left."

"That's where you're wrong, honey. This is where your ancestors came from. They arrived here almost four hundred years ago. Your history is here. You belong here. Dorsey was my second cousin. Her husband was also a descendent of one of the original islanders."

Barbara gazed at her. After her grandmother's death, she didn't feel she belonged anywhere, much less had relatives.

"It's one of the reasons I convinced you to work on the Founder's Day committee. I wanted you to gather your family's history and display it. I'll help you, of course. I have lots of information on your grandfather's side, as well as your grandmother's, and I'll give it all to you. When your great-grandmother died, I saved the information for whoever might return to the island. But you're here now and it's all yours."

"I didn't know that." Barbara was stunned. "Dorsey didn't believe in dwelling in the past. She never talked about life here."

"She was young when she left, but your roots are here, honey. I didn't want to bombard you with information as soon as you arrived. But you're also one of the women responsible for the family heirlooms."

"Family heirlooms?"

"The golden bowl, doubloons, and old coins. You, Alyssa, and Gabrielle are the ones responsible for their fate in this generation. You have to decide who gets it for the next. Anna was responsible for it and she picked the three of you to carry on the torch. But for right now . . ."

Puzzled, Barbara shook her head. "Wait a minute. I've heard people mention the bowl."

Naomi explained the heirloom's history. Barbara was astonished that she was part of this amazing history.

"But the one that originally belonged to this family is missing. I just hope we can find it. It's been in the family so long."

"It's amazing that you've kept it this long."

"And a shame if it isn't found. But I'm holding out hope that it will be."

Barbara nodded.

"And I hope you'll be here for Thanksgiving," Naomi said. "It's always at my house and I'd like you to join us. Of course, this year we're holding it at Cornell's restaurant. It's large enough for the entire family to dine in comfort. I tell you, it's nice having a grandson who owns a restaurant."

"Thank you for inviting me, but . . ."

"And, of course, Harper is invited, too. He's going to be here. With all the trouble, he wouldn't dare leave."

Barbara didn't know that. "I was going to say that my friend from New York is visiting."

"Bring her, too. Bring anyone you want. What's a few more mouths in my group?"

CHAPTER 11

Tuesday night, impatience seemed to spring from every pore in Trent's body. Nothing pleased him. He'd worked out on his equipment. He'd watched TV until it bored him to tears. He'd even gotten on the phone to talk to his sister and mother, and it made him feel even worse.

He wanted his mother's money and he wanted to move on. The sheriff wasn't watching the house as closely as before. But the man was suspicious of him. He needed to get the money and get out of there fast.

He'd already broken into the Stones' one night and found absolutely nothing. That particular night he noticed Minerva and Elliot strolling across the yard to Mrs. Claxton's house. They talked about the dinner invitation they'd received from her. And as usual, Andrew went into Norfolk. Trent spotted him walking toward the ferry earlier when he was on his way home from work.

Under the cover of darkness, Trent approached the house and slid inside unnoticed. It was easy work getting into the door using his lock picks. Even after the robbery they hadn't done a thing to increase security. Trent chuckled. An amateur could get in there without much effort.

His mother hadn't improved at all. She still refused to get out of bed except to use the rest room and to take baths when his sister forced her. And here the Stones walked around like they were good citizens.

Trent started searching in the bedroom, rifling through the closet, under the bed. His anger built as he shifted the mattresses off and slit them, just in case money was hidden in there.

Ordinarily, he wasn't destructive. His mother wouldn't approve, but the Stones destroyed lives. He felt justified in destroying their belongings. Let them see how it felt to have their home invaded. He knocked lightly on walls for false doors. He looked behind the cheap pictures.

There was nothing in the Stones' bedroom. He went to Andrew's bedroom next and gave it the same treatment, although he didn't expect to find anything there. The house was small. Only two bedrooms. No garage. He checked the living room, the kitchen, and the utility room. The money wasn't anywhere. He even climbed to the attic, pulling down the rickety stairs and shining his penlight on dust bunnies.

He didn't think they had the brains to put money into an offshore bank account or to trust banks that much. Well, if it was there, then somebody had better get it. And he couldn't fathom them burying it in the yard.

Elliot was known for his killer temper. He'd killed a guy back in D.C., but the police never even suspected. He didn't want Elliot on him when he left. The man would definitely come back to D.C. to kill him. Trent had never committed murder and wasn't about to start now.

Frustrated, when he was about to leave, he gazed

out the window to make sure no one was about. He saw someone dressed in black hiding in the bushes. He wondered if the person had seen him enter. Too short and overweight to be Andrew. Smaller than Barbara. My God, it was a woman. Could it be Barbara? People looked smaller dressed in black. Did she sneak away from the sheriff to rob the place? Was there a falling out among thieves?

Glancing around, the person started to the door.

Trent made a hasty retreat to the front door. Damn it. He didn't like going out through the front. But he quickly scanned the area, saw that it was clear, and stole out into the night. He made his way around the back and hid in the bushes for a while. In a couple minutes the woman came outside. Trent followed her for a mile to a path. She got in a boat and rowed out a short distance before she started the motor.

The way the woman moved reminded him of Sonya. She was in the bar a couple of times when he went there and they'd had drinks together. So why was she here?

Since Trent was already going in the direction of his house, he continued on home, wondering if this woman had lost money to the Stones, too.

Barbara climaxed on a scream.

"I love you," Harper said, hovering above her.

Shocked, she could only stare at him. They say you could never believe a man's profession of love in the throes of an orgasm, but Barbara believed him. Had felt it even before he said the words.

When she remained silent, Harper moved to the side and gathered her into his arms.

"Harper, don't get serious about me."

He kissed the side of her mouth. "Baby, it's already too late for that."

Barbara shifted to look directly at him. "But . . . I don't even know if I'm going to stay here permanently."

"Why not?"

"I don't know what I'm going to do. I never promised you I would stay."

He blew out a long breath. "When are you going to trust me, Barbara?"

"I trust you."

"Don't lie to me. Don't lie in my arms and lie to me."

Barbara grabbed the sheet and scrambled to the other side of the bed. Standing, she wrapped the sheet around her. "I'm going home."

Harper snatched the sheet away, leaving her standing naked—as naked as he was looming before her.

"Coward. You're not going anywhere. You're afraid of something, Barbara. So, if you go home, I'll just have to sit in the damn car in your yard all night instead of getting the sleep I need."

"I never said . . ."

"Do you really think you had to?"

Barbara remained silent.

"When are you leaving?"

"I don't know. I'm going to put the salon on the market after the holidays."

"So you'll be here at least another two, three months?"

"Longer than that. The sale will take a few months. The economy isn't exactly booming."

"Where are you going when the sale is finalized, back to New York?"

Barbara glanced away. "I don't know."

"Are you running from something?"

"No."

Harper blew out a frustrated breath. "Why won't you let me help you?" he entreated.

Barbara looked away. "It's not something you can help me with."

Frustrated, he approached her. "Is there another man?"

Barbara chuckled. "No, and there hasn't been one in a very long time."

"Do you have any feelings for me, Barbara?" When she remained silent, he said, "At least give me the truth about that, if nothing else." Hands on hips, he leaned into her and Barbara felt as if she was a villain on the witness stand. "How do you feel about me?"

A thousand denials flipped through her mind. But in the end, she could give him nothing but the truth. "I love you," she whispered.

He looked rattled, as if she'd knocked the wind from his sails. A play of emotions crossed his face— elation, uncertainty, and finally frustration. "Then I'll settle for that—for now." He pulled her into his arms and kissed her tenderly before he led her back to bed. Their lovemaking was almost desperate. Tender, wild, thrilling, each giving all, wanting to experience everything there was for as long as what they had lasted.

The Claxtons invited the Stones to another dinner with a couple from church. Afterward, Elliot and Minerva walked home.

"She's some cook," Elliot said.

"I'm some cook. I am so tired. It's been a long night and with Lambert's daughter underfoot, the days are excruciatingly long. I'm ready for bed."

"Yeah, you are," Elliot agreed. He wanted to get along tonight. He had plans.

"I thought we'd never get away from that place. It's almost eleven. Naomi just had to tell us a million stories about her grandchildren and the woman who used to live here and about her family. You'd think they were royalty the way she talked," Minerva said, and Elliot refused to comment on the jealousy in her voice.

He tightened his arms around her. "You know this is part of our research."

"It must be nice to have a stable home. I know it's paid for. Some people are so lucky. It was probably passed down from her ancestors. She probably never had to work hard a day in her life."

"She was a teacher, Minerva. Don't you remember her saying so? She taught until she retired. Handling kids isn't easy. You know that."

"But she's got a nice little piece of money coming in. And that land was handed down to her. Her family probably sent her to college. She never had to scratch the way I did."

Elliot sighed. "Minerva, you've never had to scratch. You never even worked a paying job before." Nothing he said was going to appease Minerva, so he just let her get it off her chest.

When she finally wound down, Elliot nuzzled her neck and squeezed her tighter. "Andrew went to Norfolk. It's been a while for us. I can take one of my lucky pills and we can . . ."

"You can't be acting like lovers out here. We're supposed to be sister and brother, remember?"

"I remember." He put some space between them.

"I just want sleep tonight," Minerva muttered. "I'm just too tired for anything else."

"You're always tired. It's been a while."

Peeved, Minerva slid him a sideways glance. "Maybe if you had to work, you'd be tired, too. I don't get to sit home and get a midday nap."

"That's unfair, Minerva. I've done my share of work for this family and you know it."

"Yeah, yeah, yeah."

In a fit of temper, Elliot unlocked the door and went in. He didn't want to make love to her anymore, anyway. If she didn't straighten up, he could go to Norfolk and find himself a willing woman. He had the hots for Barbara, anyway. He was too angry to hold the door for Minerva. If she wanted to be treated like a lady, then she had to be nice to him. He might be old, but he wasn't dead yet.

He flipped on the light. "What the hell?"

"What is it?" Minerva asked, pushing him aside.

"Somebody trashed the damn place."

Minerva glanced around in shock. "The money. Elliot, they stole the other half of the money! Check the hiding place."

She rushed to the bedroom with Elliot behind her. She opened the drawer with the false bottom.

"It's gone! My God. All of it's gone." Minerva staggered back.

Elliot eased down on the damaged bed. His heart was betting so fast he clutched a hand to his chest. What if he hadn't given that money to Barbara?

"What are we going to do?" Minerva repeated. "It's all gone."

"It's not gone," he finally said. They certainly would have found the place had the money been there.

Minerva looked at him as if he was crazy. "What are you talking about? It's not where you put it."

"I gave it to Barbara to invest."

Minerva swaggered as if he'd hit her. "Against my wishes?"

"Sometimes you don't make sense when you get scared. And if I hadn't given it to her, we'd be flat broke."

Trent was tired of this place. He was going to have to handle things the same way he'd handled them in D.C. Some things were the same no matter where you were. If he had to spend Thanksgiving here, he damn sure wasn't going to spend Christmas. He shuddered at the thought.

He knew that Barbara and Harper spent most nights together, either at his place or hers. Kept him too busy to be checking up on him. He also knew the asshole Andrew spent a lot of time in Norfolk. Without transportation, he usually walked the mile and a half from the ferry to home. Trent found a little pathway nearby to park his vehicle—after Harper and Barbara were well into supper or whatever they were doing for the evening.

Trent was a patient man. He was used to waiting for scum. He took a couple bottles of water and snack food, and he was good to go. He used his binoculars to spot the walkers.

Trent had to get out of the car to piss twice. The asshole waited 'til ten-thirty to get off the ferry. But he was there. Trent got out of the truck and positioned himself at a secluded spot.

When Andrew passed by, he grabbed him, clamping a hand over his mouth. Andrew's mouth moved like a fish beneath Trent's hand.

"You holler, you die," Trent whispered in his ear. "Nod if you understand."

Andrew's head swung up and down.

Trent tightened his arm around Andrew's neck, restricting his breathing. "Your family stole something from me and I want it back."

Andrew tried to nod his head again, but he couldn't move.

"No need to talk. I'll break your freaking arm again and worse if I don't get my money." He loosened his grip so Andrew could talk.

"What money?"

Trent popped Andrew upside the head and brought out his Glock.

"Oww. Jesus. Please don't kill me." He tried to move away, but Trent held him in place.

"Shut up."

"Ain't got no money."

"Your father does. And I want it back. Every last freaking cent."

"You the one who shot me?" Andrew asked.

"I wouldn't've just shot you. I would've killed your sorry ass," Trent told him and meant it. "Your daddy fucked with my mother, and I'm pissed as hell. You got one week. Or I'll kill all of you. Mama, Daddy, and you. Understand?"

Andrew was trembling in his arms. "I . . ."

"Yes or no."

"I . . . I . . . I understand."

"And you better not mention me to your mama or daddy or the police or anyone else. You just get my damn money."

"I . . ."

Trent tightened his arm around Andrew's neck.

"You got that? Yes or no?" He loosened his grip enough for Andrew to speak.

"But . . ."

"I can kill you right now." He took the safety off the Glock and pressed it against Andrew's temple. "Or I can get you from ambush any second I want to."

Andrew fainted, leaving Trent stumbling with the full weight of his body.

Trent shook his head. *Sorry-ass SOB*, he thought, leaning over and slapping the guy to see if he really was out. Andrew didn't move. He was out stone-cold.

Looking around him, Trent stuck the gun in his waistband and made his way back to his SUV.

Sooner or later, Andrew would come to and find his way home.

John Aldridge was working the night shift, making rounds, when he thought he saw somebody lying on the ground about a mile from the ferry. He called it in to the dispatcher and got out of his car to check it out.

He beamed the light from his flashlight. A young man was lying on the ground. His britches were wet around the seat. John recognized Andrew Stone.

John checked for a pulse. The man moved his head and groaned.

"Had too much to drink?" John asked.

Andrew groaned again, then winced against the light. "Please," he mumbled weakly. "Don't kill me."

"This is the police. Nobody's going to kill you. Can you get up?"

"Yes . . . yes, sir."

"Come on. I'll take you home." John put some plastic on his car seat, settled Andrew in the car, and drove him the short distance home, hoping he wouldn't puke in the squad car.

"It's not good to get so drunk that you pass out," John said. "It's downright dangerous. You could have fallen in the road and gotten driven over."

"Yes, sir. It won't happen again," Andrew mumbled.

The boy seemed extremely nervous. "You okay?"

"Yes, sir."

Andrew was older than John by at least five years. Why was he calling him "sir"? There was something pitiful about him that had John feeling sorry for him. Andrew seemed to be one of those weak souls who was easily managed by others.

"Take care of yourself, buddy, okay?"

"Yes, sir."

John parked in the yard and waited for Andrew to go inside before he drove away.

All seemed quiet in the neighborhood.

Harper was sleeping with Barbara wrapped securely in his arms when the phone rang.

"There's been another robbery at the Stones'. This time they trashed the place. Slashed mattresses. Pulled everything out the cupboards. It's a mess, Harper," John said.

"I'll be there."

"What's wrong?" Barbara asked.

"There was another break-in at the Stones'. You going to be okay here?" Harper asked.

"Of course. Go on."

He kissed her quickly on the lips and rushed to dress.

When he went into the Stones' house twenty minutes later, Harper was shocked. There was rage behind this. Nobody destroyed a house like this without a terrible passion.

The mattress was cut up as if someone were striking out at them.

"Have either of you received any threats?" Harper asked.

"None at all," Elliot responded. "We live rather quietly here."

"Did you have enemies from your previous residence?"

"No."

"Was anything stolen?"

"We went through everything and nothing was taken. They just destroyed everything."

No other houses in town were broken into and yet this house was hit twice.

"So the two of you were dining at Mrs. Claxton's house. Where were you, Andrew?"

"I went to Norfolk."

"I picked him up passed out on the road half a mile from here," John said.

"What happened?"

"I . . ." He flashed a nervous look at his father. "I musta drunk too much."

Harper controlled his disgust.

"Were you alone tonight?"

"Yeah."

"You ever catch a ride back from the mainland?"

"Sometimes."

"With whom?"

"Some dude who lives on the island. I see him all the time and since he sees me walking, he just gives me a lift."

"What's his name?"

"Gerald somebody. Never got his last name."

"Where does he live?"

Andrew shrugged. "Don't know. Never been to his house."

"Can you describe him?"

"Tall dude, little shorter than me. 'Bout John's size. Light complexion." Andrew shrugged.

That could describe a host of men. "How old?"

"Older than me. Younger than you."

Between thirty-five and fifty. *Great. Just great.*

"We can't stay here tonight," Minerva said.

"John, call Gabrielle and see if she has a room at the B and B. In the meantime, we'll process the scene."

Friday night Trent figured he needed to give Andrew another warning. He waited for him again as he got off the ferry, walking as if he'd had one too many.

Trent intercepted him at the same place, only this time he didn't touch him, just stood behind him. He didn't have to. His voice alone was enough to stop Andrew in his tracks.

"You working on getting my money, Andrew?" Trent asked, lacing his voice with menace.

"B . . . Ba . . . Barbara's got half of it, and there's no way I can get it from her."

"Half?"

"My daddy gave it to her to invest," the nervous man said quickly.

"What happened to the other half?"

"Somebody stole it a couple weeks ago. We had a couple of break-ins."

"So Barbara's working with you?"

He shook his head. "We met her when we moved to the island. And when I was dating her she told my daddy how she invested her money and made a killing."

For the life of him, Trent couldn't understand what a strong woman like Barbara saw in Andrew.

"So tell me about this stock thing."

"She's got a stockbroker friend in New York. There's some stock that's going to hit the ceiling in a few months. Barbara told Daddy she'd invest it for him."

"What kind of bullshit is this?"

Andrew turned, looked Trent in the eye, and started trembling. "It's the truth. Somebody broke in our house the night you attacked me. The only reason they didn't get the money was because Barbara already had it. It should be invested by now. Ain't nothing I can do 'til the deal's done."

Trent scowled. "You had better not ever mention my name to your daddy or anybody else. Got that?"

"Yes, sir."

"Get on outta here."

Andrew stumbled forward, and Trent made his way back to the SUV. He wouldn't accomplish a thing hurting Andrew. He'd need him if he couldn't get that money from Barbara.

So she wasn't part of the group. But something was up with that woman and he couldn't figure it out. She raked in money hand over fist at that salon. He knew those prices she charged, and although he never got near the till, he figured up in his head what she was making, and it wasn't chicken feed. He knew for sure that sharp-looking salon she owned was paid for. She wasn't renting. So what was her number? And how the hell was he going to get his money? He wasn't up for stealing from somebody who didn't steal from him. He just wanted his mama's money back.

But who the hell stole half the Stones' stash? It must have been the woman skulking to the house the night he tore up the place. She must know them and know the amount of money they had in their possession. Oh, hell. She had to be Andrew's old girlfriend. His mother mentioned her. And she was stealing the whole stash for herself.

No honor among thieves. Now he had to find that woman. He should've waited and followed her home that night, but after he'd destroyed the place, he wasn't up for sticking around and getting caught.

He'd bet she lived on the island. Or maybe it could be one of the locals. If only he'd gotten a look at her face, but he'd only seen this apparition dressed completely in black—just like him.

Barbara had given her customers a month's warning that the shop would be closed the week of Thanksgiving. Consequently, they were swamped that week, so much so that she and Trent hadn't had the time even for a break.

Barbara thanked the heavens that he'd come to work for her. She would never have been able to take care of so many customers on her own.

Late that afternoon, Liane rented a car from the airport and drove directly to the salon. Barbara hadn't eaten since breakfast and took a ten-minute break to eat and visit with her friend before Liane left for the B&B.

She finally sent her last customer on her way, locked the shop's door, and looked at Trent. They still had the shop to clean, but Trent was sitting. She couldn't blame him. She was just as tired.

"I never want to work another day like this," Barbara said.

"Me either, but I guess we better get started on the cleaning."

"Yes."

Trent had already cleaned the sink area, and now he started sweeping and scrubbing as Barbara cleaned around the hair station.

"Word around town is you're good with investing," he said.

"Are you interested in investing?"

"I thought it was about time I started. I've got a little saved up."

Barbara glanced up. "Do you own your own home?"

"No."

"Then that's where you should start. You should take care of the basics first. The price of housing is down now and it's a good time to purchase. And after that's taken care of, you can invest a portion of your savings in the stock market because that's down, too. But you have to be selective in choosing stocks. You want sound companies, those where the shares have been depressed because of the market, not the value of the stock, and one that will eventually increase when the economy picks up."

"I see."

"Are you moving back to D.C. or will you settle here?"

"Definitely D.C."

"Well, get yourself a steady job there and continue saving. Then buy your house, or townhouse or condo, whichever you prefer. Shouldn't take more than a year or so if you have good credit. Now, make sure you have a good credit record."

"I do."

Barbara nodded. "You're a good worker, you know that? You could go far. So I'll give you my number when you leave and when you've purchased your house, we'll talk about investing in stocks. How does that sound?"

"Sounds like a good plan," he said.

"Better still, after Thanksgiving, I'll give you some books to read and teach you how to select stocks."

"Even better," he said. "So when do I return to work?"

"Wednesday after Thanksgiving."

"I'm leaving for D.C. Think I'll spend the holiday with my family."

"Do they know you're coming?"

He shook his head.

"What a nice surprise. They'll be pleased to see you."

He smiled. "Yeah."

"You have a safe trip and I'll see you Wednesday," Barbara said as they left the shop.

She went home and showered before rushing to the B&B.

She and Liane hugged in the foyer.

"I thought you'd never get here," Barbara said. Some pies and wine was left over from happy hour, and they each got a slice before she and Liane settled in chairs near the fireplace.

"I thought I'd have to find you a good lawyer," Liane said. "I have one on standby for both of us."

"You're still talking about that? I told you I have it under control."

Liane's blond hair brushed her shoulders. She wore jeans and a comfortable T-shirt.

"I'm dying to meet your sheriff."

"You will. He's taking us to church tomorrow."

Liane scoffed. "Church? I haven't seen the inside of a church in months. Not since the last time you dragged me there."

"That's your problem. I'm dragging you there again."

"Don't feel you have to entertain me. I'm beat and I plan to get plenty of rest. Besides, there's this handsome guy I saw earlier. He wasn't wearing a ring. I'm going to try to strike up a conversation."

"Knock yourself out, girl." She smiled at her friend. "I'm so glad you're here."

"Me, too."

"Harper knows something's going on. I told him I was putting the shop up for sale in January."

Liane sighed. "Barbara, how do you really feel about Harper?"

Barbara clutched a hand to her chest. "My God, Liane, I love him," she whispered.

CHAPTER 12

On Tuesday, members from several churches arranged baskets for seniors and the disadvantaged. Harper dropped Barbara off that morning on his way to work since she was going with him to deliver them that evening.

The island's investigator, Alyssa Claxton, returned from her training and stopped by that afternoon to talk to her grandmother. When she was on her way out, she paused by Barbara's table. Alyssa wasn't one to beat around the bush.

"Hear that Harper's a lot happier since he's been seeing you."

"Oh?"

She nodded. "I like you, Barbara, and I'm glad he's found someone stable."

Barbara didn't know what to say to that.

"He's a good man, Barbara, and he loves you. I've never seen him taken with a woman the way he is with you." When Barbara started to speak, Alyssa held up a hand. "He hasn't said anything. He's very private. But I've known him a long time and I can tell. He needs you. I hope it works out. If you ever need anything, I'm just a phone call away."

"Thanks, Alyssa." Barbara was warmed by this tough woman's warm regard.

"Besides, you're my cousin. We're family."

Barbara chuckled. "I've met more family lately than I have my entire life."

"But I mean it."

Barbara gave her a tremulous smile. "Thank you."

"Well, I've got to go."

An hour later, Lisa stopped by. "Hey, Barbara, now that we're kinfolk, does that mean I can get my hair done for free?"

"Sure, as long as you clean my house for free."

Lisa laughed and went in search of her mother and Naomi.

Ten minutes later, Naomi approached Barbara. "Barbara, I want you to fix up a basket for three for the Stones. You know their house got broken into and destroyed inside. How do people live with themselves? It was totally unnecessary."

Barbara reserved comment.

"I don't know their financial situation, but the Christian thing to do is to offer them a basket."

It went against Barbara to have to prepare a basket for them, but she couldn't give Naomi a reason why she shouldn't. "I'll be happy to fix one for them." Now they knew how it felt to have their home invaded.

"No rush. I'm going to take it with me when I leave this evening."

After Harper got off from work, someone handed him a list of names and he gave it to Barbara when she left with him to make the deliveries. He'd driven his SUV.

"So who's on our list?" he asked.

Barbara opened it and gave him the first name. "We have a list of seniors."

"Seniors?" He looked at her in horror. "Are you crazy?"

"What's wrong with delivering to seniors? Why does it matter who we deliver to?"

Harper only shook his head. "They always sucker the new ones."

"I don't see the problem."

"That's because you've lived in New York, the land of anonymity," he said. "You'll see."

It didn't take long for Barbara to grasp what Harper meant. An experience that should have taken a couple of hours actually took five. At every house they stopped at, someone invited them inside to "visit for a spell."

"I just made an apple pie. Try a slice."

"I baked banana bread. Have a slice."

"I just made banana pudding. Have a dish."

"I make the best clam chowder on the island. Have a bowl."

And some of them even talked about Dorsey, how they attended high school with her, and the fact that she visited and was looking forward to her move to the island, and how glad they were that Barbara was now home.

When Harper finally drove into his yard and in the garage, Barbara said, "I guess dinner's been taken care of."

Harper laughed. "You'll know better next year. Hopefully, you'll choose a better list."

That stopped her. Next year. She wouldn't be here next year. So why was she suddenly sad? Even though it was tiring, it was so nice getting to meet so many of the older people who were so welcoming and grateful to see them. Who'd heard about Barbara and wanted to reveal stories about her grandparents and great-grandparents. And they all invited her back for a visit.

The garage door had closed behind them, and gratefully they went inside the house. When she started upstairs, Harper leaned against the counter and pulled her close.

"Do you ever think about the future? What you'll be doing next year, five years, ten years from now?"

Barbara looked away briefly and couldn't stop the sadness that gripped her. "I did before my grandmother died. Now . . . well . . . all my plans have changed. And I just . . . I haven't been able to plan that far ahead."

"What would you be doing right now if your grandmother was here?"

She told him about their plans of traveling, then moving to the island.

"In the house where you're living."

Barbara nodded.

"What was she like?"

"She never looked back. She did what needed to be done and kept going."

"I would love to have met her."

Barbara smiled. "She would like you."

"Did you and she travel much in the past?"

"Every year we took at least one long trip. We visited all the places she always wanted to see."

"That must be some comfort for you."

Barbara hadn't thought of that. "It is."

"Do you want to travel now?"

She sighed, wondering where he was going with this. "I don't know."

"Would you like me to travel with you after the cases are solved? I can take two or three weeks. I can't travel an entire year, but we can take some long weekends together. I haven't taken all my vacation days in years. Usually I lose most of my hours."

"I don't need to be coddled. I'm used—"

"I know," he said in frustration. "I know you can take care of yourself. It's not about being capable. It's . . ." He swallowed audibly. "I want to be with you."

She touched his face, leaned up on tiptoes, and kissed him briefly, inhaling his familiar scent, feeling warmth, contentment, and yet reservation, too, because she couldn't give him or be what he wanted. "I enjoy my time with you, Harper. More than you'll ever know."

"If you leave here next year, what would you do in New York or Philly that you can't do here?"

My God, that man was persistent. Barbara started to lie, to map out a fictional plan, but in the end, she couldn't. Not when he was looking so earnestly at her. And knowing that whatever he said came from the heart. "I don't know. I just haven't thought that far ahead."

"You know, I can live with myself and by myself. But the thing is, when my life feels fuller with you, I'd rather not. It wasn't until you moved here that I realized how empty my life really was. I work, and that gives me comfort. But I'm fifty. I won't be sheriff forever. I could get voted out at any time."

"Says the man who's been voted sheriff for the last twenty years."

"What I'm saying is, I guess I'm getting selfish, but I want something for me for a change," he said.

Barbara wasn't going to ask him to elaborate. She

knew exactly what he felt because she felt that way about him.

"I like coming home to you at night. When the lights are shining bright, knowing you're inside waiting for me. I don't care how bad my day has been, Barbara—nothing tops having you here."

"Harper, I don't know what to say. My career and my grandmother were my life. And you've given me something I never thought I'd find."

"Then trust me. I don't want to box you in. I know you enjoy your freedom, but I think we can add to each other's lives."

"I trust you."

He regarded her silently. Barbara knew that he wanted more than she could give him right now, probably ever.

"I'm going to take a shower," he finally said, disappointment lacing his words. He left her standing in the kitchen.

Sonya took a boat back to the island late that night. After making sure the police weren't staking out the place, she went to Tootsie's cottage. Now the police were looking for her and she had no way of getting that money from Barbara—especially if she died.

The only other option was the bowl. She needed to know who Tootsie was making it for. She knew it was still missing and they might have the original. Tootsie was probably making that fake bowl to get the reward. If Sonya had time, she'd make a fake herself, but she needed to get moving. Alyssa's boyfriend, Jordan, would pay a fortune to get that bowl back. She'd heard about a reward.

Word was, Alyssa still hadn't agreed to marry him. He probably thought he'd give her that bowl for a wedding gift or something. Sonya smothered a laugh. If she could get the bowl, she'd get the reward. The brother was loaded. With the money she already had, she and Andrew could escape to the island and wait on his inheritance.

Tootsie took suitcases to her car, then went inside and didn't come out for a while.

She knocked on Tootsie's door. It only took seconds for Tootsie to open the door just a scant couple of inches. She appeared nervous and kept her body in the doorway. But Sonya was twice Tootsie's size, so she just eased the door back.

"What're you doing here this time of night?" she asked.

"I told my roommate I'd help you with your sculpture if you needed it."

"I don't work this late. I'm going to visit my family. Maybe you should leave. The sheriff came around here searching for you. Nancy's been asking if anyone knew where you or your old man was."

"Did she say why?"

"No."

"I don't know why they're looking for me."

"You're supposed to be home," Tootsie said.

"Changed my mind."

Tootsie nodded. "Maybe you should check with Nancy about why the sheriff came by. It's late and I have a long day tomorrow." She yawned. "I'm getting ready for bed."

"Then why do you have your car all packed?"

"For tomorrow. I'm visiting my family."

Sonya nodded. Did she think she was talking to a fool?

"What's that you're working on in there?"

"A gift for my family. It's time for you to go," she said impatiently.

"Who are you making that gold bowl for?"

"What gold bowl?"

"Don't play dumb. You're doing a replica of the lost bowl. The one that belongs to that old lady. And I want to know what you plan to do with it. You got the real bowl?"

"Of course not."

Sonya moved forward. Tootsie stepped back. "How about we split the reward money."

"What reward?"

"I want some of that reward."

Tootsie nodded. "Sure. Come by here tomorrow and we'll discuss it."

"Oh, no. I'm not letting you outta my sight."

Tootsie looked at her as if she were crazy. "You can't stay here. The police are looking for you."

"They won't expect me to be in your cottage."

Tootsie kept backing up.

"You stand right there. I'm not finished with you."

Suddenly, Tootsie lashed out at her and cut her with the edging tool.

"Damn it." Sonya jumped back, fumbled for the gun in her pocket, and fired. The shot went wild, but by then Tootsie was on her. The women struggled. For such a small, scrappy woman, Tootsie was strong. And Sonya's arm hurt too much to do much damage. Sonya's fist glanced off her jaw. Tootsie nailed her good with her fist, dazing her. Then that whore took a statue and slammed it over Sonya's head.

For a moment, Sonya lay there dazed. By the time she came to, she was hurting like an old arthritic woman. Tootsie was gone—and so was that stupid bowl. That bitch.

Sonya heard commotion outside a second before someone banged on the door. She quickly climbed through the window and ran toward her boat.

Two things caught Harper's attention in the small room. Blood on the floor and the trail leading to a window. He'd already sent John to check it out. The other disturbing thing was the picture of Naomi Claxton's golden bowl and gold scraps on the floor. Why would this woman have a picture of the bowl? An artist at that? There was always the possibility of someone melting it for the gold.

Nancy hovered outside with many of the artists as his team went through the house.

There were no bodies, so either a body was taken off or both parties ran away after the commotion.

Harper sent John cruising around the island while he dealt with the scene.

With the shooting at the artist colony, Harper had very little sleep the previous night.

Wednesday morning he called the Philly PD. He couldn't wait any longer for Barbara to tell him the truth. He was going to do whatever it took— anything it took—to keep Barbara here even if she didn't want his interference. He knew that her grandmother died earlier that year and she was Barbara's only relative. Any trouble that Barbara was involved in more than likely had something to do with her grandmother's death.

He called the medical examiner's office and identified himself.

"I'm inquiring about the cause of death of Dorsey McNair," he said, and gave the approximate time period. After fifteen minutes on hold someone came back.

"Her death was caused by a fall down a flight of stairs. Her neck was broken. Death occurred on impact."

"Did the granddaughter contest that decision?"

"Detective Mosley was in charge of that. I can give you his number."

"Thank you." Harper copied the number and then dialed the detective, only to find he was out until after the holidays. He had left an alternate number, but Harper wanted to talk directly to him. He left a message hoping he'd hear back soon.

After his talk with Barbara on Saturday, Trent drove to D.C. He thought maybe his presence would make his mother feel better. Every day, he'd forced her out of bed. She was weak from sitting and lying around. Sunday, he forced her to walk around every hour. She leaned on his arm, walking around in a daze. No spark of life was left, and he was tearing out what little hair he had trying to think of anything that would bring her out of this melancholy state.

Same thing happened Monday, Tuesday, and all day Wednesday. Trent was at his wit's end. She couldn't give up on her life like that just over losing money. Where was the fighter he grew up with? She was the one who had always pushed him.

Even though he veered off the path, she was still pushing him.

But it was now Wednesday night and she hadn't shown any improvement. After her walks, she'd gotten right back into bed. Almost defeated, he sat by her bed and took her hand in his. She'd lost twenty pounds at least.

"I'm working for this nice lady on Paradise Island, Mama. She reminds me of you. Real hard worker. Don't get involved in messes. Don't talk bad about folks. I thought she was mixed up with that group who stole your money, but I'm thinking she moved there because they must have stolen some money from one of her relatives, because she's got a plan to get some money out of them."

His mother's eyes veered to his. She was actually listening instead of staring blankly into space.

"I'm trying to be the son you always wanted me to be. So when I get back, I'm going to ask for her advice. She's real smart. Between the two of us, we're going to get your money back."

His mother squeezed his hand.

"So, Mama, I want you to get out of that bed and enjoy the holiday with us. You're the one who always pushed us forward. You're just sixty. Your life's not over. Money doesn't define who you are. Regardless of what that lowlife did to you, you're still a great woman. That hasn't changed."

"But . . ." Her lips trembled.

Trent sighed. "The one thing I've learned from all this is there's always going to be people who want to take things that don't belong to them, thinking it's the easy way. I guess I've leaned what you've been trying to teach me all along. There's no easy way. Only the right way. But you've got to hang on and let me and Sis help you get through this."

"But . . ."

Trent wasn't listening to any of her arguments any longer. He was getting mad. She didn't let him stay home and sulk when he was growing up. He had to get moving no matter what happened. "You're still going to be able to buy your medicine and pay the bills."

"I don't like depending on anybody. I've always made my own way."

"Why can't you depend on others? Sis and I have depended on you. What's wrong with us helping you out for a change? You're not by yourself in this. The only reason I haven't killed that SOB . . ."

"Don't even think of taking a life, son. Not even for money. Especially for money."

". . . is because of you. He's still alive because of you. So he's depending on you to get better so he can continue to live. And I mean that."

Shaking her head, she squeezed his hand again. "Don't talk like that, Trent. I don't like that. And neither does the Lord."

"Well, then, you better get yourself outta that bed and get pretty so he can stay healthy. 'Cause if I don't enjoy my holiday, and let me tell you, so far I'm not, I'm taking it out on his behind once I get back to that island. Trust me," he said, and he could tell by the look in her eyes that she believed him. Trent slid his chair back. "Me and Sis are gonna start the Thanksgiving cooking. We shoulda started days ago."

His mother's eyes widened. "You cook? This is Thanksgiving, son. We've got to have a proper dinner. I could never tie you down long enough for you to learn to cook properly."

"Then I guess you're gonna have to come in the kitchen and give me some instructions. Never too late to learn."

Trent held his breath until his mother shifted the covers back and sat up without assistance.

He started toward the door. "Holler if you need help."

Breakfast Thanksgiving morning was quiet at Harper's house.

"Are you going to work today?" Barbara asked.

"I have to meet with Alyssa for a while. It shouldn't take long."

Before he left Barbara gave him a sweet kiss.

"I'm always leaving you, when I actually want to be right here with you," Harper said.

"I understand. Your job is important. We'll spend this evening together. Let's see if we can make up for lost time."

Harper groaned. "I'm going to hold you to that," he said.

While Harper worked, Barbara thought of their conversation the night before. But what would she do if she stayed on the island? She was serious about selling the shop. And she couldn't really use her investment skills here. She was considering returning to Wall Street, although she really didn't want that hectic life again. At least it gave her purpose. But what kind of purpose? The truth was, it kept her busy. It did not give her life purpose or meaning. If she decided to work in her career, she could be a broker in Norfolk.

Barbara cleaned the kitchen, then went to the B&B and visited with Liane, eventually bringing her back to Harper's house. They spent time in the hot tub, which Liane just loved, and then talked before they dressed for dinner.

Most of Barbara's days were spent with Liane. They toured in Virginia Beach and Norfolk. Liane had liked Harper from first sight.

By the time the three of them made it to Cornell's restaurant Thursday afternoon, the parking lot was filled with cars. Lots of the younger people and men were hanging outside. Cornell had arranged several fire pits outside, actually a collection of old tin bathtubs stacked with wood and set ablaze.

Obviously Thanksgiving was a huge affair with the Claxtons. There were so many people. My God, it was like a family reunion. Barbara had always spent Thanksgiving with her grandmother. She'd invite a couple of people over now and then, but her holidays were quiet. But she should have known. The Claxtons were a huge family.

They passed many of the kids teasing each other around the fire pits.

Liane hunched her in the side. "This isn't just one family, is it?"

"Yeah, and I just found out I'm a distant cousin."

"No kidding."

"I couldn't believe it either. And I don't know most of them. How is it going with your businessman?" Barbara asked.

"Very good. He's coming over later. Gabrielle invited all the B and B's guests."

"Oh, well, I'm looking forward to meeting him, then."

"And scare the poor guy away? It's too early to introduce him to the family, you know."

Barbara shook her head. "I see Naomi. Come on. I want to introduce you to her."

By the time they wended their way through the crowd, Mrs. Claxton had gone into the kitchen. When they caught up to her, she was instructing Lisa on something.

"Where do you want me to put the cakes?" Barbara asked her.

"Here, I'll take them." She called one of her grandchildren over. "Put these on the dessert table. They look wonderful, Barbara."

"This is my friend, Liane. Liane, meet my cousin, Naomi Claxton."

"It's a pleasure to meet you, Mrs. Claxton."

"Everybody calls me Naomi," she said. "Are you enjoying our island?"

"Yes, I am. I can't wait for summer when I can get in the ocean."

"Oh, dear. You can't stay away that long. At least come back for the crab fest in May. You haven't tasted crabs until you've had my fried crabs. I cook bushels of them at the beginning of the season. And later that month we have our Founder's Day. It's huge."

Liane smiled. "Then I'll have to come back."

"The B and B gets booked up a year in advance for that weekend, but we've got plenty of beds for you."

"Thank you."

Someone approached them. "Excuse me. Grandma?"

"Enjoy yourselves, darlings," Naomi said, patting their hands. "And eat until you're stuffed. Don't forget to take plates home. Food will be ready in a few minutes and there's plenty of it."

The tables were already set. Barbara noticed Alyssa, Harper, and John huddled together. That man could never get away from work. She and Liane made conversation with others until Liane's businessman arrived and she introduced Barbara to him. They sat together when it was time to eat.

"Did you enjoy yourself?" Harper asked around nine that evening. Liane was at the B&B spending the evening with her new businessman.

"Very much." Harper had lit a fire in the outside pit. They sat on a swing bench in front of it, snuggled up under a blanket, gently rocking. Harper's arm was wrapped securely around her.

She glanced up at the star-filled night. A zillion stars twinkled across the sky. She could hear the tides rush against the shore and the popping of the flames as they danced in the pit. And, more importantly, she felt the warmth of Harper beside her.

She was content.

"It's so peaceful and beautiful here," Barbara said, rubbing his arm. "I wish I could bottle this moment and carry it with me for the rest of my life."

"Is that right?" He nuzzled her neck. "Maybe I can do something about that."

Barbara smiled. "Oh yeah? Do you have a magic formula for savoring special moments?"

"Maybe something better."

"What could that possibly be?"

Barbara felt him move. "Give me your hand," he said.

Since she was on his right side, she slipped her left hand from beneath the covers and offered it palm side up. He slid a diamond ring on her finger.

Barbara's smile faltered.

"Will you marry me, Barbara Turner, so we can spend the rest of our lives together? I promise you many moments like this." He kissed her cheek.

Tears rushed to Barbara's eyes as she shifted in his arms to look at him. "Harper?" Never in a million years had she expected this. There were no jewelry stores on the island. With all he had to do, he took time out of his schedule to shop for a ring.

She wanted to marry him, God knew she did, but she'd held so much from him. She was an illusion. He didn't really know her. And how could a man who'd been betrayed in the past possibly ever forgive her or trust her?

She had no idea this relationship was going to implode this way.

He wiped her tears away.

Her grandmother always told her there was no cause or reason, but life happened when you least expected it. Especially the good things.

She was torn between the people who needed the money and her desire for a future with Harper. But she knew it was already too late to gain his trust.

Finally, she wrapped her arms around him, kissed him, and cried. She was forty-five and was acting like a teenager. She didn't shed one tear at the end of her marriage.

Alarmed, Harper held her tightly against him, his heart thumping in his chest. Of all the responses he expected, this wasn't it. If it were just tears of joy, he'd be the happiest man in the world, but these were tears of distress.

Detective Mosley hadn't called him back yet. He hoped the problem wasn't too big to solve.

"What is it, Barbara? Tell me what's wrong and I'll help you. Did I ask too soon?"

"That's not it."

"What is it, then? You've already told me you love me. I won't let you take it back."

She clasped her hands on both his cheeks. "I love you. I really do."

"Then what's wrong? Talk to me, baby."

She leaned against him, unwilling to talk. Unease grew in Harper's chest.

"Tell you what. We'll have a long engagement and we won't set a date right now."

"But . . ."

"I want you to wear the ring until you decide if you're going to marry me."

"But after I wear it, you won't be able to get your money back."

"I don't care about that. I care about you." He kissed a tear that slid unbidden down her cheek.

She still didn't speak, but she didn't remove the ring either. So maybe she wanted to be with him. It gave him a smidgeon of hope.

"May I have a kiss?"

She turned her head to kiss him. Harper felt all her love pouring into him.

"Baby, you keep this up and we won't make it back inside."

Barbara wasn't listening. She was tearing at his clothes as if she couldn't get to him quickly enough. And Harper found himself tearing at hers.

"Wait, baby, we've got to . . ."

She unzipped his pants and took him in her hand.

"Jesus. We can't make love on the swing. . . ." But they were. And further objections eluded him.

He stripped her blouse off and suckled on a nipple. Kissed her neck, her stomach, and then back to her breasts, just waiting for him to feast on.

Her hands explored his back, his thighs, they were all over him, driving him insane with need.

"Baby . . ."

"Hummm?" she said, but when she came up to kiss him again, plunging her tongue deep inside his mouth and sucking on his, she stole his breath away.

She let him go, kissed his chin, his neck, grabbed his hips and ground hers against him.

A deep moan tore from Harper's throat. He parted her thighs and inserted a finger inside her. She was wet and more than ready for him. Her cry of pleasure nearly undid him.

In one swift movement, he grabbed her pants and panties together and tugged them down her hips, her legs. He kissed his way up her legs, her thighs, kissed her intimately, stopping to caress her stomach, her breasts, and found her mouth again.

He stepped out of his pants, leveled himself over her, and sank into her with one swift plunge. They moved together in a rhythmic beat that swayed with the tides.

Cries of pleasure tore from Barbara's throat and he answered them in turn. Pleasure built to unbearable limits and when release came, it was cataclysmic.

Minutes later, Harper moved aside and pulled Barbara up beside him.

"Did I crush you, baby?"

She laughed. "Are you kidding?"

"Out in the freaking open where anybody with a boat and binoculars could get a peek."

"They'd have had an eyeful."

Harper laughed. "You got that right."

There was no way on God's green earth Harper was going to give all this goodness up.

He stroked Barbara's shoulder, then lifted her hand and rubbed the ring on her finger.

He'd find a way to keep her.

CHAPTER 13

While most Americans went shopping on Black Friday, business owners on the island hustled to finish getting their Christmas decorations up. Paradise Island was fifty years behind most of the country. Naomi was also on the community planning committee and she'd deemed it sacrilegious to have Christmas lights up before Thanksgiving. It was a holiday that needed to be celebrated without the interference of another.

Business owners were out in full force putting final touches on Christmas decorations, instead of heading to Norfolk and Virginia Beach to shop. And those who did escape to shop were sure to be back before sundown when the lights went on in the town square.

Barbara was a business owner now. For the most part, her decorations were up, but they wouldn't be lit until tonight. Trent had hung the lights before he left, but Liane helped with the last minute details.

"Harper's Santa?" Liane asked.

Barbara nodded.

"All that muscle and a washboard stomach? Guess he'll be wearing a pillow."

"Guess so."

"He's tall enough. I'd sit on his lap. God knows he's handsome."

Barbara laughed. "We won't see much of his face, though."

When dusk came, hundreds of people gathered in front of the courthouse waiting for the mayor to light the tree. Parents pointed out to their children the live reindeer in its pen.

Even Santa's chair was waiting for him, and "elves" served hot chocolate and apple cider, cookies, and brownies to raise money for Harper's youth program.

When the mayor lit the tree, the crowd erupted in cheers and lights began to go on all around. Even some of the boats in the harbor had lights strung on them.

Children ran to the Santa line. One of Alyssa's brother's had been harangued into taking pictures.

Barbara, Liane, and Liane's friend, Steve, walked around.

When the last child had sat on Harper's lap, Barbara approached him.

"Santa, I have a long list of things I want for Christmas."

"Oh, do you now? Come closer and whisper them all in Santa's ear."

Barbara laughed but moved closer.

Harper grabbed her and swung her onto his lap. She squealed, drawing everyone's attention.

"Harper!" She was so embarrassed. The crowd clapped and cheered around her.

"So, what do you want Santa to bring you?" he asked with a wicked grin.

"It's a long, long list," she said, just as she heard the camera snap. She turned around and several people were snapping pictures. She also spotted Andrew at the edge of the crowd, scowling, before he turned and walked toward the ferry.

Barbara debated what to do. It was Monday, and at seven she had breakfast with Liane at the B&B before Liane's flight back to New York.

Liane lifted Barbara's hand for a better view of the ring. "Harper has very good taste."

"He's very good at a lot of things, Liane." She inhaled before saying, "I've decided to tell him everything. I might lose him, but that's the chance I took from the beginning when I took this path. I never, not in a million years, expected to find a man like him to love me. And the wonderful thing is I love him, too."

Liane quirked an eyebrow. "What did your grandmother say about doubting Thomases?"

"What she said was I didn't trust in the Lord enough. That miracles happened when you least expect them. Liane, I hope I'm not too late for my miracle."

"There you go again with all the doubts. Who says you'll lose him? He loves you, honey. You're human. He can't expect perfection."

"He's been betrayed before and he'll see this as another betrayal."

"Hey, he's no spring chicken . . ."

Barbara smiled. "You've never seen him in action."

Liane rolled her eyes. "What I'm saying is he's old

enough to know life isn't perfect. If he's expecting perfection from you, then he's not the man for you. Because he's going to make a few mistakes along the way, too, and he expects you to forgive him."

Barbara shook her head doubtfully. "Men are . . ." Barbara searched for a descriptor.

"I know they can be asses, but some are good. And it looks like Harper's a winner."

"Until you get on the wrong side of his ethics."

"Here," Liane said, placing both of her hands palm up on the table. "Give me your hands."

Barbara clasped her hands.

"I've spent so much time with your grandmother that I feel I know her."

"She loved you," Barbara whispered, giving Liane's hand a little squeeze.

"Okay, this is Granny talking. Trust. Trust love, trust that what you have is true and you were sent here at this moment in time for a purpose. This move didn't just happen out of the blue. Your grandmother's time was up. She lived a wonderfully full life and you enhanced that life. . . ."

"But . . ."

"Even though you'd made plans to be together after your retirement, she didn't wait around for life to happen. She lived every day, every moment to the fullest. How many hours did she spend in soup kitchens after her retirement? Look at the work she accomplished in church. She was a scrapper to the very end. I know she gave the Stones hell for taking her money and that's why they killed her. And they're not going to get away with it."

"No, they aren't," Barbara muttered, her chin lifting.

"The two of you took vacations every year to

places she would have never seen without you. You were a blessing for each other. And she gave you wisdom. Now she's sent you home. Home to Paradise Island to meet your future. Embrace it with both hands. Forget all the doubts. Forget the 'what ifs.' You've almost accomplished your goal. Let Harper help you. Let Harper be a part of this. I'm glad you're going to talk to him, because it's letting him enter into a segment of your life you've kept closed from him, and that shouldn't be."

Seconds ticked by as they regarded each other. Barbara could imagine her grandmother saying just that. She'd thought she'd let her grandmother down by not being there, not helping her when she needed help most in her last hours. And she was angry that her grandmother went after the Stones without telling her, without waiting for her. But it wasn't her grandmother's way to sit back and wait when she felt the need to take action.

Liane was right. By telling Elliot about this place, her grandmother had sent the Stones here and thereby sent Barbara here, too.

"Thanks for being my friend, Liane," Barbara said. "I miss you."

"Yeah. well." They unclasped hands and Liane sipped her coffee. "There's a certain man I met who's spending a couple of weeks here during Christmas. You better believe I'll be back."

Barbara laughed. "I'm looking forward to it. Any chance in talking you into staying in my house this time? I might not be there."

"Not on your life. You're a fabulous cook, but after you cook, I'd feel responsible for the dishes. But never fear. Mrs. Claxton informed me that the rooms are all booked in May for the crab fest, so I'll have to stay with you then."

"I have a dishwasher. I know how you feel about housework. I won't make you do dishes. Promise. You'll be my pampered guest."

"At the B and B, I get fed and don't have to feel guilty. And I wouldn't have met Mr. Charming if I'd stayed with you."

Barbara raised her eyebrows. "You're going to have to tell me more about Mr. Charming. You didn't give up your goodies to this guy already, did you?"

Liane pursed her lips. "I'll never tell."

Barbara laughed.

"Besides, if I don't get moving, I'll miss my flight. We have to have something to talk about on the phone. Are you going to tell Harper about the money?"

"Yes, but I'm not handing it over to him. It's still in the safety deposit box. I'm going to divide and distribute it next week."

The women embraced before Liane left. Then Barbara went to get breakfast to take to Harper.

When she drove by the sheriff's office, his car was parked out front.

She rehearsed what she'd say to him, the way she'd often done for difficult clients.

The secretary was on the phone. Barbara pointed toward Harper's office and the woman waved her back. Of course she was one of her clients, and when she saw the bag from the B&B, she made an "okeydoke" sign with her hand.

Barbara laughed and continued on back to knock on his door. With the terse "Come in," she opened it, then stopped when she saw officers in there with him.

"Come on in. We're finished here," he said, standing.

The officers cleared out and the last person closed the door behind him.

"Have a seat," Harper said.

"I can see you're busy. But I wanted to bring you breakfast and tell you that tonight we need to talk."

Harper nodded. "About what?"

"I love you," she said. "But there are some things I need to tell you and then you can decide if you still want to marry me."

"That sounds ominous. But whatever you tell me won't change my love for you, Barbara. It's solid."

"I need to talk to you about the reason I came here. And that will take time. There are some things you don't know about me, and if we move forward . . . well." She paused. "We'll talk tonight."

He nodded. "I'll leave here at five."

"Enjoy your breakfast." She kissed him again, lingered over it, and he wrapped his arms around her waist. She felt comforted by his touch, but nervous, too, because she was taking a chance on losing all this. But that was exactly what she had to do.

"I love you," she said, then left.

Finally, Harper thought as he watched the sway of Barbara's backside as she walked away. It had taken a while for her to trust him, but finally.

Belatedly, he glanced at the container of food she'd left for him. The aroma mixed with her pleasing perfume.

He opened the top. Plain toast, one scrambled egg, and cinnamon oatmeal. He liked the B&B food, but Barbara's oatmeal couldn't be beat. She'd complained that the three-egg omelets he devoured were too much. Harper sighed. He was going to have to get used to healthier food.

Small sacrifices.

She'd been in bed when he left earlier than usual that morning. It had felt good knowing she was safe there. He took the plastic fork out of the package. That's what Barbara didn't understand. He wanted someone who cared about him, and whom he cared about, too—concerned enough to take the time to bring him food when he was perfectly capable of getting it for himself.

He dropped the fork onto his plate, dialed Sam's place, and put in an order to have a nice arrangement of flowers delivered to his house. Barbara would be there today.

Trent left D.C. late Monday morning. He was driving against the D.C. rush-hour traffic, thank goodness. It was eight and the traffic travelling north was still bumper to bumper. By the time he would reach Hampton and Norfolk, the traffic in that area should have diminished.

With his pedal to the metal, he pushed forward, thinking about his mother's progress. It was going to take time for her to gain her weight and strength back, but at least she was finally moving forward. They'd enjoyed a wonderful Thanksgiving dinner— even if it wasn't quite as tasty and elaborate as her dinners usually were. And he'd walked with her through the neighborhood each day. Some of her neighbors had come out to tell her how glad they were to see her out and about.

As soon as he got to the island, he was going to

have that talk with Barbara. He was sure she'd help him.

Dinner was almost ready. Barbara had prepared an easy cassoulet without the fuss and fat of the original French dish. While the dinner was in the oven, Barbara wrote letters to the women Elliot had bilked, telling them she had a portion of the money and would be mailing it to them within a couple of weeks. The money was still in the safety deposit box. She wished there was a way for her to get more. But this was better than nothing.

After she finished writing the letters, she went outside to clean up a little around the fire pit and placed some soft pillows she'd purchased earlier on the wooden swing where Harper and she made love. Her backside had gotten a couple of splinters the other night. Hopefully they'd sit outside in Harper's favorite place after dinner and after their talk.

Then she went inside to shower and dress. On her way downstairs the doorbell rang. She peeped through the window. Sam's florist truck was in the yard. Frowning, Barbara opened the door.

It was Sam standing with a humungous bouquet.

"I was given specific instructions for this," Sam said. "That there would be dire consequences if I didn't get it right." He offered one of his rare smiles. "To Barbara Turner. Are you by chance Ms. Turner?" he asked when she still hadn't spoken.

"I can't believe it. What did I do to deserve these?"

"Only you can tell," Sam said. "They're heavy. I'll take them in for you. Where do you want them?"

"On the kitchen counter."

After placing them there he handed her a bud vase with two roses, a fern, and baby's breath. "This goes with it."

"Oh, thank you. Let me get you a tip."

"Nope. I charged him enough for these."

"Thanks, Sam."

"Enjoy," he said, backing out the door.

Barbara closed the door and rushed to the kitchen, pulling the card out of its stand. It read: *To a special woman.*

Barbara stood for a moment, letting the words sink in. She would not second-guess the outcome of tonight. He loved her. He'd help make this work.

Candles would look wonderful on either side of the flowers. Harper should be home in an hour, she thought, then remembered they'd used all the candles. It was closer to drive to the grocer than to her house, so she made a quick trip.

Elliot was walking toward his car when she spotted him at the supermarket.

"How you doing, Barbara?" he asked. "Got those shares invested?"

"Sure do. My friend was here for Thanksgiving week, but she took care of it before she arrived."

Elliot nodded. "As soon as you cash them in, we're moving on, I think."

"So soon?" Barbara asked with a surprised expression. "I thought you liked it here."

"It's a nice place, but expensive. Dollar doesn't stretch as far as it used to."

"Isn't that the truth? Where are you moving to?"

"We were thinking Arizona. Minerva's arthritis, you know. But we haven't made a final decision yet," he said cautiously. "Been looking through magazines about the most favorable retirement places in the country."

Barbara nodded. "It's cheaper in some southern areas. But they're getting well-populated, too. So it's hard to find reasonably priced locations."

"That's the truth."

"Well, give my regards to Minerva," Barbara said.

"I'll do that."

Barbara was just about to continue into the store when she heard a very loud pop and felt tremendous heat and pain knock into her. She dropped her purse and placed her hand on the pain, looking down at the area. Blood oozed through her fingers. Puzzled, she touched her shoulder. Blood flowed over her hand. She heard people screaming and felt herself falling.

Elliot saw a kid do a nosedive in the body of a pickup truck just before he hunkered down between two cars and glanced around nervously. This wasn't the first time he'd heard gunfire. The asshole peppered the area, bullets hitting the side of the car. Was the asshole aiming at him? Or was it Barbara?

"Stay low," Elliot said to Barbara, expecting her to be hovering beside him.

People in the parking lot were screaming and shouting, some crying. Maybe somebody was hit.

"Maybe we oughta ease round back. Stay low to the ground," he said. But when Barbara didn't respond, he said, "You okay, Bar—"

And then he saw her. Five feet away, she was laid out on the pavement in the wide open. "Barbara?" Elliot shouted, panicked. He crawled on his stomach to reach her, a knot forming in his stomach. If she died, they'd be broke.

When Elliot reached her, he saw so much blood pouring out and covering her shirt. Oh, my God. Was she even breathing? He saw the shallow fall and rise of her chest, but he had to get her out of the line of fire. If he moved, though, the crazy SOB could shoot him. But he had no other option. He had to take the chance. She had his money. All of his money. She couldn't die on him now.

Easing up on his knees, Elliot gathered Barbara beneath her arms and pulled, but she didn't move. Grunting with the strain, he gathered a breath and pulled again, and this time he managed to slide her back a foot, then lay her flat to take a breath, before he continued. By the time he had her safely by the truck with him, he was tuckered out. He was an old man, for chrissakes, too old for this.

Since no more shots fired, the shooter must have taken off.

And then he heard the blessed sound of sirens. Thank the Lord.

"Hold on, Barbara. Help's on the way," Elliot said, taking his coat off to stem the flow of the blood. It was still gushing out like a fountain.

"Don't you die on me now."

Slowly, people started coming out of their rabbit holes.

"Anybody hurt?" he heard somebody call out. "The police're on their way."

"Over here. Barbara's been hit," Elliot returned.

Harper was getting ready to leave work a little early when Alyssa said there had been a shooting at the grocer and Doc had already been contacted. She was on her way there.

He ran out behind her. He tried to reach Barbara on his cell to tell her he'd be late as he tore out the parking lot. He was only a couple minutes away. A crowd had already gathered.

John was moving the crowd back and Alyssa was stooping over someone lying on the ground.

"Hang in there, honey," he heard her say as she pulled out her phone to make a call.

"Harper?"

Harper got his first glimpse of Barbara. Barbara? His heart jolted as he went down beside her. My God, she was covered with blood. Was she alive?

Doc got there, pushing him aside.

It seemed hours before the chopper arrived, but it was only fifteen minutes.

"Who was with her when it happened?" he bellowed.

"She was talking to Elliot Stone," someone said.

Elliot stepped back. "I didn't do it. We were just talking," he said.

Alyssa went to Stone. "I've got everything covered here, Harper. You take care of Barbara."

Harper was torn between staying and beating the truth out of Elliot or going to the hospital with Barbara. He was losing it and he knew it. He had to focus, to think.

"I'm going to the hospital. I want you to lock up every damn Stone on this island. You got that?" Harper ordered.

"I got it," Alyssa said.

"And do a gun residue test on him."

"I am. Now go. Barbara needs you."

* * *

As they airlifted Barbara away, Harper was on the chopper with her.

Just before the shooting, Detective Mosley had finally called him back to tell him that Barbara had accused the Stones of pushing her grandmother down the stairs. That Dorsey had been spying on them.

So she was here attempting to retrieve her grandmother's money and to exact revenge. Had she shot Andrew? She had been with Harper that night, but there was that small window of time when he couldn't contact her.

But she didn't trash the Stones' home. She was in bed with him when it had happened. What role did Elliot play in this shooting? They'd said he was talking to her when it happened. Was the shot meant for him and not Barbara?

Harper scraped a frustrated hand over his head.

Barbara had become his world. He pounded the carpet in the waiting room.

Within the hour, Claxtons who lived or worked on the mainland began to pour in. Within two hours, Naomi and Alyssa's mother arrived with Vanetta and Lisa.

"Hoyt and the boys are checking all the cars getting on the ferry," Naomi said. "Nobody's going to get off the island without them knowing."

Harper nodded. As soon as Barbara was out of danger, he was going to drag the truth out of the Stones, by any means necessary.

Elliot was pacing the floor when Minerva arrived at the station.

"Heard there was a shooting," she said. "What are you doing here?

"Barbara was shot," he said.

"But . . . how is she?"

"Don't know. I was talking to her when it happened. At the grocery store." He swiped a hand over his head. "They grilled me for hours, Minerva. For hours. Even checked to see if I had gun residue on my hand. They still won't let me go."

"She's got all our money," she whispered.

Elliot's legs gave out on him and he flopped down on the chair. "Every last penny."

"What are we going to do?"

"Minerva, I just don't know. I've got to think about this." His world was caving in on him.

"Look where your thinking has gotten us so far. We've lost everything, everything we've made. We can't make that money back."

"Just hold on. You're acting like she's not going to make it. It's not over yet," Elliot said. "You know she's going to have the best doctors working on her. Lord knows they're used to dealing with gunshot wounds in the hospital they took her to."

"Elliot, you're full of shit," Minerva said, and got up to go home.

Disbelieving what he'd just heard, Elliot gazed at her backside as she left. If she kept that up, he'd teach her a lesson she'd never forget, brothers or no brothers.

Everything around him had gone crazy. Now Andrew appeared.

"Daddy?"

"What are you doing here?"

"John came and picked me up. Said he wanted to talk to me."

"About what?"

"How should I know?"

Elliot swiped a hand over his face. What in God's name did they want with Andrew?

Elliot leaned close. "You keep your mouth shut, you here? You don't know nothing. You didn't do nothing!"

CHAPTER 14

Harper paced back and forth in the waiting room waiting to hear from the doctor, his cell phone pressed to his ear.

"Did you interview Trent?" he asked Alyssa. "Don't give those Stones any slack. It's got to have something to do with them. Stay on them, Alyssa."

"I've got it under control, Harper. Trent was on the ferry when the shooting occurred. Did you call Liane?"

Harper pinched the bridge of his nose. "Not yet. I don't have a number. Didn't think to check Barbara's cell phone."

"I have her purse. I'll call. Just take care of Barbara. I've got things covered here."

"The couple at the artist colony. Pick them up and interrogate them, too. Find out where they were at the time of the shooting."

"I will."

Harper flipped the phone closed. Take care of Barbara. He hadn't done such a good job of that so far.

He barely noticed others sitting in the room waiting for loved ones or waiting to get service themselves.

Trent dumped his duffle on the bed. He'd wait until tomorrow to call Barbara. Maybe tonight would be a good time. A helicopter was taking off just as he arrived, and Harper was probably busy. She'd have time to talk. He wondered about all the activity at the dock, but he didn't stick around to ask questions.

Hearing a knock at the door, Trent wondered who it could be. He didn't get visits—except for the sheriff. His heart leaped. He just got back on the island, for chrissakes. He debated pretending he was away, but his car was parked in the yard. He had no option but to answer. He peeped through the curtains. It wasn't Alyssa or the sheriff, but the woman he met at the bar a few times. She was dressed in all black, just as she'd been that night he'd torn up the Stones' house.

He jerked the door open. "What are you doing here?"

"Can't get off the damn island. What happened? They're checking everybody who gets on the ferry."

"I just got here. How the hell would I know?"

Without waiting for an invite, Sonya passed by him to slump on the couch. "This place is always in an uproar."

"I don't have time for company," Trent said, scrubbing his hands across his whiskers. He needed a shave.

"Can I crash here for a couple days?"

"Hell no. I don't know you that well. If they're

questioning everyone on this island, I don't want to get mixed up with it."

"And I just don't want to get mixed up in some mess that's none of my business."

"Look, I don't need any trouble."

Sonya crossed her legs. She patted the couch. "I'm no trouble. I'll sleep right here."

Trent was momentarily distracted by Sonya's delectable body. She had the potential to be a good distraction, but he shook his head. Never mix sex with business, and he had business to take care of, the business of talking to Barbara, and he certainly wasn't going to leave this woman in his house. He didn't know a thing about her. You didn't get to know a person by sharing a few drinks.

"Sorry. You've got to go."

She looked startled. "You're kidding, right? I could have popped your behind when I caught you spying on the Stones."

"You could have done a lot of things." Trent backed to the door and opened it.

"I can't fucking believe this. There's no place to go on this stupid place. I don't know why we came here in the first place."

"Not my problem." Who was this *we* she was alluding to? Trent wondered but wouldn't ask. He knew there was more to her than met the eye. Didn't trust her from the beginning. He nodded toward the door.

In a temper, she hopped off the sofa and stomped out.

Trent shut the door after her, then tried to reach Barbara. But she didn't answer and he didn't leave a message.

* * *

It was nine-thirty that night when the surgeon met with Harper and Naomi, Naomi being the next of kin.

"The bullet was lodged close to her heart. The next few hours will be critical," he said, then answered questions Harper peppered at him.

Harper retrieved the bullet as evidence before he went to recovery to see Barbara. Seeing her all doped up, with tubes and machines attached, broke his heart and made him mad as hell.

He took a deep breath. At least she was alive. That was something to be grateful for. Harper stayed most of the night and he didn't leave until she had regained consciousness.

Naomi had left for a while to stay with one of her sons who lived in Portsmouth, but she returned early that morning.

"I'll stay with her," she said. "You go take care of what you need to. She won't be alone. I'll call you with her progress."

Barbara was still in ICU when he left in the wee hours of the morning.

The last ferry had already run and he got a taxi to the medical examiner's office to drop off the bullet for them to produce an analysis for him, then got a water taxi to ferry him back to the island.

The night deputy picked him up and dropped him off at the office where he got his car. Harper looked at himself in the rearview mirror. He looked bad enough to scare himself. He scrubbed a hand across his chin and headed to Trent's place. He needed a shave badly. It's a wonder Barbara recognized him.

He pounded on the door. When Trent answered it, he could smell sausage cooking.

Harper moved inside. "Why are you here?"

Trent stepped back. "What's going on?"

"Don't bullshit me. Why are you here? Barbara was shot late yesterday afternoon."

"Barbara? The helicopter was lifting *Barbara* to the hospital?"

The guy seemed genuinely shocked, but he could be a good actor, too.

"I'm not going to repeat myself."

Trent sighed. "I came here to get my money from the Stones," he said. "They stole most of my mother's retirement."

"And Barbara?"

"I thought she was working with them at first because I knew Andrew had a girlfriend. But I found out it wasn't her."

"Did you shoot Andrew?"

"No, but there's a woman who's been watching their house."

"How do you know?"

"Because I've been watching it, too. We ran into each other one night. Yesterday after I returned from D.C., she came by here telling me she couldn't get off the island and asked if I'd put her up."

"Why would she come to you?"

"I've had drinks with her a couple of times at the bar, but that's all."

"And you don't think she lives here."

"No."

"Do you know where she lives?"

Trent shook his head.

"What's her name?"

"I only know her first name and that's Sonya. At least that's what she told me."

The elusive Sonja again. "Did she have a weapon on her?"

"I don't know."

"You tried to reach Barbara several times last night. Why?" Alyssa had toggled through the numbers on Barbara's phone.

"I was going to ask her if she knew a way for me to get my mother's money back. At the first break-in, some of the Stones' money was stolen."

"How do you know?"

"Andrew told me."

Harper was skeptical. "He just told you?"

"I gave him some inducement."

Harper didn't even want to think about what the inducement might be.

"You mind if I visit Barbara in the hospital?" Trent asked.

Harper shook his head. "You might want to wait a day or so. She's still in ICU and pretty much out of it right now."

From there Harper headed to the office.

"Jesus, Harper. Some men don't do well without a shave," Alyssa said. "You're one of them. I've got a razor in my desk."

Harper ignored her. "What do you have on the Stones?"

"Minerva was at Hughes's place. Grandma saw Andrew at the house just before the shooting. And Elliot was with Barbara. Witnesses were pretty confused about where the bullet came from, but a couple people thought they heard the shot coming from the woods."

"Find anything there?"

"Footprints. We made casts."

"The Stones are a family of con artists—actually,

confidence people. They may have killed Sarah so that Minerva could get her job with Hughes."

"I found an abandoned boat tied up not far from where the body was found. It was reported stolen a month ago in Norfolk."

"Where is it now?"

"Impounded."

"Let's see if we can lift some prints," he said. "I talked to Trent. He said a woman approached him seeking shelter last night soon after the shooting. He'd caught her casing the Stones' residence."

"Did he get a name?"

"Sonya. She might be the woman from the artist colony."

"I found some footprints in the area where the shooter was standing. Size eleven foot," Alyssa said. "I think it was a man's. Somebody in that area saw a boat taking off shortly afterward."

"Let's get some fingerprints. See if we come up with anything. Where are the Stones?"

"In a holding cell."

"Did you pick up the couple from the artist colony?"

Alyssa shook her head. "They've disappeared. We've searched the island for them."

"Get Andrew to the interview room."

"You're not starting with Elliot? He runs the show."

"Andrew. He's the weakest link." Harper could get info he could use against the others.

"Okay . . ."

Harper made a few calls, including to the hospital to find out Barbara's progress, before he went down the hall to the interview room.

Andrew was standing by the interview table.

Alyssa glanced at him. "Harp, I'm thinking I

should do this interview. I don't think you can be objective."

"You can come in if you like. But I'm leading this interview," he said with finality and shoved the door open. Harper rounded the table and stood with his hands on his hips looking as mean as he felt. Alyssa leaned on the door, blocking the exit.

Andrew shot a look at Alyssa, then at Harper.

"Have a seat, Andrew," Alyssa offered.

The younger man glanced at Harper and eased into the chair in slow motion.

Harper hit the desk with his fist.

Andrew fainted.

Alyssa rushed over to Andrew and shook him. "Jesus Christ, Harper. What're you trying to do? Give him a heart attack before you get your answers? Honestly. You're going to get nowhere this way." She opened the door and called out.

"Somebody get some smelling salts, will you?"

"Smelling salts? I don't think we have any," the secretary called.

"Cleaning ammonia. Anything that'll wake him."

Alyssa glared at Harper. "Have you looked at yourself lately? You look like the leader of some biker group. You need a shave. You look like hell. No sense in me bringing him to if you're going to tower over him. He'll faint again."

Harper rounded the desk again and took a look at Andrew. "He seems to be coming around. I'll send John in to help you." He left the interview room and had John bring Minerva to the conference room before he joined Alyssa.

"Sheriff, I'm really upset that I've been kept overnight like I'm some criminal," Minerva began. "I was with Lambert when the shooting took place, nowhere near Barbara. She's a nice young lady and I hope she pulls through just fine."

"May I get you a cup of coffee?" Harper asked.

She looked surprised. "A cup of tea would be nice. And a muffin to go with it."

Harper barely contained his incredulity. Where did she think she was? "Ellen, could you please bring Mrs. Stone a cup of tea and the muffin out of my office, please?"

"Okay, Harp," she said.

Satisfied, Minerva leaned back in her chair. "You need to get a nap. It won't do Barbara a bit of good if you wear yourself out."

"Have you been read your Miranda rights?" he asked.

She nodded. "Am I under arrest?"

"Not at this time, but I want to make sure your rights had been read and that you know you have the right to an attorney."

He made small talk with her until Ellen rushed in with tea in a white Styrofoam cup and the muffin still in the wrapper. She handed them both to Minerva with a stirrer and a couple of packets of sweetener, then hurried out.

Minerva added both packets to her tea before she sipped it, then sighed. "This is the first decent thing I've had since I got here."

"I'm glad you're pleased. Tell me about the money that was stolen from your house during the robbery."

The cup slipped, sloshing tea on Minerva's dress.

"Careful," Harper warned. "The money?"

"No . . . nothing was stolen. They just trashed the house."

"I'm talking about the first break-in. That's when the money was stolen."

"How did . . ." She pressed her mouth together. "You're mistaken. How did you come up with that conclusion? We don't have money. If we did, I wouldn't be working at Lambert's as his companion."

"Oh, but your goal is to become much more than a companion, isn't it? Lambert Hughes is a wealthy man by most standards."

"No more than we will be."

Harper arched his eyebrows. "Elaborate."

"Andrew will come into money in a few years, so you see, we don't need to steal from anyone."

"How may years?"

"In five, when he's forty."

Now Harper understood why they kept Andrew around and why he never had to work. They'd browbeat the poor guy so much that he couldn't make one decent decision on his own. So when the money came to him, they'd take over without him questioning them. What a sorry bunch. For the first time, he began to feel sorry for Andrew. With parents like those, no wonder he regularly drank himself under the table, and they probably encouraged it.

"So you can just let us go, Sheriff. All of us. My . . ."

"Husband?"

"Brother," she snapped.

Harper shifted the papers in front of him. "Elliot's your husband. One Minerva Smith married Elliot Stone thirty-five years and four months ago in Detroit," he read and glanced up, staring directly into Minerva's eyes. "Just in time for your dear son to be born with his father's name," he said. "Now, do you want to revise your statement?"

"I've never stolen money from anyone. That's all

I'm saying," she said, tea and muffin forgotten. "I was with Lambert when the shooting occurred. If you don't believe me, ask him or his daughter."

They already had.

"Harper?" John poked her head in the door. "Can you come here a minute? There's an emergency."

Harper followed him into the hallway and shut the door behind him. "What is it?"

"Somebody broke into Barbara's house. Lisa went to get some clothes and things for her. Looks like somebody's been living there."

"How's Andrew?"

"He came around. Alyssa gave him something to eat and drink. He's okay for now. But he's still waiting in the interrogation room."

"Take Minerva back to a cell. But don't let her see Andrew."

In five minutes, he was at Barbara's place.

Alyssa had left a minute before them and was canvassing the area on foot. Lisa was sitting in her car.

Harper checked his watch. The next ferry was due in fifteen minutes. He called the night deputy and told him to get up and go to the ferry to check the cars leaving, especially those he couldn't identify. "And in particular a brown Ford Taurus."

"Secure the place with cones," he told John. "I'll be back soon."

Alyssa was on foot. Whoever was there had made a mad dash out the back door when Lisa came in the front. They could have had a car parked someplace nearby. Harper looked around at the thick woodlands on the other side of the road; then he got into his car and drove down the path.

Just an old barn remained where a family house

used to be. That property belonged to Barbara, too. He drove down the severely potholed path. It opened onto an inner island road. A car had recently driven through there. Harper drove alongside of the tire tracks, hoping to find a place to get a cast to determine who drove through. He spent an hour cruising the island searching for the culprit and ended up at the ferry.

"No strangers came through here," the night duty deputy told him.

The entire sheriff's staff was exhausted. He called a couple of retired deputies and had them help with the ferry search. "As soon as they arrive, let them know what we're looking for and you get some sleep," Harper told the deputy and called Nancy at the artist colony.

"Has that couple returned yet?"

"No, but I know they will in a couple days. They always do. They've left all their things here."

"They could be dangerous. If they show up, give my office a call," he said, and headed back to Barbara's house.

He put on crime scene bootees and plastic gloves before he went in.

The scent of bacon hit him as soon as he entered. It pissed him off that someone had invaded her space while she was fighting for her life in the hospital.

Someone had cooked breakfast and hadn't bothered or had time to wash the dishes afterward. He bagged a glass and fork for DNA analysis.

Quickly, he walked through the house, room by room. He couldn't tell if anything was taken. At least they hadn't trashed the place, but they could have stolen things.

In the den, the drawers were opened, all of them. He knew that Barbara usually kept them locked. He's seen her use the key to retrieve something. He rifled through the drawers, but he couldn't tell if anything was missing.

A picture of an older woman looked at him from the desk. He did not see that when he was here before. It must be her grandmother's photo.

"I want prints lifted," he said, "especially in here, in the kitchen, and the bedroom where this scum slept."

"We're already on it," Alyssa said.

Andrew had said the stranger usually gave him rides from the ferry or from bars in Norfolk. Everybody wanted something from Andrew. His parents wanted his money. He thought of Trent. He was around the ladies. Minerva went to the shop. Did he fit into this mess? Harper worked until dusk.

"You've got to get some rest, Harper. And you need a shave," Alyssa told him.

"I'm going to shower and shave before I visit Barbara. I'll probably catch a nap there."

When Harper arrived at home, none of the lights was on to greet him. No smell of food or Barbara's smiling face. His home felt lonelier than ever. He showered, changed, and even took the time to shave.

The next day, they got the results of the fingerprints of the person who'd handled the boat.

"Do you know a Sonya Davies?" Harper asked Elliot.

"No, never heard of her," he said. "Why do you ask?"

Harper saw the shift in his eyes. He was lying. "I'm asking the questions."

Harper moved closer, got right in his face, and

loomed over him. "You want to think about your answer?"

Elliot leaned back and shook his head. "I don't know anyone by that name."

Harper interrogated Elliot for an hour but didn't get any useful information. Harper had nothing to hold him with, but he held Elliot and Minerva an extra couple of hours and was forced to let him go, even though he didn't want to.

CHAPTER 15

Barbara felt like Sleeping Beauty must have felt after her extremely long nap. Then the pain hit her and she groaned.

"You just can't do things the easy way, can you?"

Barbara tried to open her eyes, but she felt as if she was in a fog. "Liane?" she whispered, but it couldn't be. Liane was on her way back to New York. And what was wrong with her?

"I'm here."

"What . . ."

"You were shot."

Her fuzzy memory began to return. She had been talking to Elliot and suddenly something hit her.

She remembered waking up a couple of times and people talking or barking at her. She remembered hearing Harper's voice. But he wasn't there now. Liane looked worried.

"I'm glad you're finally pulling out of this."

Her mouth felt dry. "Who shot me?"

"They don't know. Did Elliot do it?"

She shook her head. "Don't think so. We talked.

I was going into the store and he was leaving. Didn't see a gun."

"That doesn't mean he didn't have one."

The nurse came in, took her vitals, and gave her medication. Barbara couldn't keep her eyes open for very long before she slept again.

When she woke up the next time, the nurse was there and Harper was sleeping in a chair near her bed. His face was lined with exhaustion.

He moved close to the bed. "How are you?"

"Okay." Barbara wasn't one to say the obvious. Anybody looking at her knew she felt like hell.

Barbara was looking a little better, but she was still in ICU.

"How are you feeling, babe?"

"I wasn't trying to get out of our conversation, honest," she said hoarsely. At least her breathing tube was removed.

It was too soon for Harper to find levity in the situation. Not the way she was hooked up to tubes and beeping machines.

"You could have trusted me."

"I do trust you. So who shot me?"

Harper squeezed her hand. "I don't know yet." He pulled up a chair. "So you were here to retrieve the money the Stones stole from your grandmother." Harper knew this but felt like repeating it. Liane had given him an abridged version. How much she left out was questionable.

"Elliot killed her."

"Detective Mosley said she fell down the stairs."

"She called me when she—" Barbara coughed, alarming Harper.

"Don't talk now," he said. She was worn out from the conversation, but she gripped his hand.

"I know he killed her. And I know he killed Sarah."

He stroked her forehead. "Get some sleep. I'll be here when you wake up."

When Naomi came in, Harper left and called Alyssa for an update. None of them was getting much sleep. When he returned, he straightened the covers over Barbara.

"Someone broke into your house."

"Did they steal anything?"

"I can't tell."

"Did they damage anything?"

"Looks like they knew you weren't there and were looking for a place to stay. Your grandmother's picture was on the desk."

"But I left it in the back of the drawer."

"Why? You don't have any pictures around."

"In case Elliot broke in."

"You want to tell me what's going on?"

"It's part of what I was going to tell you. Elliot courted my grandmother and ultimately stole money from her—a lot of it." She told Harper about the five other women the PI had found.

"They were all women and all seniors?"

Barbara nodded.

"So you came here to get your grandmother's money back."

"He operated a little differently with my grandmother. Because her signature wasn't on the CDs, the bank was responsible. Dorsey wouldn't just hand them over for any reason. She wore huge floppy hats and Minerva wore one pretending to be my grandmother. She did a pretty credible job of the signature, too."

"So how did you plan to get the money from Elliot?"

Barbara was silent. "You don't want to know. Suffice it to say, Elliot killed Sarah. I can't prove it, But he did."

"How do you know that?"

"Because Lambert Hughes was their next mark. The only reason they can't get money from him is that I called his daughter to give her the heads up. She was able to get power of attorney over his assets. But Elliot had no problem with killing Sarah to get her out of the way."

"And you think he shot you?"

"No, he can't get his money back. . . ."

Harper scrubbed a hand over his face. "Barbara, what have you done?"

She clamped her mouth closed.

"Barbara."

"One woman they stole money from can't afford to buy her medicine. These women are alone, Harper. They have no other resources. Social Security doesn't pay enough to take care of all their expenses. They are in their seventies and eighties, and often alone."

"Why didn't you tell me this in the beginning? I could have helped you."

"How were they going to pay for their expenses if lawyers got most of their money? By the time any court case is over, they'd be dead and still wouldn't have their money," she said, then coughed. Jesus, the pain shooting through her chest felt like somebody stabbed her.

"Take it easy," he said, concerned. "Take a couple of breaths."

It took several moments for the pain to abate. When Barbara had calmed down, she said, "These women are not going to resort to eating cat food to exist, and they will be able to buy their medicines."

As angry as Harper was, he couldn't help but feel a touch of pride. His tigress was laid up in the hospital and still fighting. But this was dangerous, too.

"So obviously Elliot gave you the money. And since you were a broker, then he expects you to invest it."

"He doesn't know I was a broker and it's not *his* money."

Harper blew out a long breath. "What did you expect to do once you got the money? Did you think he'd just walk away because you spanked him?"

"I expect you to put him in jail where he belongs and I won't have to deal with him."

"With no information? You didn't say one word, not one . . ." Harper restrained his temper. He'd wait until she was well before he laid into her, but good.

"You know now, don't you?"

Harper grabbed his temper. "What else can you tell me? Can you give me the names of the other women?"

"It's in my credenza. The file folder says 'Marks'."

"Let's hope your thief didn't destroy it."

"If he did, I'll give you the name of the PI. He can give you names and addresses. I also have them in Dorsey's house in Philly, but that would take more time."

"Why don't you give me the name of that PI?"

"It's in the same folder. His phone number is also on my cell phone."

"Did you break into the Stones' house the first time?"

"No."

"Trent mentioned some woman was watching the Stones' place."

"I don't have a clue. I haven't been there."

He could see she was tiring. "Get some rest," he said. He kissed her on the forehead.

"Take my ring back."

He looked at her sharply. "Why?"

"I can't wear it in here. I'd rather you kept it until I go home."

He nodded.

"The info on the contact lens came back," Alyssa said late the next morning. "The ophthalmologist identified Elliot Stone as the one he made them for."

"Book him for the murder of Sarah Rhodes." About time they got a break.

"And for the attempted murder of Barbara?"

"I don't think he shot her."

Alyssa and John left to pick Elliot up again. It had really bothered them when they'd had to release him.

Trent had visited Barbara while she was in ICU, but a couple days later they moved her to a regular room. He got there around eleven that morning.

"You're looking better," he said, standing in the doorway.

Barbara smiled. "I feel better."

He carried a bunch of flowers in his hand and had the foresight to put them in a vase.

"The flowers are beautiful," she said. "Thank you."

He searched around for someplace to put them

and noticed the available space was already covered with flowers, so he set them on the floor and dropped into a chair near her.

"Your customers been sending their regards. They want you to get well soon." He encountered people everywhere—the cleaners, the grocery store, the Greasy Spoon.

Barbara smiled. "How was your visit with your family?" she asked.

"Very good. My mother's doing much better. Got her up and moving again. I talked to my sister and she hasn't regressed."

"I didn't know your mother was ill."

Trent glanced at his hands. Seemed to choose his words carefully. "She's the reason I came here. When you get outta the hospital, we'll talk."

"I've got nothing to do here. Why don't we talk now while we have a quiet moment?"

"You just get yourself well. This can wait."

"You can do manicures and pedicures in the shop if you want to. The customers will want their nails done for Christmas parties."

"I might. Give me something to do."

"I'll have Harper give you a key. It seems everyone has a motive for being here. So tell me, why are you really here?"

"The Stones stole my mother's life savings."

"Oh, Trent. No wonder she's heartbroken."

He shook his head. "Didn't think anything could knock her off her feet. She's a proud woman. Reminds me of you."

"She's lucky to come out of it with her life. I believe Elliot killed my grandmother. But I can't prove it."

Trent frowned. "What about that women they found near my place? You think they killed her, too?"

"Yes, or at least Elliot did, so that Minerva could take her job as Lambert's companion. He's very wealthy and I believe they planned to bilk him for everything they could. I called his daughter before that could happen, and she now has control of his money."

"What about you? You think they shot you?"

Barbara shook her head and sighed. "I don't know. I was with Elliot when it happened. I can't see Andrew having the gumption to shoot anyone."

"Andrew has a girlfriend."

"Girlfriend?"

"Yeah, my mother told me about her. Then there's this woman who was spying on their house."

"How do you know this?"

"'Cause I was spying, too. Trying to find a time I could get my mama's money back. Mama went to the police department. They couldn't do nothing." He sighed in disgust. "No wonder people take care of things themselves. Especially when the law won't do a thing."

"They have to have proof."

"I've got proof. A mama who's sick to her soul for what they did. Look at you laid up in the hospital. That bullet coulda killed you." Trent stood. "If the law isn't gonna take care of it, I will."

"Trent, give Harper a chance. You know he'll do a thorough investigation. It's their main priority. They have to make sure that the information they find holds up in court. It does no good if they do a shoddy job. And I don't need to be worrying about you."

"You don't have to worry about me. I can take care of myself. I'll get a confession out of 'em."

Barbara leaned over to grab his hand. Pain stabbed her chest and she groaned. It hurt so bad she couldn't breathe.

Trent gently laid her back. "Don't you be moving like that. Take it easy."

It took a minute for her to get a breath. Trent pulled up the chair and patted her hand awkwardly, not knowing what to do. "Want me to call the nurse?"

Barbara shook her head. Finally, she spoke in a weak voice, "Promise me you'll leave the investigating to Harper and Alyssa."

He could see she was tired. She couldn't talk about this any longer. He gave her a curt nod, but it was evident she didn't believe him.

"What will it do to your mother if you end up in jail? Do you want to worry her more than she already is?"

Frustrated, Trent leaned back in the seat. That's the last thing he needed. If he couldn't get that money back, he might have to help her pay the bills. He couldn't do that in jail. He regarded Barbara. She was upset when she should be concentrating on getting well. He didn't want her worrying about him.

"Okay. I'll let your man take care of things. You get a nap now. I'll be back to visit you."

"I may be able to get some of her money for her," Barbara said. "I'm considering different options, such as setting up a trust that I manage and sending each woman a monthly check. With the money invested, they'll eventually get all of it back."

"You can decide that later. Just get some rest now."

Barbara nodded. "Okay."

* * *

Elliot was dead. Murdered with a single gunshot.

Jesus Christ, Harper thought as he drove toward their house, lights blinking.

He had every deputy and even the retired ones canvassing the island, the shore, and the ferry, but already they could be too late, depending on how long ago Elliot was killed. Having drank himself nearly unconscious, Andrew had either slept through it all or it happened before he got home. Minerva had slept through it. Andrew had found him that morning when the phone woke him. Lambert had phoned the house when Minerva didn't show up for work. Minerva had overslept. Elliot usually woke her.

Andrew and Minerva were now with Naomi Claxton.

That house was going to get a reputation for bringing bad luck. First the Flemings and now Elliot Stone. He doubted anyone would want to live there after this. Soon they'd be including it on ghost tours.

Crime scene cones and tape had already been put up. It was going to take the rest of the day to process the scene. Harper really wanted to know the whereabouts of the couple living at the artist colony.

At the hospital the next day, Barbara was sitting up in bed eating, but only picking at her food.

"Oh, Harper, I can't believe it. That Elliot was killed. I mean, I was very upset at him for Dorsey's death, but I never expected this."

"Do you know or have you ever heard of Boyd Xavier?

Barbara frowned. "He's my ex-husband."

"When was the last time you saw him?"

More than puzzled, she said, "More than a year ago. When I was in Manhattan, and I only saw him in passing then," Barbara responded. "Why?"

"His fingerprints were on the boat we found on the island the day you were shot.

"Boyd is here? On the island?"

"His fingerprints were also in the cabin at the artist colony where he was staying with another woman—Sonya. We don't have her prints on file. Does he hold a strong enough grudge against you to kill you?"

"Kill me? Why would he want to kill me? He has nothing to gain by my death. He doesn't get one cent if I die. Besides, our marriage was over fifteen years ago. It makes no sense that he would try to kill me now."

"And this whole case makes sense?" he asked, tongue in cheek.

Barbara shook her head. "I can't imagine why Boyd is here. He was always jealous. But he remarried twice after me. I think he's divorced again, but he and I parted fifteen years ago, Harper. If he wanted to kill me, why not do it soon after we divorced? As far as I know, he's never been involved in criminal activity."

"So it's just a coincidence his fingerprints showed up on a stolen boat on my island."

Barbara frowned. "No, but I don't know what his purpose is."

"Okay. Let's discuss the divorce. Whose idea was it?"

"Mine. Like I've told you, he was cheating and offering nothing to the marriage. I wasn't going to put up with that crap."

"Did he fight it?"

"I told him if he fought it, I'd use his infidelity as the reason. If he didn't, we could go with irreconcilable differences. It took less time and I didn't ask for alimony."

"And the apartment?"

"I owned the condo before we married. I had already tossed his stuff into garbage bags and changed the locks on the door. Anyway, I paid the mortgage. And since I owned it before we married, I considered it mine. It was also part of the prenup."

"How did he feel about that?"

"The prenup was his idea. He wanted to keep his assets in the event of a divorce, and I felt I should, too. There was nothing he could do."

"How has his career progressed in the last fifteen years?"

"I don't keep up with him. Quite frankly, I didn't care enough. As far as I was concerned, it was over."

Harper nodded. He slid out of his jacket and draped it on the back of the chair before he dropped into the seat. Fatigue coated his face like paint on a canvas.

There was no hello kiss. No intimate touches.

Her secrecy stood between them. Barbara had never let fear hold her back. The one thing she knew was that she had to face her fears to overcome them. This wasn't going to be easy, but she needed to know if they had a future.

"Harper, I know I should have told you . . ."

"That conversation's over with. We won't discuss it again."

Barbara tightened her fist into the blanket. "I think we need to talk about it."

He gave a tired sigh. "Everything that needs to be said has already been said. So drop it, okay?"

The nurse came in, interrupting the stilted conversation. Barbara wanted to have that talk now. She didn't like not knowing how things stood. Lord knows she never understood the male mind. She knew enough about men to work with them and get what she wanted, but her dates had been sparse since she didn't put up with crap. Most men couldn't handle the truth.

But Harper wasn't like that.

By the time the nurse left, Harper had fallen asleep.

Barbara regarded him slumped in the chair. His legs were spread wide and his hands were resting on his knees. The hands that had given her such pleasure. He looked relaxed in his sleep. More relaxed than she'd seen him since he grew suspicious of her.

For the first time, a man was in her life who didn't want her money, or to pick her brain about a stock, or for any selfish reason. He loved her for her. Overweight and all.

Was it too late? His parents and brother had visited her over the weekend. He wouldn't have told them she was ill if he was planning to break up with her, would he?

CHAPTER 16

Lisa got up early to clean Barbara's house the day before her release from the hospital; then around noon, Alyssa told her Barbara was staying at Harper's place and she had to spend her afternoon cleaning there. It was late before she could make it to the hospital.

"It's all ready for you tomorrow," she said. Barbara was looking a little better, but she still looked as if she needed to spend a couple more days in the hospital. But they got you out of there in a hurry now. At least Lisa's cousin, Regina, was a nurse and she'd be looking in on Barbara.

"I'll pay you . . ."

"You're kinfolk. I can't take money from you."

"Remember your business. You can't . . ."

"This isn't business. I'll keep things straight until you're on your feet again. After that, it's business."

People were always underestimating Lisa, but Barbara had always seen another side of her. Trent had told her that Lisa often stopped by the shop to make sure it was properly cleaned, although he cleaned up after himself. Lisa had said she didn't want dust to pile up.

What a huge, giving heart, Barbara thought. She knew Lisa didn't have very much money, and Lisa could make extra money cleaning for someone else rather than clean Barbara's place. Santa was going to have to put a little extra under her Christmas tree.

"Thanks, Lisa."

"What are cousins for? I'm taking Grandma home with me tonight. Harper is going to check you out tomorrow, and I'll see you when you get to the island."

Liane had taken the next flight back to Norfolk after Harper called her. After Barbara was out of ICU, she'd left to tie up some things in New York so that she could spend the next couple of weeks with Barbara.

"Thought any more about that cleaning business?" Barbara asked Lisa.

Lisa looked sheepish. "Vanetta's helping me make a business plan. We'll see."

"Good for you."

"She's working with Jordan a couple of days a week in the hotel. And that's good."

"That is improvement," Barbara said. "I know she feels better doing something constructive. How did you talk her into that?"

"Just kept telling her she should get involved. It's her business, too. She can't depend on others to take care of things for her when she's fully capable." She glanced up at Barbara. "I can't believe I said that. But I think she likes it."

"Gives her purpose."

Lisa started straightening the bedside table and

covers. Put water in the flower vases. "You've got enough flowers to start your own shop."

"People have been so kind. I sent most of them to the children's ward and to some of the seniors." That was a lot for someone who thought she was virtually alone in the world. She'd gotten flowers from people at her old job, as well as from Liane's family. The Claxtons had sent enough to supply the entire children's ward. What a huge family. There were flowers from her customers as well and cards of well wishes.

But she did not know where she stood with Harper. He'd visited her every day. He was warm and worried. But she didn't know if the offer of marriage still stood. She'd sent the engagement ring home with him. Her fingers swelled in the hospital and she didn't want to keep it there. He hadn't objected.

All his conversations were about her health and the case. They didn't discuss personal issues. Maybe he felt duty bound to stick by her until she was well.

Barbara sighed. Maybe she should have trusted him. Perhaps she should have come clean from the very beginning about the Stones even if she couldn't retrieve the money for the families who so desperately needed it. But hindsight always offered a clearer view.

Barbara shook her head. She couldn't have done it. Those people needed the money, and by the time the lawyers and the court finished with it, it would have whittled down to a pittance. She wasn't dealing with the wealthy, but everyday people who sacrificed to sock away a few dollars at a time.

* * *

Barbara came home the next day. When Harper headed toward his house, she said, "We're going to my house, right?"

"Liane's already at my house."

"Harper, I'd be more comfortable at my house."

He was silent a moment. "Well, you aren't going there. You were shot with the same gun that was used to kill Elliot."

"So the bullet that hit me was meant for him."

"I don't know that and I'm not taking chances."

Barbara glanced out the window. It seemed a lifetime ago when she was last at his place. She wondered if he'd eaten the meal she'd prepared.

"No argument?"

"I'm not crazy. I want to live."

He shook his head.

"What happened to our dinner?"

"It ended up in the trash. I haven't been in the fridge since you left and Lisa found it in there when she cleaned."

Barbara nodded. "How is Andrew?"

"Not good."

"You're going to have to take him in hand," Barbara said. "At this point, he isn't capable of taking care of himself. But with a little help, I think he can make it."

"That was done intentionally to get control of his trust fund. But, Barbara, he was part of the conspiracy. He's going to jail along with Minerva."

"Harper, you know Andrew didn't scam anyone. He's been mentally beat to death by his father his entire life. It was Elliot doing the planning and Minerva worked with him."

"But he knew."

"Alyssa said he fainted when you tried to talk to him. Do you think he could stand up to Elliot?"

"Too bad I can't put some of that fear in you," Harper mumbled.

"In your dreams."

"Andrew can't get off with nothing after all the scams they pulled."

"*They* pulled, not Andrew."

"I can't pick and choose who gets punished. Why have you become his champion suddenly?"

"Because he's just pitiful. They'd eat him alive in jail. That's not the place for him," Barbara said. "I can't see justice being served by locking him up."

"At least he's going to have to be put on probation."

Satisfied, Barbara nodded. "And you can keep an eye on him."

"Me?" He looked at her as if she'd lost her mind.

"Yes, you."

"For as much trouble as you're in, you're asking a hell of a lot, woman."

Her eyes widened. "I haven't done a thing."

"Right."

"Besides, he's not going to accept help from me. I broke his arm, remember?"

"You should be happy to know the cast is off. He's getting some therapy. I'm sure he'll forgive you in a year or two," Harper said.

"His trust fund might be the reason Elliot was killed."

"I've thought of that," Harper said, turning into his driveway. "The girlfriend could have killed him, and after the dust settles, she plans to return. She'd have complete control over him."

"Where is this elusive girlfriend?" Barbara asked.

"That's what I have to find out."

He drove into the garage and helped Barbara out.

Liane and Scott, the retired deputy, were in the kitchen. Harper and Scott lugged in her things while Liane helped her settle in the bedroom.

"I guess Harper can calm down some now that you're home. He's been a real bear with you away."

"Thanks for being here, Liane."

"Where else would I be? Now you go get in bed. Do you need help?"

"No."

Harper came into the bedroom with her luggage. A huge flower arrangement was on the dresser.

"Oh, Harper. The flowers are beautiful."

"From Sam and Regina."

"That's so sweet of them."

"I want you to keep the curtains closed. I know you'll feel like a prisoner, but until we find this couple, we have to take precautions."

Barbara nodded. She noticed he'd installed a security system.

"Scott will be with you all day until I get home."

He helped her settle in before he left.

Harper went to the Claxtons' to talk to Andrew. Minerva had been arrested for collusion in Sarah Rhodes's death.

"How is he?" Harper asked Naomi.

"As well as expected. Doc gave him a light sedative. He's in the living room with Hoyt watching TV."

Harper peeked through the door. Andrew was sitting in Naomi's recliner. Hoyt had kicked back in his own, sleeping.

"Andrew?" Harper said. He moved into the room, found a chair, and pulled it close.

Andrew glanced at him and sighed deeply.

"I want to contact your girlfriend, Andrew. I'm sure she'll want to be with you at a time like this."

Looking hopeful, Andrew sat up. "I forgot. She calls once a week."

"Is there any way I can contact her?"

"I don't know."

"How does she contact you?"

"She calls me on my cell phone."

"May I see it?"

Andrew dug into his pocket for it and handed it over.

Harper flipped through the numbers. "Which one is hers?"

Andrew took the phone and toggled, then handed it to Harper. "That one."

Harper frowned. "Her name's Sonya?"

He nodded.

"Where did you say she was?"

"In the Bahamas."

"How long has she been there?"

"Couple months."

"You mind if I keep this for a while?" Harper asked.

Andrew frowned. "I'll miss Sonya's call."

"I'll make sure she reaches you."

Harper left wondering how this could get any worse. Andrew's entire world had shifted. Not only was his father dead, but Minerva couldn't give him directions while she was locked up.

At the station, Harper tried Sonya's number several times but was unable to reach her. He didn't believe she ever went to the Bahamas.

An area-wide all-points bulletin had been put out on Sonya Davies and Boyd Xavier.

In the meantime, he had a funeral to attend.

Elliot's funeral was held at Naomi's church. Since she did the planning, the turnout was good.

Even Harper and Alyssa were there to see if Sonya and Boyd would show up. Harper had left two retired officers at his house just in case they took it as an opportunity to get to Barbara. But they didn't appear at either place.

Barbara had visitors every day. Naomi visited her with information about her family's history, and Barbara was exhausted with a deluge of information.

Harper came in after Naomi left.

"Minerva made bail."

"How?" she asked.

"She got an attorney from Norfolk and he's saying there's no evidence indicating that she knew Elliot was going to kill Sarah. He ran things without telling her what he was doing." Flight risk was the main problem with bail.

"I can't believe she could get off with that lame excuse."

"According to her, unknown to her, Elliot played the scams. The prosecutor has to prove her complicity in court."

"What about all the money?"

"She claims there's no money."

It was a week before Christmas and Barbara was restless from being cooped up in the house for two weeks.

Boyd and Sonya were still out there, but Harper had told her to dress for an outing and she was happy to finally leave the house. He'd moved some of her clothes into his closet, and she selected wool pants and a sweater. Liane helped her dress.

It was warm in the car. Barbara thought they'd go to the B&B or drive around to look at the houses and boats decorated with Christmas lights, so when he headed to the ferry, she was surprised.

"Where are we going?"

"To see the decorations on the Boardwalk in Virginia Beach. It's a drive-through," he said. "They'll give us a CD and it plays music to fit the various scenes as we drive forward. I think you'll like it."

When they got there, there was a long line of cars moving at a snail's pace on Atlantic Avenue waiting to go on the Boardwalk.

"When is your family arriving?" Barbara asked.

"Wednesday night. They're waiting for the kids to get out of school."

Finally, they were on the Boardwalk. There were overhangs and sidebars of beach-themed decorations.

They rode under the Little Mermaid display.

"This is so cute. You need to bring your nieces and nephews."

"I have," Harper said, smiling. "Last year."

As the music played, they rode under jumping fish. The Twelve Days of Christmas displays revealed one day's scene at a time as they rode forward. Farther up on the far right, Santa waved from a boat.

"This was nice, Harper. Thanks for taking me out."

"Now see, in the old days, I would have taken you to an outdoor movie. We would have made out rather than see the movie," he said, running his hand down her arm and leaning over to kiss her sweetly. "But they're a thing of the past."

They hadn't made love since before the shooting and Barbara missed his intimate touch. "There's something to say for days past."

"Do you think they're still here?" Barbara asked, referring to Sonya and Boyd. It was Wednesday and they were eating supper. Harper's family wasn't expected until midnight.

"No, I think they're long gone out of the state or maybe they even left the country. If they still haven't found what they're looking for, they're probably stowed away on somebody's boat. Or found a boat belonging to the summer people."

Harper's cell phone rang. It was Mr. Hughes complaining that someone was coming in to shore near his house.

"I'm going to have to leave, babe," Harper said, giving her a brief kiss before he left.

It was a perfect opportunity to pick up a small gift for Harper. The stores were open, not that there was much on the island to choose from, but some of the artists were quite good. Perhaps she could get him a sculpture or painting.

She called Liane.

"Harper doesn't want you going out."

"It's just on the island, and he even said Sonja and Boyd probably aren't here."

"But still . . ."

"I'll go by myself if you're afraid."

"I can't let you do that."

"Either way, I'm going."

In five minutes they were backing out the driveway but came up short when someone pointed a gun at Barbara's head. "Open the door," she said.

Barbara had never seen the woman before. Could this be Sonya?

"Should we make a run for it?" Liane whispered, still backing up.

The gun shot the side-view mirror off, making their decision for them.

"Stop the car and open the damn door," Sonya yelled. "Or the next one will be in you."

Liane stopped and popped the lock.

The woman opened the door wide. "Okay, smart-ass, get out."

"Wh—"

"If I want sass from you, I'll ask for it. Get out of here."

"Just go, Liane," Barbara said.

"You get in that driver's seat," she said to Barbara.

"She can't drive," Liane responded.

"She's driving tonight. Get yourself behind that wheel."

Barbara got out, walked around the car, and slid behind the wheel.

"Where are we going?" she asked. "Why do you need me?"

Sonya pointed the gun at her. "You've got some money I need."

"The bank isn't open this time of night."

"I'm not looking for a few hundred in cash. Those investments you made with Elliot. I want you to cash 'em in. I need that money," she said with a desperate air. "That cheap-ass sonofabitch. We ain't got all day. Get moving."

"To where?"

"We're leaving this island."

"You want me to go to the dock?"

"Hell no."

"Where am I supposed to drive?"

"Toward your house."

Was this woman crazy or what? The first place Harper would look was her house.

Harper drove along the ocean road, but he didn't use his blinkers. Halfway between Hughes's place and Barbara's, he turned his lights off and looked toward the ocean to see what was there. Sure enough, not far from the Hughes place there was a small boat pulling in to shore. There was a light on it shining into the darkness.

Harper got into his car and called for backup, just in case. There was one figure and he pulled the boat to shore, stowing it in the tall grass. Dressed in black, he stealthily made his way down the beach as Harper unhooked his gun and advanced. Was he going to break into Barbara's house, or Hughes's?

To the right was marsh and to the left was sand. He veered toward the right.

Harper moved forward. He heard cars approaching in back of him and veered toward the bushes in the marsh for cover. Harper was almost on him when he turned back toward the boat.

He pointed his high-beam flashlight at him. "This is the police. Raise your hands," he called out.

Someone took off in a run and Harper streaked after him, catching up to him just as he dragged the boat to the water. Advancing on him, he saw something point toward him; he ducked and dived just as a shot rang out. Harper rolled on his side and fired, police academy style, holding the gun in both hands.

Someone ducked behind the boat, quickly pulling

it toward the water, but Harper peppered the boat with shots until the perp ran toward the marsh, taking cover in the tall grass. Picking himself up, Harper charged after him.

He couldn't point the light or use himself as a target, so he scurried around in the dark.

"Harp?" Alyssa called out.

"Over here."

Alyssa approached. They could only hear the wind, the waves, and the swaying of branches. They stood still, trying to assess where the perp went and accustom their eyes to the night.

Several minutes passed before they heard movement.

Both he and Alyssa advanced stealthily through the mud and bushes.

He must have heard them, because he ran like a rabbit. Alyssa and Harper charged after him. The perp turned, and Alyssa and Harper ducked as a bullet whizzed by. They returned fire and the guy dove in the mud, giving them an opportunity to get closer.

Finally, they pinned him down.

"Okay . . . Don't shoot. I'm coming out."

"Hands in the air," Harper called out.

He stood gingerly. They could barely see him against the darkness of the night.

Quickly, they cuffed him, walking him back to shore.

"Boyd Xavier, I presume."

The man didn't speak.

"Where's Sonya?" Harper asked.

"I'm not saying anything until I see my lawyer." Boyd was bleeding, but it wasn't a major hit.

Alyssa read Boyd his rights, put him in her back

seat, and slammed the door. "Doc's going to love this," she said.

"Harper?" the dispatcher's voice came over his radio.

Harper responded. "What is it?"

"That Sonya woman just took Barbara."

CHAPTER 17

Barbara saw flashing lights ahead.

"Turn onto that path," Sonya said. "And cut those lights."

"It's pitch black out here. I can't see if I turn the lights off."

"Cut those lights or I'll shoot you this minute and do it myself."

Barbara switched the lights off and made a left onto the path, driving gingerly down the rutted road. She could barely make her way, it was so dark.

"Just drive far enough that they don't see you when they pass."

Barbara stopped the car with the engine idling. *God, please let Harper look this way.*

"Why did you kill Elliot?" she asked.

"You ask too many questions."

So she did kill him. Barbara shivered. Boyd wasn't much, but she couldn't fathom him committing murder. Did this woman trick him? Was he so head over heels in love with her that he'd do anything for her? Did he even know what she was doing?

"They're gone. Back out to the road," Sonya said.

Barbara flipped the lights on and backed out, wondering if she was going to live through the night.

"Park near your house," Sonya said.

When Barbara complied, she ordered, "Now get out."

Barbara found herself wading along the beach, through the tall marsh grass, the water soaking through her shoes. Her shoulder started to ache.

"Move faster."

"I can't. You shot me, remember?"

"Get your butt into gear," she said, looking around.

Before, Barbara walked along the beach without even getting winded. What a difference a bullet and a few weeks made. She trudged ahead, every bone in her body aching. They finally made it to a boat pulled to shore.

Sonya flashed a light on it. "Get in."

Barbara glanced around, hoping to hear sirens and cars coming back, but nothing. She climbed in.

Sonya got in with her. "Damn it. Can't anything go right in this freaking place?"

There was no motor on the boat.

"What did he do? Take the damn thing with him? Get out," Sonya barked.

Thank God.

Harper was out of his mind with worry that Barbara would be another of Sonya's victims. Clearly she didn't have a problem with murdering people. He'd notified the coast guard to watch for boats leaving the island. He'd gotten his dispatcher to call all the part-time officers in for the search, as well as the citizen's police, which numbered more than their tiny department.

Alyssa met Harper on his way to interview Boyd.

"Jordan just called. He put out a reward for Naomi's golden bowl and someone just called him with an offer."

"Why am I just hearing about this reward?"

"Because I'm just hearing about it."

"You deal with Jordan."

"The bowl can wait. Barbara's more important."

"I'm banking on them still being on the island. I'm going to check the area where we left the boat," Harper said. "You check the artist colony. Sonya should have more sense than to go there, but we have to cover all the bases."

Harper had Boyd brought to the interrogation room. "Where is Sonya taking Barbara?"

"I don't know. I was following her but lost her on my way here."

"I'm supposed to believe that?"

"Look, she's been very secretive lately. I wanted to know what was going on."

"Listen here, scumbag. You're already an accessory to two murders."

"I didn't murder anyone. And where did you get two from?"

Harper got in his face. "So you're admitting to one? Don't forget Sarah Rhodes. . . . ."

"I didn't know anything about that. It was probably Elliot's doing. Look, man," he stammered. "I wasn't even here when that happened."

"You're an accomplice. That means you'll get the same punishment as Sonya."

"I'm telling you I didn't kill anyone."

"What about the gun? The same gun was used to shoot Barbara and Elliot."

Boyd grabbed a shaky breath. "She told me she shot Barbara by mistake. She was aiming for Elliot. But Sonya lost the gun. If she shot Elliot, it wasn't with that gun."

"Lost the gun?" Harper asked, incredulous.

"I know it sounds ridiculous, but she lost it when she was trying to get away." Boyd scrubbed a hand across his face. "I'm telling you the truth. I don't know where she's taking Barbara. I didn't know she was going to kidnap her."

"That's the best you can do?"

"I'm telling you everything. I've never been mixed up in stuff like this. I've never hurt anybody in my life. I don't even know how I let myself get involved. But I didn't kill anybody."

"Tell it to the judge."

When Harper stormed out, Boyd was still screaming his innocence.

But was he lying? Had Sonya lost the gun? If so, who killed Elliot? Who had anything to gain? The gun was wiped clean of fingerprints. Would Sonya have taken the time when the gun was still in her possession? Then, too, she could have ditched the gun without telling Boyd. Seems he wasn't really in her confidence after all.

And then there was Trent. Barbara had an ulterior motive for being here, so could he.

But Trent didn't kidnap Barbara, and she was shot while he was on the ferry. No. Maybe he didn't like Trent, but his focus was on Sonya.

"Lambert saw lights near the boat again."

Harper couldn't brush it away as just a crazy old

man. The first time he'd said he'd seen lights, they were definitely there.

"Let's go."

"Why don't we just go to my house?" Barbara asked Sonya.

"You think I'm crazy?"

Barbara thought she was. "I'm tired. I can't go much farther without rest. And if I have a relapse, you can forget about getting any money."

"Shut up and let me think. Just keep moving to the car."

Sonya was breathing hard behind her. If Barbara had kept up her walking regimen and hadn't been shot, she could easily lose Sonya. But she had been shot, and she hadn't exercised since then. She was ready to collapse at Sonya's feet, but she couldn't give up. Never.

The car was still shrouded in the trees. Barbara got in on the driver's side. Sonya opened her door and hefted herself up on the seat. Before Sonya could get into position, Barbara pushed the red emergency "OnStar" button and hopped out, fell to the ground, and shut the door at the same time. Hovering close to the ground, she dived into the trees. Bullets peppered the air around her, but Barbara kept running.

"Get your ass back here or I'm going to kill you," Sonya yelled.

Fat chance. Barbara didn't stop long enough to consider giving up. She hurt all over, but especially where she'd been shot. She knew she was moving slower than Sonya. Every footstep was leaden. Sonya had stopped shooting, maybe to reload, and was gaining on her. Barbara stopped and hid behind a knarled oak, its branches picked as bare as a chicken bone.

"Damn it. Don't make me keep running after you," Sonya yelled.

Barbara clutched a hand to her heart, gathering huge breaths. What to do? If she moved, the ground cover would crackle like popcorn. Whatever people believed, you couldn't move quietly through a dense forest. She heard twigs snapping, underbrush rustling every time Sonya moved—and she was moving closer by the second. Barbara had to get out of there.

She looked for a branch big enough to use as a weapon. Finding one, she quickly grabbed it and darted off.

She must have reloaded. Bullets sprayed again. One hit a branch that fell on Barbara. She swiped it away.

"Move and I'll kill you."

Barbara froze. Sonya was right behind her.

"I ought to kill you anyway for making me run this way."

Barbara was too winded to talk. She hid the stick at her side and hoped it was too dark for Sonya to see.

"Now lead the way back to the truck. And don't try any tricks," Sonya ordered.

To tell the truth, Barbara just walked. She didn't know which direction the truck was, but neither did Sonya.

"I mean what I said."

They'd walked several yards when Barbara bumped into a tree. "Umph."

"Watch where you're going."

"I can't see."

"Keep going," Sonya urged.

Barbara went a few feet before she tripped.

"What the hell's wrong with you?"

"If you can see better than I can, you lead the way."

"If you hadn't acted so stupid, we'd be in the truck. Now get yourself into gear."

Barbara picked herself up, making sure to keep hold of the stick. Sonya bent to rest. Barbara stood and swung with all the strength she had left. Sonya dropped the gun and Barbara took off running again.

"Damn it. I'm gonna kill your ass this time. You hear me, bitch? Fuck the money."

She'd obviously stopped long enough to retrieve the gun, but Barbara kept running, although she didn't know where the heck she was going.

Sonya found the gun. Bullets started firing, but Barbara ran and ran until she plowed into a solid wall.

And screamed.

A hand covered her mouth. It took her a few seconds to realize the wall was Harper's chest. He eased her behind him.

"Barbara?" Sonya's voice blasted the night air. "What the hell's going on? Barbara?"

Barbara struggled to catch her breath. She was standing next to another of those knarled oaks and scrunched down behind it.

A few more bullets peppered the air as Harper moved away.

Barbara wanted to scream for him to be careful, but the sound would carry. So she did what her grandmother taught her from an early age. She prayed.

She is safe. That was the litany running through Harper's mind. That she was unharmed.

He'd heard the bullets when he got out of the car

near Barbara's house just before the OnStar people notified them, directing them to Barbara's location. Seconds later, he found his truck, with no Barbara. His worst fear was that she was already dead.

He stood beside a tree as Sonya slowly came toward him.

"Barbara?" Sonya called out. "I'm not going to kill you. Okay? I need that money. I'll let you go as soon as I get it. I didn't kill Elliot. I don't know who did."

Sure she didn't, Harper thought. As if anyone was fool enough to believe that. She was almost beside him now. Close enough for him to touch. He gave her a single chop on the neck and slammed her to the ground.

"Police," he said belatedly. "You're under arrest." In seconds he cuffed her and dragged her to her feet. He retrieved her gun where she'd dropped it, then read her her rights.

"I didn't kill Elliot. I can prove I wasn't even here when he was killed."

"Yeah, yeah, yeah," Harper said. "That's what every murderer says."

"Harper?" Barbara called out.

"I've got her."

"Thank God."

Harper had dragged Doc out of bed to check Barbara thoroughly before he'd take her home. With some painkillers in her system, she'd slept through the rest of the night.

"We arrested your ex last night," Harper told Barbara while she dressed for breakfast. "How are you feeling, sweetheart?"

She smiled up at him. "Fantastic."

"After the night you had?"

"I'm alive."

He kissed her. "And gorgeous as ever."

She felt all hot inside when he said things like that.

"I'm going to work after breakfast. I want you to take it easy today."

"Liane won't let me do anything."

"That's the way it should be," he said with a satisfied grin.

"You are too much, Harper."

"Uh-huh. But you love it."

"Yeah, I do." Since her shoulder was throbbing, he helped her dress.

"It's hard to believe that Boyd really came here. I want to see him."

"Are you crazy?"

"I have a right to know why he tried to kill me."

"You're not seeing him," Harper said with a finality that would have a lesser woman retreating.

"Why not?"

"You're sick."

"Harper, don't be ridiculous. Sonya had me trouping all over this place."

"Which is why you need to rest now."

"Harper . . ."

"Damn it, Barbara." He jerked the door open. "Come on."

"Can't we have breakfast first?"

Harper shook his head. "I can't believe I let you get away with this," he said as he drove Barbara to the jail.

"I've got a right to know why he tried to kill me."

"You're getting away with too much. You always get your way."

"I never understood the male species. And you haven't done anything for me to change my opinion."

"Don't even think about lumping me in with everyone else."

They arrived at the jail and went inside. Harper escorted Barbara to the visiting area. A screen separated Barbara from Boyd.

"I want to know why," Barbara said.

"Why what?" Boyd asked with the same sullen look she remembered so well.

"Why did you try to kill me?"

"I didn't."

"They've got shoes, fingerprints, and the gun. You were at my house. You may as well tell me."

"I didn't shoot you."

"Why did you get your girlfriend to do it? I'm nothing to her."

Boyd remained silent.

"You know you're the same sullen boy who was too lazy to work for what you wanted fifteen years ago. You haven't changed a bit."

"If you say so," he said with a bored air.

"Why Dorsey? She never hurt you."

"Elliot killed Dorsey," he whispered.

"But Sonya says you led him to her."

He leaned forward and whispered again. "You had enough money to spare."

"You killed my grandmother for money?" Barbara wanted to jump through the partition and wring his neck. "I hope you rot in hell."

"I didn't kill anybody. And I didn't know he was going to kill her."

"They may not be able to tie Dorsey's murder to

you, but you're going to go down for two murders. Sarah and Elliot, right along with Sonya.."

"I didn't kill either of them."

"Doesn't matter. You were part of the conspiracy and you'll get the same punishment."

"In your dreams."

Barbara stood. She knew just the buttons to push to rattle him. "You know what? You never were good enough. I don't know what I ever saw in you."

"Bitch."

"Is that the best you can do?

He came forward. But Barbara had already started out of the room. And what could he do through the partition anyway?

Before Barbara left the building, Boyd was asking for a plea bargain.

But later, Harper kept thinking about Elliot's murder. Andrew had moved back into the house with Minerva. Who would gain from Elliot's murder? Sonya would if she could snatch Andrew, but Sonya insisted she didn't kill Elliot. She'd shot at him, but she'd missed and shot Barbara. She'd sworn she'd lost the gun and that she was with someone else who'd left Norfolk for the holidays. The gun she'd held on Barbara hadn't killed anyone.

Harper raked a hand over his head and went to the evidence room.

Harper and Alyssa knocked on Minerva's door.

Minerva peeked through the curtains and opened the door wide for them.

"Evening, Sheriff. Naomi told me you caught Sonya and that guy she's been hanging with. I'm glad you caught my husband's murderer. I feel a whole lot better now."

Andrew lumbered into the room.

"How're you doing, Andrew?" Harper asked.

Alyssa came forward. "Minerva Stone, you're under arrest for the murder of your husband."

Minerva took a step back. "Are you crazy?"

Alyssa turned her and clipped on cuffs as she read her her rights.

"Mama didn't kill nobody," Andrew said.

"Stand back," Harper ordered.

"Mama?"

"They're wrong, son. Call my lawyer. There's no way I killed your father. You know how much I loved him. You can't tie me to Elliot's murder."

"Your fingerprints were on the clip," Harper said. "You wiped them off the gun, but you forgot the clip. You see, it's the little details that mess you up every time."

"Mama?" Andrew looked puzzled. "How could you kill Daddy? He loved you . . . I thought . . . Why?"

Looking at her son, all the fight drained out of Minerva.

"Don't you understand? Your daddy never did right by you. He was just using us. Sitting around, planning all this mess while he waited for you to get your money. You'd never have control of it," she said. "I was going to take you to Detroit to live with my family. My brothers would have been good to you, not put you down all the time like Elliot."

"But, Mama."

"I was tired of him messing up things. Getting us in trouble. With him gone, we could stop this nonsense."

She shook her head. "Dear God. It worked for Wanda Fisher. Why couldn't it work for me?"

Harper looked at her, incredulous. She used Wanda as her guide? The crazy woman who chopped up her husband to fit in the freezer? "You thought you'd get away with it because of Wanda?"

"It sounded real good when Hoyt Claxton told us about it at dinner."

Harper shook his head. Who would have thought this was a copycat killing?

After they booked Minerva, Alyssa turned to Harper, shaking her head. "It pays to treat your women folk right."

"Don't worry. I'm going to treat Barbara like a queen."

"Jordan called. The person with the bowl didn't show up."

"Where was he supposed to meet her?"

"In Virginia Beach. I've already called my contact there, but she didn't give him much to go on." She sighed. "Now that these murders are tied up, I'm going to try to find Grandma's bowl before she disowns me."

"I thought she already did that."

Later, when Harper returned home and had taken his shower, Barbara had started the fire in the outside fireplace. A bottle of wine was chilling and two glasses were on the table along with a midnight snack. And she was already wrapped up in the blanket. He smiled. She was definitely the woman for him.

He snuggled in beside her and drew her against his chest, enjoying her pleasing scent and her softness.

This was the life, he thought as he nuzzled her neck before he kissed her there.

"Umm." He turned her in his arms, kissed her long and hard. "Did I tell you how happy I am to spend the holiday with you?"

"You must have forgotten."

"Let me remind you," he said, drawing her close again and kissing her.

"Oh, Harper. I'm so happy."

For a while they enjoyed being with each other while they gazed toward the ocean.

"Okay, talk to me. I've been hearing rumors."

Harper sighed, hating to release this good feeling. "This is the most bizarre set of crimes." He told her about Minerva. "It seems Boyd turned them on to your grandmother. Sonya was Andrew's girlfriend, but she'd tried to do a con on Boyd. But he acted like he was wealthy and he has family members with money, but Boyd actually was broke. He and Sonya got involved in a relationship and decided to put their heads together to scam the Stones after they conned your grandmother.

"But Sonya knew about Andrew's trust fund and knew she'd never get her hands on it while Elliot was alive. Plus, Elliot was holding out on her. If Minerva hadn't killed Elliot first, she would have killed him."

Barbara shook her head. "It is so much easier to work a legitimate job than to go through all that. And why didn't Minerva just leave Elliot and take Andrew with her?"

"Elliot would have never let that happen."

Barbara shook her head.

Harper's mother, sister-in-law, and Liane were cooking Christmas dinner while Barbara and Harper talked.

"You're going to have to turn the money over to me," Harper said.

"First you have to prove it isn't my money. Elliot's dead. It's in my account and I can do what I want with it."

"You're being unreasonable. You know that money belongs to those women."

"Of course I do. And it's going to them, just not through the court system. I still need the rest of the money, Harper," Barbara said. "I want you to find it."

"If I find it, I have to turn it in. Along with your money. You know that."

"You can't do that," Barbara said.

"Why not?"

"You know why."

Incredulous, Harper glared at her. "I'm an officer of the law. I can't turn the money over to you to distribute as you see fit."

"You asked me to trust you. I trust you to do the right thing, and you know the only option is to give that money to the people who need it."

"Are you crazy? It's my job to uphold the law, not break it. I can't do that. Even for you."

"What would you do if somebody did it to your mother?"

Harper sighed heavily. "That's hitting below the belt."

"Well?" When he didn't respond, she said, "Fine. Just stay out of my way because if I have to dig up this entire island, I'm going to find that money for those seniors."

"You are the most impossible . . ." Harper hopped off the chair, then paced back and forth in front of her. "You are out of your damn mind," he shouted.

"Now you know."

Suddenly, he turned on her. "If I do this, I want a New Year's Eve wedding."

"What?"

He loomed over her, every muscle of his body tense. "Either put up or shut up, Barbara. New Year's Eve. Yes or no."

"You know you aren't being fair."

"First you want me to show leniency with Andrew. Now I'm supposed to find that money and turn it over to you."

"Not to me. To the people whom it belongs to. You might be the law, but I'm going for justice."

"I don't give a damn about the reason. It's still against the law. If I'm going against the law, I'm getting something out of it. You." He kissed her with all the pent-up emotions storming through him.

"Yes or no."

"You are crazy, Harper," she said, but he only glared with a stubborn façade. Barbara sighed. "Yes. But you know giving the money to the seniors is the right thing to do, Harper. And giving me an ultimatum isn't fair."

"You always got to have the last word, don't you? The only one I'm hearing is the 'yes.' And you need to get yourself a wedding dress, sweetheart. Time is passing." He stormed off.

Barbara heard the motor rev and tires peeling out the driveway.

"Did I hear Harper say something about a wedding dress?" Liane asked, coming outside.

Barbara rolled her eyes. "Yes."

"So, when are you getting married?"

"New Year's Eve."

Liane was silent as she gazed at Barbara suspiciously. "You're referring to a year from now, right?"

"A week from now."

"Are you crazy?"

Anger rode Harper as he drove toward the artist colony. Barbara was the most impossible woman he'd ever met, Harper thought. Of course it was right for those seniors to get their money, but there was a right way to do things—through the legal system. Laws were made for a reason.

The thing was, the legal system would take years. And the women needed the money now. But you couldn't bend the law every time it didn't suit you. Chaos would reign.

Then he smiled, the anger rushing out of him. He was getting married. He'd have her right under his thumb where he wanted her.

Get real. Barbara would never be an easy woman to live with. But that didn't matter. He loved her. And everything else was just collateral.

He'd thought about Sonya and Boyd a lot. They were coming *to* the island. Not leaving. Why would they come to the island when they knew everyone was searching for them—unless they'd left the money here?

And since they were caught near Barbara's house . . . Harper changed directions.

EPILOGUE

It was close to midnight New Year's Eve. Barbara wore her white suit and Harper looked handsome in his black suit. Their wedding was held in the B&B's magnificent living room and the reception was a sit-down dinner in Cornell's restaurant.

Barbara thought they would have a small, intimate celebration, but it turned out to be huge. How they'd decorated the place so beautifully and prepared a dinner for three hundred people on such short notice, Barbara couldn't imagine. Sam had done a wonderful job with the flowers. And Cornell had pulled out all the stops for the dinner.

While she was getting her strength back, Barbara still wasn't up to par and hadn't been much help.

A few friends had come from New York and Liane's parents arrived, too. The room was full of islanders.

"Mrs. Porterfield," Harper said later while he poured glasses of champagne for them both. They were now at his house.

"Revenge can be so sweet," he said.

"You, Mr. Porterfield, didn't complete your part

of the bargain. I didn't get my money. Yet, you insisted on going through with the wedding."

"I did what you asked. I looked for your money."

"But you didn't *find* it."

With a self-righteous look, he asked, "Are you pleased with the outcome?"

She nodded. Truthfully, she loved Harper and she was exactly where she wanted to be.

"I still haven't given you your wedding gift," he said.

"Oh, Harper. You've given me so much. And I haven't given you a thing."

"You've given me more than I've ever dreamed for." From the closet, he retrieved two boxes wrapped in gold and white wedding paper and set them on the comforter.

"What's this?" she asked, as she began to tear the paper.

"Take a look."

Barbara tore the paper completely away and opened the first box.

"Harper? Oh, my gosh. You found it."

"Yes, I did," he said with a smug look.

"Where?"

"At your house."

"My house?" she asked, puzzled.

"They'd left the money there when they made the mad dash away."

"Oh, the seniors are going to be so happy."

"Are you happy?"

She pulled his head to hers and kissed him. "I'm very happy."

"I'm not talking about the money. Are you happy to be married to me?"

Barbara's smile was open and warm. "You are perfect for me. I couldn't be happier."

"That doesn't mean I'm going to let you boss me around, woman."

"Oh?" She ran a finger along his collar. "What if I ask you nicely to take me to bed? Would that be considered bossy?"

"Absolutely," he said, his eyes darkened with desire. "And your wish is my command."

Barbara laughed.

Dear Reader,

I hope you enjoyed Barbara and Harper's story, the third title in the series "Quest for the Golden Bowl." I wrote a plus-sized woman into *Island of Deceit*. I wanted a strong character secure in herself and her capabilities. She makes no apology for her size and doesn't take crap from anyone else about it either.

The first title in the "Golden Bowl" series, *Golden Night*, featured Gabrielle Long and Cornell Price. The second title, *Long, Hot Nights*, featured Alyssa Claxton and Jordan Ellis. The theme of the series is family history, so I hope you are talking to your older family members to gather your family's interesting stories or writing your own family history.

Stay tuned for the fourth title featuring Lisa Claxton, a troubled character from *Golden Night*. In book four, Lisa comes into her own and we discover the cause of her sour disposition. We've already seen her making changes, but her story is truly a transformation.

Please visit my web page: *www.CandicePoarch.com*.

You may contact me at: *readers@CandicePoarch.com*.

Or write to me at: P.O. Box 291, Springfield, VA 22150.

With warm regards,

Candice Poarch

GREAT BOOKS,
GREAT SAVINGS!

When You Visit Our Website:
www.kensingtonbooks.com
You Can Save Money Off The Retail Price
Of Any Book You Purchase!

- **All Your Favorite Kensington Authors**
- **New Releases & Timeless Classics**
- **Overnight Shipping Available**
- **eBooks Available For Many Titles**
- **All Major Credit Cards Accepted**

Visit Us Today To Start Saving!
www.kensingtonbooks.com